Bluebells in
the Mourning

KaraLynne Mackrory

Meryton Press
Oysterville, WA

Bluebells in the Mourning

Copyright © 2013 by KaraLynne Mackrory

All rights reserved, including the right to reproduce this book, or portions thereof, in any format whatsoever. For information: P.O. Box 34, Oysterville WA 98641

ISBN: 978-1-936009-23-7

Graphic design by Ellen Pickels

Acknowledgments

It is a truth universally acknowledged that a girl in possession of a story must be in want of a few good friends with whom to share it. I owe a great thanks to many friends and family members who encouraged and persuaded this story from me.

A particular thanks must go to Ron and Kayla for their endless excitement for this endeavor and for me. Like Miss Bennet, I similarly have many sisters who also were steadfast in their support. In addition, I would like to acknowledge my dad, who gave me such a charming, adorably tender inspiration to draw my Mr. Bennet. (Seriously, the cutest old man in the world!)

Many thanks also for the darling ladies at Meryton Press who made this possible: Michele Reed and Ellen Pickels. Of course, a most devoted thanks to my editor, Christina Boyd. Her uncanny ability to see the potential of a moment made the book better than I had dreamed possible.

Lastly, to Jane Austen. Now, there is one diva I have on my bucket list of people to meet in the afterlife. I will probably give her at least a high-five!

Chapter 1

Elizabeth stared blankly out the window of the carriage as it jostled its way toward London. The shock she had received the day before had yet to abate, and her mind ached in turmoil. Her heart still beat, almost traitorously, despite her overwhelming grief. Her unseeing eyes roamed the Kent countryside as she leaned against the windowpane, the cool glass soothing her throbbing head. Disbelief colored her thoughts, overwhelming her emotions. She was wild to see Jane and be with her family once more.

"Are you well, Miss Elizabeth?"

"As well as can be expected, Colonel, I thank you." She smiled wanly for his evident concern. She then turned to look upon her other traveling companions. Mr. Darcy, seated directly across from her, was holding his book. When her eyes met his, she was stunned to see compassion. She quickly looked away. The tenderness she saw warred with her opinion of the man, and contemplating the variance only added to her headache. Miss Maria Lucas's head was bowed as she silently wept. Elizabeth handed her handkerchief to her friend, who gratefully replaced a sodden one. Elizabeth had not cried since the day before—not since *he* came to the parsonage.

While walking with Colonel Fitzwilliam the previous morning, Elizabeth had been angered when her suspicions were confirmed that Mr. Darcy had indeed separated her sister Jane from his friend, so she complained of a sudden headache and begged to return to the parsonage. The colonel had boasted of his cousin's loyalty to Mr. Bingley and his triumph in separating his friend from a most imprudent marriage. Fury rose inside her again at his preposterous interference, now compounded by the loss she was feeling.

She wished she had not accepted his offer to escort her to London, but at the time, she was distraught and anxious to reunite with her family.

The colonel nodded his head in understanding, and Elizabeth said, "Your concern is much appreciated, sir. My heart is indeed grieved, but I am most concerned for my sister and my mother, who are no doubt suffering greatly."

She was startled to hear Mr. Darcy's reverberating voice. "Miss Catherine was very close to Miss Lydia if I remember correctly."

Elizabeth's gaze met his, and displeasure flashed in her eyes. "Yes she was, but it is my sister Jane for whom I most worry." He looked out the window briefly to control his surprise. "She has suffered another great loss this year. I fear for her compassionate heart. Her emotions, though little displayed, are fervent and tender. She will suffer not only her own loss in this tragedy, but her kind heart will keenly feel the grief of our family."

Elizabeth watched in satisfaction as her allusion towards Mr. Bingley's abandonment caused Mr. Darcy to wince. *You think I do not know, Mr. Darcy, but I do.* He turned and nodded briefly towards her before picking up his book. "I am sure your company will bring her great comfort, Miss Elizabeth."

Elizabeth turned her head towards the window again. His kind response in the face of her sharp words lessened her anger, and it frustrated her that she felt remorse. Again, her eyes glazed over as she watched out the window and thought back to the day before. Her emotions were raw and turbulent; she wondered how she would ever gain control of herself once more.

AFTER THE COLONEL HAD LEFT her at her cousin's parsonage, she had ascended to her room where she spent no little time reviewing all Jane's letters from London. Although Jane never expressly declared her anguish over the loss of Mr. Bingley, her general tone lacked its usual grace and lightness. *If only Jane would write again! I have not heard from her in over a week.* She worried anew for her sister and wondered at her lack of correspondence.

When it came time to ready herself for dinner, Charlotte knocked softly on her door. She breathed deeply and checked her countenance in the mirror before opening it to her friend.

"Mr. Collins asked me to remind you that we are to dine at Rosings tonight, Lizzy."

A groan escaped Elizabeth's mouth before she could check herself, and her friend's concern was immediate. "Lizzy, are you unwell?"

Elizabeth was silent. She was desperate to avoid the Great House and its occupants that day. Perturbed with her own lack of imagination, she sighed, "'Tis only a slight headache, Charlotte; I shall be fine."

Mr. Collins, on his way to change for dinner, interrupted when he heard of his cousin's indisposition. "Cousin Elizabeth, surely you are not considering staying home from Rosings because of your headache. Lady Catherine would be most displeased!"

"Well..."

"You cannot, Cousin! Her condescension in extending the invitation forbids it. You will dress immediately and rest until it is time to go. I insist!"

He spun on his heels and left the ladies standing open-mouthed. Elizabeth looked to her friend for help, and Charlotte reached for her hand as she said, "I will see what I can do, Lizzy. In the meantime, rest and see if you do not feel better by the time we must leave."

The door to Mr. Collins's bedchamber opened abruptly as he said, "Make haste, Charlotte, make haste! We cannot be late; you know how her ladyship detests delays."

"I am coming, dear." Charlotte rolled her eyes and squeezed Elizabeth's hand.

Elizabeth closed the door to her room and fell upon her bed. After a groan into her pillow and the subsequent flight of said pillow through the air towards her bedchamber door, Elizabeth sat up and dressed for dinner with the overbearing Lady Catherine and her officious, meddling, arrogant and presumptuous nephew.

When she reached the parlor, her cousin was pacing with impatience. Her appearance caused him to exhale with great relief as he hurriedly put on his gloves. Just then, the maid entered and handed two letters to Elizabeth. "The mail's come, ma'am."

Elizabeth smiled down at the letters in her hand. "They are from Jane!" she exclaimed with happiness and relief. Her brow frowned briefly as she studied the envelopes. "Well that is why I have not heard from her: the address on this one was written very ill and was misdirected at first." She sighed again and looked to her friend with entreaty.

Charlotte understood her wishes to remain at home and read her letters. Her husband was again anxious to leave. She walked towards Elizabeth, eyeing her friend. "Lizzy, dear, you are flushed." She placed a hand on her friend's brow and said, "You are a bit feverish too! I hope you have not caught a cold!"

Elizabeth looked at her friend in puzzlement before understanding. "Yes, I feel a bit warm."

Mr. Collins hastened to her side. "Charlotte, it would not do to expose Miss de Bourgh's fragile constitution to a cold." He pulled his wife's arm, imploring she keep her distance less she catch the malady and take it to Rosings as well.

"Cousin Elizabeth, I insist you stay here tonight. I will give your regrets to Lady Catherine."

Elizabeth stifled a smile as she curtsied to her cousin, "Thank you, Mr. Collins; I will stay here as I would not want to expose myself to her ladyship or Miss de Bourgh."

"Yes, yes, well we should be going," Mr. Collins said as he pulled out his watch from his pocket. "My dear Charlotte! We must make haste. Now!" He pulled his wife towards the door. Charlotte gave her friend a wink before she turned to leave with her husband and sister Maria.

Elizabeth sank gratefully into the chair as she looked over the two letters and determined to read the misdirected letter first.

The beginning contained an account of the various engagements and parties Jane had attended with her Aunt and Uncle Gardiner in London, but the latter half, which was evidently written a day later and with obvious distress, contained more important intelligence. It read:

My dear Lizzy, since writing the above, I have obtained news of a most serious and distressing nature. What I have to relate, I fear, will worry you excessively. Be assured we here are all in good health. What I have to relate pertains to poor Lydia. We have heard from our father at Longbourn. An express came to our uncle's house late last night detailing that Lydia and Kitty, in the company of officers, in truth Mr. Wickham and Mr. Denny, were out for a walk. They were near the ravine at Oakham Mount, when her footing slipped near the edge and she fell down the slope! She is very badly injured. Our father reports that when the officers brought her to the house, she was conscious and speaking Mr. Wickham's name restlessly. After the apothecary came and treated her, she slipped into a deep sleep. I am willing to hope for the best, that of her speedy recovery, as her consciousness in the beginning cannot but mean she did not suffer a serious blow to the head in her fall. Our father asked that I write to you. Our mother, as you can imagine, keeps to her bed; the news quite distresses her. I must conclude; I cannot be long from packing. I am to return home tomorrow with our aunt and uncle to be of help where we can."

Without anytime for consideration and being scarcely able to know how she felt, Elizabeth reached for the other letter and broke the seal immediately.

By this time, dearest Lizzy, you will have received my hastily written letter detailing Lydia's accident. I hope this one may be more intelligible; though I am not pressed for time, my head and heart are so weary that I know not how to write what I must. I hardly know where to begin, for I have bad news. Distressing as Lydia's accident was, we are now greatly grieved, for our poor Lydia soon became feverish. Oh, Lizzy, my heart breaks when I must tell you this news and cannot be there with you when you receive it. Our poor Lydia is gone! Her fever did not subside despite our endless ministrations to her. Soon an infection took over. I take comfort to know that in the end she slipped peacefully into the eternal sleep in which she now resides. Our poor mother is inconsolable and keeps to her room still. Circumstances are such that I know you would want to be with your family as soon as may be, and I beg that you make all possible haste in coming home. In truth, I long for your comfort as we grieve the loss of our dear sister."

The tears were now streaming down Elizabeth's face as she stood quickly, in all eagerness to alert her cousin and friend. "Oh, where are Mr. and Mrs. Collins!" As she approached the parlor door, it opened, and Mr. Darcy walked in. "I beg your pardon, but I must leave you. I must find Mr. and Mrs. Collins on business that cannot be delayed. I have not a moment to lose!" Her pallor and tears commanded his immediate concern. Mr. Darcy hastened to her side and steadied her shaking shoulders as she nearly collapsed against him in her distress.

"Good God! What is the matter?" he cried with more feeling than politeness as he carefully settled her on the sofa. Calling for the servant, he bellowed instructions for her to retrieve the Collinses from Rosings immediately.

Elizabeth tried to rise again, but he said, "No, let the servant go. You are not well enough; you cannot go yourself."

Elizabeth assented. Her shoulders folded inward as she covered her face and let grief wash over her. She looked so miserable and fragile that Mr. Darcy could not leave her and, without forethought, sat beside her, taking her hand in his.

"Miss Elizabeth, can I get you something for your present relief: a glass of wine perhaps? You look truly ill." His voice rang with such emotion and true compassion that Elizabeth's eyes rose to meet his.

"No, I thank you." As she endeavored to compose herself, she was taken aback when he quietly offered her his handkerchief. "I am well; I am only distressed by some dreadful news from Longbourn."

Elizabeth rested her head against the carriage windowpane as the memory swept over her again. She did not know what compelled her to spill her grief to Mr. Darcy that evening, but she told him all. Her eyes again brimmed with tears as she felt the loss of her youngest sister. *Poor, vibrant Lydia! Gone in the youth of her life.*

Mr. Darcy had been kind and solicitous, saying little and allowing her to speak freely. She succumbed to the weight of her grief and cried unaffectedly on his shoulder as he gently held her, murmuring incoherent sympathies. Now, as she traveled in his coach, she could not deny his kindness in offering to escort her and Maria back to London. His gentle understanding clashed with the arrogant, interfering character she knew he possessed. She battled between gratitude for his generosity and resentment at the pain she knew he inflicted on Jane's heart by separating Bingley from her. Before receiving the news of Lydia's death, she had been determined that, when she next encountered Mr. Darcy, she would confront him about his cruel treatment of both Jane and Mr. Wickham. With the wounds fresh from the news from Longbourn, she had, of course, never challenged him.

She closed her eyes and let the tears roll gently down her cheeks. The sway of the carriage matched the waves of pain surging in her breast. She opened her eyes when she felt a gentle pressure on her hands. Maria and Colonel Fitzwilliam had both fallen asleep, and Mr. Darcy was again handing her his handkerchief. She was about to refuse his offering until she remembered she had given hers to Maria. She swallowed thickly as she accepted it with a faint, "Thank you."

His eyes were kind, and his face softened in sympathy as he nodded to her.

Mr. Darcy was at a loss to describe what he felt when he saw her thus pained. He felt powerless in bringing her relief. If he could take away her agony and carry it himself—if only to see her smile and the light in her eyes return—he would do so in an instant. He had suffered the loss of his parents, and he knew her misery, albeit he could not formulate the words or the actions to assuage hers. He felt stunted, paralyzed in how to comfort her. *If only the post had been delayed one day!* he thought before castigating himself for his own self-interest. He had gone to the parsonage that evening to tell her of his ardent love and admiration, and to seek her hand in marriage, forever binding them together the way his heart demanded. If the post had come but a day later, they would have been an engaged couple, and he could have offered his sympathy and support in a more tangible way.

True, he had held her in his arms the previous evening, and it had been sweet torture. Her small frame had fit perfectly in his arms, and he had selfishly wished she could remain that way evermore. When her hand had contracted around the lapel of his jacket as she sobbed, he felt guilty for taking such satisfaction in her embrace when she was obviously in despair.

He knew it was further proof of his selfishness that he had immediately offered to escort her and Miss Lucas back to London to her aunt's house in Cheapside. He had told her and himself that, as he was leaving Kent the next day anyway, it was the most logical solution and would save her the trouble of securing passage by post in such haste. In truth, he did not want to separate from her so soon.

As he gazed at her staring out the window, he was reminded of the barbed comment she had made earlier in the journey about Miss Bennet. It puzzled him, for she said that her sister had suffered 'another' loss earlier this year. *Surely, she could not be referring to Bingley?* Yet there was that implication in her voice—almost an accusation. He dismissed the idea that Miss Bennet had felt Bingley's loss. He had observed her most acutely at the Netherfield ball. Her manners were as open, cheerful and engaging as ever, but they were without any symptom of regard. He was sure that, although she received his attentions with pleasure, she did not invite them, and her heart did not seem easily touched. And yet…what had Elizabeth said? *"Her emotions, though little displayed, are fervent and tender."*

Mr. Darcy shifted his weight in his seat, stunned by the meaning of her words. In his disbelief, his eyes darted again to her. *How did she know?* He realized that not only was he likely wrong about his friend but that somehow Elizabeth had learned of his interference. For the first time since encountering her at the parsonage, Mr. Darcy felt relieved that he had not paid her his addresses. In that instant, he remembered that his cousin Colonel Fitzwilliam had seen her earlier in the day and told him he accompanied her back to the parsonage when she fell ill with a sudden headache. He must have told her about his involvement with Bingley! He now sat wide-eyed with the realization that she must have stayed away from Rosings that evening to avoid him! He was never more thankful that he had not proposed. He shuddered to think what could have happened.

As relief rushed through him, he realized with extreme disappointment—and no little aggravation—that he could not in all propriety pay his addresses to her for at least three months as she would be in full mourning. *However, I might use the time to persuade her to my cause and change her opinion of me.* At almost the same moment, he felt disgusted anew at what seemed to be his proclivity for slipping into a selfish disdain for the feelings of others. *Have I always been thus?* he thought in frustration as he clenched his teeth. He hit his head against the back of the carriage to force his thoughts into a more charitable direction. *For God's sake, she has lost a sister, and all you can think about is how soon you can marry her!*

"Is everything all right, Mr. Darcy?" Elizabeth queried.

And with that, he fell in love with her all over again as he looked across at her tear-stained face. She was asking after his well-being even in the midst of her grief! *You thoughtless cad.* "Pardon me, Miss Bennet. I did not mean to disturb you." He watched as she simply nodded her head and turned her attention once again to the view outside. *'Til this moment, I never knew myself.*

As their caravan rolled closer to London and the sounds of the city began to compete with the creaking of the carriage wheels, Elizabeth sat up to straighten her dress. But when she was about to give Mr. Darcy the address of her aunt and uncle in Cheapside, she realized with a start that they would not be at home! They had left for Longbourn with her sister earlier in the week. Suddenly, she felt bereft and absurd at the same time.

"Ohh..." She moaned as she sat back into the seat and brought up a hand to cover her face. A frown contorted her brows as she thought of what she was to do. "Mr. Darcy, I...that is, with the turmoil of the moment...I neglected to realize..." She twisted her hands together in her lap before raising her chin and continuing, "Mr. Darcy, would you be so kind as to procure Miss Lucas and myself a room at an inn for the night? We will, of course, need to borrow a manservant for protection." Her voice drifted off; she was embarrassed that she lacked the foresight to have a plan.

The colonel spoke first. "Miss Bennet, I understood that you had an aunt and uncle in Cheapside?"

Elizabeth colored at her stupidity once again. "You are correct, Colonel Fitzwilliam. I only just realized that they would have left town with my sister Jane several days ago for Longbourn. I can only blame the distress at the news of Lydia's passing..." Her voice faltered briefly. "I failed to remember...to realize..."

Mr. Darcy's voice caused her to lift her head to him. "Miss Bennet, that will not be necessary. You and Miss Lucas will be welcome at my home tonight. As tomorrow is the Sabbath, we can journey onto Longbourn on Monday. I will be happy to accompany you as your relatives are not available to do so."

"Mr. Darcy! Certainly you cannot expect me to accept such a proposition!" Elizabeth was aghast at his indelicate suggestion.

Mr. Darcy was puzzled at her fervent declaration. "I fail to understand your meaning, madam. My house is large, and my staff is proficient enough that it would be no imposition."

Elizabeth looked with astonishment from Mr. Darcy to Colonel Fitzwilliam. The latter also seemed unaffected by his cousin's offer. *Are the two of them mad? Have they lost all sense of decency?* Elizabeth took in a slow, steadying breath to lessen her feelings of offense as she stated flatly, if a little coldly, "Must I remind you? It would not be proper for Miss Lucas or myself to stay the night at the home of an unmarried gentleman without a proper chaperone."

Mr. Darcy attempted to hide a smirk at Elizabeth's adorable ire as she properly chastised him. After a moment of matching her steady gaze and relishing the feelings coursing through him, he said, "You are correct, Miss Bennet. Your modesty commends you. However, you do not need to worry about your reputation. I never would compromise—"

"That is hardly the point, sir!" she interrupted him, astonished at his audacity to continue in that vein and coloring at the implication.

Mr. Darcy's lips twitched in amusement before he drawled, "If you will allow me to continue, Miss Bennet, I was saying that I never would compromise your reputation by putting you in such a situation as you suggest. My sister, Georgiana, and her *widowed* companion, Mrs. Annesley, are both in residence currently at Darcy House. Her companion is of an appropriate age and status to offer proper chaperonage."

"Oh," was all the response Elizabeth could manage in her discomfiture.

Mr. Darcy was secretly thrilled for the opportunity to have Elizabeth in his home. He allowed himself a moment of self-indulgence as he savored the fact that he would be welcoming, hopefully, the future mistress of Darcy House and Pemberley to his home.

Feeling frustration with Mr. Darcy despite his proffered kindnesses, Elizabeth tried to regain some of her dignity and said, "I thank you, Mr. Darcy, but after all the benevolence you have already bestowed, I do not think we could possibly accept."

"Miss Bennet, I understand your hesitation. However, I would recommend that you accept my cousin's proposal as you would be in far better comfort as well as better protected in his home than in a strange inn for the evening," Colonel Fitzwilliam argued.

Elizabeth drew a slow breath. *I do not want to stay at Mr. Darcy's house! I do not even like the man!* She wanted to scream. She was irritated that she could not simply be angry with him. Anger was easier than the disconcerting gratitude and disgruntled admiration for his unparalleled compassion. She opened her mouth to speak, but Mr. Darcy forestalled her.

"Miss Bennet, my cousin is right. You have been through much these past twenty-four hours. You cannot deny that the restful solitude of my home would benefit you far greater than the noisy, coldness of an inn. If you do not wish it, you do not even have to leave your bedchamber. My staff will do all that is necessary to ensure your comfort."

The thought of a quiet setting to grieve for Lydia would indeed be a comfort. She looked at the younger girl next to her and could see that Maria might need the same. If it were not for its being Mr. Darcy's home, she would not hesitate. Suddenly she felt very tired and over-taxed. "I thank you, Mr. Darcy; we will accept. You are too kind," she whispered.

"You are most welcome in my home, Miss Bennet," he said and as almost an afterthought, "and you too, Miss Lucas."

The ladies murmured their thanks.

"If there is anything we can do to bring you comfort, you need only ask. It will be granted with all due haste and consideration." His voice was gentle, and Elizabeth gazed briefly at him, surprised to note that compassion rendered a certain attractive quality to his face. She nodded slowly before turning her tearful countenance away from the beguiling man and toward the mind-numbing relief of the moving landscape outside.

Chapter 2

Elizabeth drew in a long, steadying breath and closed her eyes. They had arrived at the home of Mr. Darcy in Grosvenor Square, a fashionable part of town. She held her breath, willing herself to endure the next two days — praying she would be home with her family soon.

"Miss Bennet?"

She squeezed her eyes tighter when she heard *his* voice from outside the carriage. Slowly she opened her eyes to see Mr. Darcy peering inside, his hand extended to help her descend. She wondered why the colonel could not assist her out of the carriage.

She reached for her reticule and begrudgingly allowed him her hand. She kept her eyes to the ground, but instead of releasing her hand afterwards, he tucked it into the crook of his arm and walked her towards the house. With reluctance on his part and great relief on Elizabeth's, he released her arm only upon crossing the threshold of his home.

When he turned to address his butler, Mr. Carroll, she looked up and caught her breath. She barely registered giving her pelisse and gloves to one of the servants as she admired the distinguished elegance of his home. It was stately and refined — like its master — with the same reserve and grace. To her embarrassment, she could not conceal her awe.

"Miss Elizabeth Bennet," he said, then flicked his eyes away to Miss Lucas for a moment, "Miss Maria Lucas, this is my housekeeper, Mrs. Carroll. If you require anything, you need only ask, and she will see to it. Welcome to Darcy House."

After acknowledging the small, kind-looking woman, Elizabeth detected an almost supremely satisfied look about him. *Insufferable man!* she thought before censuring her unchristian thoughts. He had been kindness itself in the face of her grief and had admitted her gracefully into his home. She determined she would not give him another reason to find fault with her.

"Mrs. Carroll, I apologize for presuming upon your staff without notice. I assure you, we will not trouble you at all."

"Nonsense, child! It is nothing; we of Darcy House are at your service." Mrs. Carroll had a kindhearted, motherly way about her that caused Elizabeth to smile and swallow quickly before tears could form again.

"Mrs. Carroll, please escort Miss Elizabeth to the Blue Room and Miss Lucas to the Rose Room, and see that a tea tray is sent. I would speak with you afterwards in my study then, ma'am."

"Yes, sir," the housekeeper affirmed. She then brushed a bit of the road dust off Mr. Darcy's jacket in such a familiar way that Elizabeth had to hide a smile when she saw his embarrassment. "And you, sir, must rest from your traveling too," she said sternly.

"Mrs. Carroll, am I to be forgotten?" Colonel Fitzwilliam was almost comically petulant.

Elizabeth covered her mouth with her hand as she spied the butler, Mr. Carroll, rolling his eyes discretely. She was amazed to see such ease with the staff. There was always a slight detachment with the servants at Longbourn. Surprisingly, she found this rather sweet.

"Of course not, Colonel! I shall have some of Cook's biscuits sent up to your room; will that do? We cannot neglect a member of His Majesty's army, can we?"

Colonel Fitzwilliam smiled charmingly. "Thank you, Mrs. Carroll." He shot a teasing glance at the butler. "You know just how to take care of me, ma'am. It is good you are married; I am afraid my heart would be in quite some danger otherwise!"

Elizabeth was truly diverted now. She watched the butler roll his eyes again, his wife blush sweetly while swatting the colonel's arm, and Mr. Darcy shake his head in amusement. This was obviously a familiar scene. Being at home added an ease to her host's features, fascinating Elizabeth until his gaze fell upon her. She quickly averted her eyes to her own shoes and chastised herself for momentarily forgetting her dislike of him and being distracted by his handsome features.

Just then, a commotion brought all their eyes to the landing above where a graceful, womanly figure stood. She paused briefly before calling out, "William!" and rushing down the stairs into Mr. Darcy's arms. Elizabeth's brows rose when she heard his deep chuckle as he wrapped his arms around his sister and assured her that he missed her too. Then Georgiana turned and greeted her cousin, though less exuberantly and in a more genteel fashion.

"Georgiana, may I introduce to you our guests, Miss Elizabeth Bennet and Miss Maria Lucas of Hertfordshire. They are to stay with us for a few days. Ladies — my sister, Miss Georgiana Darcy."

Georgiana, acknowledging their presence for the first time, immediately turned white then red in her embarrassment. Her modesty surfaced, and she looked to her brother for guidance. Mr. Darcy responded with a small smile that showed the tender regard he held for his sister. Suddenly, Elizabeth was caught by Georgiana's recent youthful animation, so like her deceased sister, even if displayed with more decorum than Lydia was wont to do. With unshed tears, Elizabeth curtseyed and managed a stifled greeting to Miss Darcy. The brief familial scene had been a lovely diversion, but the force of her loss hit her once more, bringing with it again the weight of the past few days.

Georgiana looked at her brother with creased brows, and he shook his head infinitesimally before turning to his housekeeper. "Mrs. Carroll."

Immediately Mrs. Carroll walked to Elizabeth and linked her arm in hers before leading her towards the stairs. "Come, dear. I'll take you to your rooms; you must be very tired from your journey." She motioned to a maid to help Miss Lucas, and together they ascended. Elizabeth found the housekeeper's touch a comfort. Certainly, she was not expecting Mr. Darcy's servants to be so familiar, but at that moment, the tender, soothing words served only to ease the ache in her heart.

MR. DARCY WATCHED ELIZABETH REACH the landing of the stairs and turn to go up the next flight. His eyes never left her person until she disappeared from sight. He was torn by the joy he felt at having her in his home and the sorrow he felt for her melancholy spirits. He turned to his sister, who was clearly befuddled by the situation with their sudden guests.

"Come, Georgie," he said as he led her to his study. Georgiana sat quietly on the settee while he walked along the perimeter of the large, book-filled room to his mahogany desk. He sat warily in the leather chair behind it and rubbed his eyes. Together they sat without speaking until there was a knock at the door and Mrs. Carroll appeared.

"You wished to speak to me, sir?"

"Yes." Darcy rubbed his face again before standing. "Mrs. Carroll, Georgiana, I wanted to speak to you both about our guests." He looked towards his housekeeper. "I trust they are comfortably being taken care of in their rooms?"

"Yes, sir. I have ordered baths—and tea and hot chocolate."

Darcy sighed heavily. "Thank you, Mrs. Carroll. Miss Bennet and Miss Lucas are acquaintances of mine from my stay with Mr. Bingley in the autumn. I encountered them again while I was at Rosings. They were visiting with Miss Lucas's sister and Miss Bennet's cousin, Lady Catherine's parson. Yesterday, Miss Bennet received news that her sister had suffered a terrible fall and passed away. She was not sixteen."

Georgiana's face froze in horror as she realized that the girl was her age.

"Oh, Brother! How awful for her! And I—" She covered her mouth as she thought of how her exuberant greeting for her brother might have looked insensitive to the solemn situation.

Darcy walked around his desk and kneeled next to his sister, taking her hand. "Do not worry, my dear. Miss Bennet is simply longing to be home. I will accompany her there on Monday."

Both ladies nodded their heads slowly. Mrs. Carroll stood straighter, determining to ensure that the two grieving ladies received every possible comfort. She excused herself to see to it personally. Darcy smiled appreciatively at her as she left.

"Georgiana, you must not assume… If Miss Bennet or Miss Lucas do not join us for dinner…you must not think it is you. They will likely not be inclined for company."

Georgiana nodded and threw her arms around her brother again. She was filled with gratitude for his presence in her life. They had suffered the loss of their parents, and he was all she had left. Darcy, feeling much the same, returned her hug with equal fervor.

ELIZABETH STOOD HUMBLY, TAKING IN her surroundings. The graceful room before her was fitted up in calming shades of blue. Its furniture was massive; the heavy pieces made from cherry wood complemented the soothing shades of the wallpaper and linens. They neither dwarfed the space nor felt intimidating. It was a comforting apartment, and she was grateful for the delicate strength she could draw from it. She barely had time to take in the beautifully appointed surroundings when she heard a knock from the dressing room door. She reached into her pocket for her handkerchief to dry her eyes and recognized the "FD" embroidered on the corner. Sighing heavily as she remembered its owner, she threw it on the bed and called for the maid to enter.

A small, slim girl about her age reverently walked into the room and gave a quick curtsey. "Ma'am has ordered ye a bath, miss, if ye like. I've been sent to help ye ready for it."

The thought of soaking in a warm bath after her travels—and indeed after all she had endured—sounded heavenly. The maid hummed as she took out Elizabeth's pins and began to brush her hair. Elizabeth shared one maid with all of her sisters. Having someone brush her hair was a luxurious comfort, and for a moment, she closed her eyes and believed she was back in her room with Jane.

"What is that tune you are humming?"

The maid stopped humming and bowed her head. "Pardon me, miss."

Elizabeth turned in her seat at the dressing table. "No, do not stop. It was nice. I simply wanted to know what it was called."

Nodding, the maid quietly replied, "I don't rightly know, miss. 'Tis a song my mum would sing to me."

Elizabeth turned around again, and the maid continued brushing. After a moment, she began humming again. A knock on the dressing room door signaled the bath was ready. Elizabeth sank gratefully into the warm water as the maid quietly bustled about the room, adding soothing scents to the water. When she began to wash her hair, Elizabeth quietly asked, "What is your name?"

The maid seemed to hesitate for a moment, worried that she had displeased the pretty miss. "My mum says Penelope, but I goes by Penny, miss."

Elizabeth smiled wanly. "My name is Elizabeth, but my sisters call me Lizzy." Then she closed her eyes and leaned back against the tub. Her tears disappeared into the bath water. When the maid finished washing Elizabeth's hair, she quietly retreated out the servants' door, leaving her alone with her depressed thoughts. She missed her family terribly and could not wait to be with them. She thought of the warm welcome the staff and Miss Georgiana made for Mr. Darcy. It was a side of him she had not seen before. Here, he was loved and respected. To have the approbation of his servants in such a familiar manner spoke of their regard towards the man, and she marveled at it. She hated to be indebted to him for his profound kindness. He had seen to her every comfort, and she could see that he understood her grief. He had lost both his parents after all. Thinking of Mr. Darcy in that light was humbling. She was suddenly grateful to be at his house instead of a lonely, cold inn.

Although she could not forgive him for his interference with Jane, she could at least repay him for his hospitality by attempting civility. *After all, if it were not for all this sorry business with Lydia, he would not tolerate my presence.* It was some consolation that her low esteem for him was equally met by his towards her. *Humph! At least in that we are equals!*

She wondered at Mr. Wickham's contrary description of Miss Darcy; he had said she was much like her brother — exceedingly proud. Elizabeth did not see that at all. She had been spirited when she greeted her brother and cousin, and she only became excruciatingly shy upon realizing the presence of guests. Elizabeth could easily see that. Despite her own grief, she felt sorry for the girl. Why would Mr. Wickham paint her as proud when it was obvious she was merely timid?

Elizabeth held her breath and sank below the water. She was determined to think no more of the Darcy family. Instead, she thought of Jane, somewhat alone at home without the comfort of her favorite sister. Oh, how she longed to be with her! Her lungs burned as she continued to hold her breath. Her loneliness felt oppressive. She squeezed her eyes tighter and felt relief; the blackness was soothing, inviting.

Suddenly, she felt herself pulled out of the tub. Gasping for breath, Elizabeth allowed Mrs. Carroll to wrap a warm robe around her.

"Come now, miss," she said tenderly.

Elizabeth could not hold back any longer in the face of such sympathy, and she fell against the woman in searing sobs. Mrs. Carroll assisted her into bed still wrapped in her robe where she curled up on her side facing away from the kind woman. Mrs. Carroll began to dry her hair.

"You do not have to do that, Mrs. Carroll," she murmured after several long, silent minutes. She was mortified to have been found so broken and weeping with little dignity in front of the household staff.

"Hush, child. Master says you are to be taken care of; I intend to see you are. Do not worry yourself now."

"He told you, did he not?" She ought to be upset that Mr. Darcy had not kept her troubles private but then could not find the strength. He was certainly solicitous of her comfort.

"Yes, dear. I am sorry for your loss." She was quiet for a moment and then added, "It will get better."

But Elizabeth could not believe the housekeeper's words. Just as she seemed to come to terms with her grief, she would feel it all over again. It was not as if she was so very close to Lydia. In fact, they had rarely understood each other. But she loved her. And she knew her family was suffering, and she could do nothing to ease it.

She closed her heavy eyes. Mrs. Carroll continued her ministrations, drying her hair with soothing strokes of the cloth. Before she knew it, Elizabeth drifted off into the first sleep since learning of Lydia's death.

Mrs. Carroll finished with Elizabeth's hair, stoked the fire and prepared to leave the room. From the doorway, she looked back at the girl. She knew her loss well, for her own dear sister was gone those twenty years. She puzzled at the behavior of her master towards this young miss. He was always a generous, kind master, especially towards those in need. But the happy glint in his eyes when he entered Darcy House with Miss Bennet on his arm had not gone unnoticed. His nervous energy was suspicious, too, in the way he looked for the young lady's approval of his home. She had also seen his satisfaction at Miss Bennet's admiration.

Mrs. Carroll smiled knowingly to herself as she exited the room, securing the door quietly behind her. *Perhaps, this is not some ordinary visitor,* she thought. Motioning to the footman stationed in that wing of the house, she ordered that Miss Bennet not be disturbed and that she was to be called personally if the lady needed anything. With that, she left to check on her other guest.

Chapter 3

When Elizabeth awoke the next morning, she felt much improved. After falling asleep the previous afternoon, she had only woken once to find Penny sitting nearby. Much of the previous evening was a blur, but she did recall that the maid had curtsied quickly and left through the dressing room door. A few minutes later, Mrs. Carroll came to her bedside and, with matronly persuasiveness, requested that she eat. Although she had little appetite, she consented to the oddly compelling woman, and a series of servants entered with tray after tray of food.

When the servants left, Elizabeth had exclaimed, "Mrs. Carroll, certainly you do not expect me to consume all of that?"

The housekeeper laughed and shook her head. "I should think not! I simply did not know your preferences." She paused then continued, "I was not sure whether Master Darcy would know them either."

Elizabeth's eyes narrowed unconsciously. "I do not believe Mr. Darcy would notice my preferences."

"Ah, well then, shall I help you dress?" *So this is how it stands then! I wonder what Miss Bennet would think if she knew that the majority of these dishes were chosen specifically for her by the master.* "Here you are, miss; now I must have you eat something."

Elizabeth smiled genuinely, eyeing the generous spread. "You have done well ma'am! Nearly everything here is a favorite of mine."

"Yes, well, how lucky for me," she returned with a wry smile.

Elizabeth had not been hungry before, but seeing all the delightful foods, her appetite returned; having gone a long day without anything more than tea, she was grateful for this bounty. Afterwards, she was very nearly forced back to bed by Mrs. Carroll. In the darkened room, with a full stomach and a heavy heart, Elizabeth soon fell easily back to sleep.

She woke the next day, stretched her limbs and smiled to herself at the thought of Mr. Darcy's housekeeper. The image of Mrs. Carroll managing him in the same motherly way as she had Elizabeth was almost comical. When she returned from the necessity closet, Mrs. Carroll was there fluffing her pillows. Elizabeth chuckled then stopped herself. She was surprised at the lightness she felt compared to the day before. A full night of rest did her body and soul much good—as did the insistent machinations of the lady before her.

"I could get used to this kind of treatment, Mrs. Carroll," she warned with mock gravity.

The woman turned and looked at the young woman. She looked rested—not quite happy but less sad. Satisfied with her progress, Mrs. Carroll said, "It is a pleasure, Miss Bennet. Shall you dress today?"

As Elizabeth opened her mouth to speak, Penny quietly entered with a breakfast tray, curtsied and left just as swiftly. Elizabeth nodded to the housekeeper and teased, "I shall be useless when I return home, Mrs. Carroll." She walked over to the tray and lifted up the lid of one of the dishes.

The warm rolls and eggs smelled heavenly, and she breathed deeply before sitting down. She watched Mrs. Carroll pour her some tea and accepted it gratefully. Elizabeth was wary of venturing from her room as she knew not how to look at Mr. Darcy after all he had done. Her determined dislike of the man was taking a decided step in the opposite direction.

As she picked up a sweet roll, she tried to steady her voice. "And has the rest of the household risen?"

Mrs. Carroll spoke over her shoulder as she set Elizabeth's toilette items in an orderly fashion on the dressing table. "Mr. and Miss Darcy are at Sunday services, and Miss Lucas keeps to her bed."

"Oh!" Elizabeth looked towards the windows as Mrs. Carroll pulled the drapes open to reveal the sun was already quite high in the sky. "I had not realized it was so late."

"Phooey!" The housekeeper waved her hand dismissively. "What would you like today?"

Elizabeth decided that a book might be a welcome distraction. Although still deeply grieved, she needed to be strong for her family the next day. It was time that she composed herself. Therefore, she finished her breakfast and dressed with the help of Mrs. Carroll; then she was left with Penny to pin up her hair.

"Penny can direct you to the library when you are ready."

"Thank you, Mrs. Carroll—for everything."

Mrs. Carroll patted Elizabeth's hand and smiled before she exited the bedchamber. When Elizabeth's hair was finished, she had Penny take her to Miss Lucas. Before entering to see Maria, Elizabeth asked, "Penny, after I check on Miss Lucas, where might I find the library?"

"'Tis simple; it is to the left off the main hall, miss."

The young girl curtseyed and bobbed her head before leaving Elizabeth at Maria's door. Elizabeth visited with Maria for a solemn hour as they reminisced about Lydia. It was difficult but good practice for condoling with her own family as she could see her young friend needed to talk. Elizabeth knew those at Longbourn might be in need of a listener. She could do that.

Upon reaching the main hall, Elizabeth looked around her and thought briefly on their reception the day before. The house was quiet except for the occasional housemaid. Elizabeth admired the elegant home as she ran her hand along the ornate cherrywood baluster. When she looked up, she saw the butler, Mr. Carroll.

"Can I be of service to you, Miss Bennet?"

"No, I thank you. I was just on my way to the library."

"Very good, miss. It is just around the corner there, first door on the left."

"Thank you." Elizabeth hurried around the corner, feeling conspicuous and not a little grateful that the master of the house was attending services. She was thankful not to worry about encountering him.

As she walked down the hall, she admired the handsome décor of Darcy House. Never had she seen such refinement. It was neither garish nor ostentatious as Rosings had been. The richness of the wood paneling was warm, and the furniture, though suited to the fortune of their proprietor, seemed to have real purpose rather than simply to draw attention to an awkward taste. Having her attention thus occupied, she missed the first door, the door she sought. Upon reaching the second door, and believing it the library, she opened it gingerly and looked inside.

She smiled widely at the richly appointed room and the long wall of bookcases filled with immaculately tended books. At one end of the room was a large mahogany desk with a couple of plush leather chairs. Opposite were large windows that overlooked the square. Elizabeth took a moment to admire the view and to breathe in the warm leather smell of books. *What a beautiful library.* She walked along the wall of books and ran her fingers across their bindings.

Wordsworth, Donne, Shakespeare—all my favorites. She smiled at the variety in the collection. There were many titles she had enjoyed and a few others that now caught her interest. She reluctantly acknowledged that the collection spoke to the excellent taste of their owner. After choosing a book, she walked towards the large desk. She laughed to herself at Mr. Darcy's choice of that particular piece of furniture. *Mr. Darcy and his love of order. Ha! Of course, he would have a desk in his library.* She walked to the large, leather chair and felt its softness.

With contentment she had not felt for days, she sank slowly into the chair. It had a lovely lemon and sandalwood smell mixed with the scent of the leather. As she tucked her legs under her dress, she was reminded of her favorite chair in her father's library. That thought comforted her as she settled in to read her book. Before she knew it, however, the soothing scents of the chair, combined with its warm embrace, lulled Elizabeth into a pleasant sleep.

Upon returning from Sunday services, Mr. Darcy leaned towards Georgiana and gave her a parting kiss on her cheek, whereupon she skipped up to the music room. Darcy turned to his butler. "Mr. Carroll, might you know how our guests fare this morning?"

Mr. Carroll nodded his head and gestured up the stairs. "Miss Lucas, I believe, still keeps to her chambers." He noticed Mr. Darcy was keen to hear his next words. "And Miss Bennet is in the library, sir."

"I am glad to hear it. Thank you. I shall be in my study if I am needed."

Upon reaching the library door, Mr. Darcy considered whether to greet Elizabeth. He wanted to — oh, how he wanted to! — but he was not certain whether he should intrude upon her solitude. He remembered how she had kept to her room the evening before and was still abed when he inquired after her that morning. He stood for a moment with his hand hovering over the doorknob. Finally, he sighed and dropped his hand. As much as he yearned to be near her, he thought it best to wait for her to find him — if she ever did.

With a low murmur, he continued to his study, all the while tugging restlessly at his cravat. He had managed to conquer it just as he reached his study door. He opened the door, pulling at his collar buttons and shrugging out of his tailcoat. He tossed the garments onto a nearby sofa as he passed it. Groaning and rubbing his face, he walked to the window overlooking the square.

It was wonderful to have Elizabeth in his home. She was so near and yet not near enough. He had barely a wink of sleep for the thought of her being so close. He wished again that he had managed somehow to come to an understanding with her before the news of her sister. Whenever he saw her tears or heard a report from Mrs. Carroll, his chest clenched, and he struggled not to go to her room immediately. His mind drifted to their embrace in the Hunsford parlor. He was sure she had been too overwhelmed to care about propriety, but it was a stolen pleasure he would not soon forget.

Elizabeth awoke with a start and froze upon seeing Mr. Darcy walk into the library. She realized soon enough, as she felt herself flush, that he did not know she was there. *Why else would he undress so casually?* She was paralyzed watching the muscles of his arms move under the thin lawn of his shirtsleeves as he ran his hands through his hair. Her eyes flitted to his discarded cravat and tailcoat only to be lured, dragged really, back to his form. She swallowed hard and attempted to recover her composure as she stood.

"I can do this!" he vowed aloud.

"What can you do, Mr. Darcy?" She smiled coyly, pleased with her ability to keep her voice level.

Mr. Darcy spun around on his heels with a shocked expression on his face. In the short moment it took for him to come to his senses and speak to her, she noticed two things: first, his eyes were blinking rapidly as he gazed over the entire length of her form standing behind the desk; and second, she could see his neck. Both observations wreaked havoc on her senses. She clasped her hands behind her back in an attempt to distract herself and to feign a calm she did not feel.

"Miss Bennet!"

As a slow smile spread across his face, she was struck again by his fine features. He stepped forward and bowed. "Good morning! I trust you are well... that is you look well... Are you well this morning?" he stammered.

Elizabeth bit her cheek as she lowered her head for her curtsey. "I am much improved today; I thank you."

They stood there in a pool of awkward silence, glancing about at anything but each other. *This is like the dance at Netherfield all over again*, Elizabeth thought. She was wild for a neutral topic to introduce, anything that would ease her rapidly beating heart—anything that might allow her traitorous eyes to study his face, indeed, and his bare neck with equanimity. But her wits failed her miserably.

She would have been surprised to know Mr. Darcy was struggling as well—struggling not to smile like a buffoon at the pretty picture she presented standing serenely behind *his* desk, in *his* study! *What is she doing here? Pull yourself together man. You look like a bloody fool—a mute fool.*

"Please"—gesturing to the chair—"will you not be seated, Miss Bennet?"

She nodded and began to resume her seat when she shot up. "Oh, this must be your seat, sir."

He forestalled her movement by holding out his hand. "No, please. Indeed you are charmingly placed." His lips twitched as he motioned to one of the seats in front of his desk. "Do you mind if I join you, Miss Bennet?"

Elizabeth swallowed the lump in her throat as she stiffly resumed her seat. She felt as if she were now sitting on his lap, realizing that it was his accustomed chair. "Of course, Mr. Darcy, do be seated."

Darcy took his seat. She was uncommonly affected by his casual attire and ease as he threw one leg over the other and laced his arms across his chest. She tried not to stare. *What is wrong with me?* She forced a polite smile.

"You have a lovely library here, sir."

Mr. Darcy's lips smirked and humor lit his eyes. "Thank you."

He is laughing at me! Her courage was bolstered, and she raised her chin. "I have looked through your vast collection and must commend your taste." She swallowed again as she saw the edge of his mouth turn up. *Hateful, mocking man! What amuses him so?*

"Indeed! Well, I am glad you approve. These are some of my favorites from my collection."

Mr. Darcy was using all his powers as a gentleman not to grin at her error and reach across his desk to kiss her soundly for it. She did indeed paint a charming picture sitting in *his* chair; he knew he would never sit in it again without recalling that moment. It occurred to him that he had never sat on the other side of his desk before! However, he did not mind the change. He found the view rather arresting.

"Your favorites? Are you saying, sir, that you have more books than this?" she asked incredulously, finally distracted from their awkward meeting.

Her eyes roamed the bookshelves in his study. He had never been in her father's study, though he must assume it did not contain such a collection as this.

"Indeed, I do. Many, many more." He was tempted to take pity on her and guide her to the real library but decided against it; he was enjoying seeing her at his desk more than he ought and was not ready to end their tête-à-tête.

He studied her as she continued to contemplate his collection. The silence grew deafening, and Elizabeth keenly felt the awkwardness return. She felt his dark eyes upon her in that glaring, disapproving way. Her gaze fell to the desk and noted before her two large tomes in rich, leather bindings. Curiosity colored her features suddenly, and before she knew what she was about, she reached for one. She almost opened it when Mr. Darcy's voice caused her to pause.

"Are you interested in estate management, Miss Bennet?"

There was that wry humor in his voice again. She arched her brows. "I have never studied it, Mr. Darcy. Is that what these books cover?"

His reply was a half step too slow as he held desperately to the last vestiges of his self-control. He watched her thin, delicate fingers spread across the binding of his estate books.

"Yes, I find those books essential to the smooth running of my estates," he finally said evasively.

Elizabeth nodded. His pleasant manners were making it difficult to remember how she disliked the man. And then there was the mesmerizing way his throat moved when he talked. Usually covered by his shirt and cravat, his neck was altogether distracting. Collecting herself, she looked down at the tome in her hands and thought, *Well, estate management ought to be boring enough to clear these insufferable thoughts.*

Mr. Darcy held his breath. He knew that, in the next moment, she would realize her mistake. He watched her gently open the cover of the book and look at the first page. She seemed frozen, staring blankly.

Pemberley House, Derbyshire, Estate Accounts, 1811. The words shouted out at her from the page, crashing violently through her mind. *No, no, no!* Slowly, her eyes stirred from the shouting page to discover a miniature of

Georgiana on the desk, next to an ink and pen stand. Her head shook in disbelief as she came to terms with where she was. *Not his library—his study!* She snatched her hand back from the book as if it were on fire. She looked at Mr. Darcy, who was sitting expressionless across from her. *At his desk,* she thought, *his chair!* She flung herself out of the chair and backed away. Her mouth opened, and her hand moved numbly to cover it.

Mr. Darcy sensed the time for him to take action was upon him; he could see her face contort in mortification. He moved cautiously to her.

"Do not be alarmed, Miss Bennet. You could not have known. For myself, it was a delightful misdirection on your part, one in which I was the benefactor."

Elizabeth finally found her voice. "Mr. Darcy, believe me, I would not have ventured into your private study had I known... I thought it was the library!"

He reached for her hand and tucked it into the crook of his arm as he led her across the room. "Shhh. I know you would not have, Miss Bennet, but I cannot find it in me to wish it otherwise."

"Thank you, sir," she murmured, still red with embarrassment and grateful he was not upset with her breach of his privacy.

"Shall I repay you for this pleasing interlude that you have bestowed upon me and guide you to the real library, Miss Bennet? I assure you, with my navigation you shall not get lost again."

She laughed with little humor but determined to redeem the remnants of her dignity. She needed her wit to dispel the thickness of the moment and distract her from the thinness of his shirtsleeve beneath her fingers. She did so by saying archly, "I should certainly hope so Mr. Darcy, or else we would be a sorry pair, indeed, to get lost in *your* house."

His eyes darkened, and she had to look away. *I should like to get lost with you in this house, Elizabeth.* "Sorry, indeed. Right this way, madam."

He walked her to a door at the opposite end of his study that opened directly to the library and ushered her in. He watched delightedly as her eyes grew big with childlike wonder as she scanned the cavernous space of his library. The room was easily three times the size of his study and filled with books on all four walls.

He leaned against the door frame, appreciating the sparkle in her eyes, a light he had not seen in several days, as she slowly turned in a circle taking in the scene. He looked at the walls around them, humbled that she should take such joy in something so commonplace to him. *Wait until I take you to Pemberley, Elizabeth.* He smiled at the scene she made and likened the silence of the moment to music when added to the enchanting smile spreading across her features.

He stepped forward when she stopped turning and walked further into the room. He watched as she neared a rug on the floor; its raised edge always caught people unawares. *I really should replace it*, he thought absently as he prepared to warn her. Before he uttered a word, she turned and walked the perimeter of the room, grazing the books with her fingers as she went.

Her voice wafted back to him, breaking the spell. "Mr. Darcy, this is the most beautiful room I have ever seen!" she said, laughing. Transfixed, his smile grew wider as she almost skipped down the remainder of the room, her hands still on the books beside her. When she got to the end of the room, she spun in a circle and laughed quietly.

Too beautiful. It pained him that the moment could not last forever. "Thank you, Miss Bennet, though I admit I almost wish you remained under the assumption that my study was the library."

Elizabeth stopped and looked at him quizzically. "Why ever for, sir — to keep such a secret as this?" She motioned to the walls around her.

He swallowed, unsure whether he should be so bold. "Because then you would forever be in my study with me rather than in here" — *When you come to live here* — "whenever you visit Darcy House."

Elizabeth stood stock-still. *When shall I ever come back to Darcy House?* she thought in bewilderment. She was taken aback by his forward pronouncement, and she could not make out his meaning — that he should presume she would return to this house! *He does not like me. I do not like him.* The proverbial sentiment began to sound stale in her mind, so she brushed it away, not wanting to think why.

In an attempt to dispel the sudden awkwardness, she teased, "Ahh, but sir, I am afraid that would not do, especially if you are in the habit of dressing so casually in your study."

Mr. Darcy's brows furrowed as he looked down at himself and realized for the first time since discovering Elizabeth in his study that he was in just his waistcoat and shirtsleeves. His head shot up, his eyes wide with shock to see her smirking face. "Forgive me, Miss Bennet. I had forgotten . . . what with the surprise of your presence in my study... Please excuse me."

He turned abruptly and returned to his study. She privately enjoyed witnessing the usually controlled and elegant Mr. Darcy in complete disarray when he recognized his blunder. She walked slowly into the center of the room and looked about again. She had truly never seen a more magnificent room in all her life. She thought, *To be mistress of such a home, to have access to all these treasures!* She stopped in her tracks. *Where did that come from?* Unfortunately for her composure, at that moment the master of the house returned, once again impeccably dressed with his tailcoat and cravat reassembled.

'Tis a pity; I think I preferred the other look. Elizabeth blushed scarlet and slapped her hand across her mouth as she realized too late from the surprised yet amused look on his face that she had voiced her thought aloud.

Mr. Darcy bowed to her. "I shall endeavor to remember that, Miss Bennet."

Mortified for the second time in a half hour's expanse, Elizabeth hastened towards the exit, wishing she did not have to walk past him to leave. "Excuse me, but I think I must be goin— Oomph!"

Darcy grinned. Elizabeth was in his arms, having tripped on the rug. *I shall never replace that rug,* he vowed.

Elizabeth's eyes squeezed shut, praying for a moment that it was all a terrible dream. *Sandalwood and lemon,* she thought. *He smells like sandalwood and lemon. Ohhh, it is not a dream.* She cringed as she attempted to step out of his embrace.

When she began to pull away from him, she found, much to her increasing embarrassment, that the chain of her garnet cross necklace was caught on one of the buttons of his tailcoat. With growing exasperation and need for escape, she tugged fiercely at the offending jewelry, the process made more graceless by the shortness of the chain.

"Miss Bennet, if you please. I rather like this jacket. Allow me." He chuckled when she obliged him, her hands clenched into fists at her side. He took his time as he unclasped the chain around her neck, relishing the feel of her soft skin. "There, you are free."

Elizabeth backed away immediately and sat heavily in the nearest chair, her mind reeling from the disastrous morning! *First, I stumble upon Mr. Darcy's study and then attach myself bodily to his person.* A more horrifying morning she could not imagine.

While Mr. Darcy worked to release her necklace chain from the button on his coat, he spied through his lashes a stunned Elizabeth. He worried suddenly for her mental strength after the past few days, combined with the extreme embarrassment he knew she must feel.

Her shoulders began to shake, and he thought she was sobbing. *Oh no! Anything but your tears, my love!* When he kneeled beside her, he heard a noise from her mouth and then another. He watched in amazement as she fell into hysterics, holding her arms across her middle with tears streaming down her face.

In her amusement, she turned to him, dazzling him with her unaffected beauty. "What a disaster today has been! I should have taken your suggestion from yesterday and never left my chambers!"

He was laughing now, too, as he joined her on the seat. Together they shared a few moments in companionable mirth. When their laughter stilled, Mr. Darcy handed Elizabeth his handkerchief to dry the tears.

She took it with a smile. "I am collecting quite a pile of these, Mr. Darcy."

He laughed once again. "There are plenty more should you have need of them."

Elizabeth knew at that moment that he was not just speaking of handkerchiefs but of his willingness to provide any comfort she might need. He leaned towards her and deftly secured the clasp on her necklace around her neck. She blushed and whispered a quiet "thank you."

"My pleasure," he whispered back.

It really was unfortunate, she thought, that he was capable of behaving so despicably with regard to Jane and Mr. Wickham as she began to comprehend that he was exactly the man who in disposition and talents would most suit her. She sobered, remembering his past offenses. However, she could not forget his kindness and thus spoke sincerely. "Thank you for allowing us to stay here and for accompanying us home tomorrow. It is far more than you need do."

"Again, my pleasure, Eliz— Miss Bennet."

Wishing his misdeeds were untrue, she said, "And thank you for the laugh. I think I needed it more than anything else."

"I cannot take credit for that, Miss Bennet. You provided all the folly."

"Indeed, it seems I did."

They sat companionably in silence before she stood and smoothed her skirts. "I believe I shall return to my rooms now, Mr. Darcy. It seems venturing out this morning has been rife with unparalleled dangers to my dignity. Before it is completely destroyed, I fear it is best I retire."

"Though I am sorry to hear about the demise of your dignity, I cannot repent the pleasures I experienced at its expense. Good day, Miss Bennet. It has been a pleasure." He took her hand and kissed it.

"Good day, Mr. Darcy." Making an obvious effort to step over the edge of the rug, she walked out of the room, leaving a smiling, contented master of the house.

Chapter 4

Mr. Darcy stood in front of the chair Elizabeth had occupied just a few hours before. A smile pulled at the edges of his mouth as he remembered the delightful picture she presented sitting there. Her small frame looked engulfed in the large, leather chair, and yet it seemed also to fit her just right. He lowered himself into the chair. It was cool, the heat from her body long gone. He looked at his estate books in the center of the desk where she left them, the book on top still open. Closing the book, he traced the outline of the binding just as her fingers had.

Shaking his head, he laughed at himself for behaving the besotted fool.

A knock at the door interrupted Darcy's pleasant ruminations, and he hoped that perhaps she had returned. Standing eagerly, he bid the visitor enter.

The door opened to his butler who stepped to the side to reveal another gentleman. "Mr. Bingley to see you, sir."

Mr. Darcy tried to hide his disappointment but was not quick enough before his friend caught his falling countenance. "I say, Darcy, thank you for the warm welcome," he said with good humor.

"You will excuse me, Bingley. I had not expected you. You are, of course, welcome."

"Yes I can see that!" Bingley laughed. "It seems you were anticipating someone vastly more appealing."

Mr. Darcy shifted uncomfortably before offering his guest a seat. "To what do I owe the pleasure of your company, Bingley?"

Bingley took the seat across from him, causing Darcy to smile at the memory of having occupied that seat himself earlier. He quickly pushed the thought away.

"Have you forgotten? We had plans today to go to White's."

"Of course!" He had forgotten. Before leaving for Kent, he had arranged to go to his club with Bingley the day after his return. That was today. "I suppose I did forget."

"That is not like you," Bingley observed. "How was Kent?"

Darcy was grateful for the change of topic and answered without forethought. "It was pleasant enough. My aunt was, as always, a bit tiresome. Her new parson—you remember we met in Hertfordshire—is lately married to one of our acquaintances from that neighborhood."

Darcy, having thought he was simply relaying news of no consequence, realized his mistake when he saw his friend's countenance fall. The two of them sat in an uncomfortable silence. Bingley had not been quite himself since leaving Netherfield. Until that moment, Darcy had refused to believe that Bingley might still feel the loss of a certain lady there. It occurred to him that perhaps he had done a great disservice to his friend.

Bingley swallowed his rush of emotion at the mention of Hertfordshire. It was a topic that Darcy had studiously avoided and had not brought up in some months. His last words finally registered in Bingley's mind: '*lately married... our acquaintance... Hertfordshire.*' Bingley looked up at his friend with anxious eyes.

"Is that so?" asked his friend with a barely discernible shake to his voice. "And this acquaintance from Hertfordshire would be...?"

Darcy heard the controlled panic and quickly spoke to relieve his friend. "Yes, I believe you will remember her as Miss Charlotte Lucas."

Bingley drew in a deep breath, collapsing into his chair. Recovering himself, he affected an air of languor he did not feel.

"I am glad to hear it. And did you find her well?"

Guilt crept into Darcy's heart as he saw the transformation in his friend at the reference to Hertfordshire and the clarification on the maiden identity of Mrs. Collins. He imagined what he might feel had he come to the parsonage and found Elizabeth married to the man. Suddenly, he felt sick at the mere thought of Elizabeth with such an odious man—any man! He felt all the weight of his presumptuous dealings. He needed to think in peace without the miserable countenance of his friend before him.

"I did find her well." He stood, indicating the end of their visit. "Bingley, I am sorry to have forgotten our engagement, but I am afraid I must beg off. I have some matters to attend." He knew it was boorish of him to cancel their plans, but Darcy could not bear the guilt as he looked at him. *What might be done to make amends?*

If his friend noticed his poor manners, he made no indication and simply rose from the chair blankly. As Darcy accompanied Bingley to the door, Colonel Fitzwilliam walked in. Darcy groaned to himself as he had forgotten that his cousin had stayed the night. He prayed he would not mention the current presence of Miss Bennet or Miss Lucas.

"Darcy! Oh, hullo, Bingley. I left early this morning to visit my mother and so have not seen Miss Bennet or Miss Lucas. How do they fare this morning?"

Darcy closed his eyes and clenched his teeth. *Damn you, Fitzwilliam!* He opened his eyes and glanced at Bingley who looked at him oddly before becoming red in the face.

"Uhh... yes, Miss Lucas I believe has not left her chambers but..." Darcy stammered and cleared his throat as he awkwardly continued, "Miss Bennet was down earlier to select a book from the library and looked much improved."

Bingley spoke through clenched teeth. "Miss Bennet is here?"

The colonel spoke before Darcy could. "Yes, she and Miss Maria Lucas were in Kent. We accompanied them to town. Sad business, the whole lot," he said, shaking his head.

Bingley turned to his friend. "Is that so?"

Darcy had never seen Bingley livid before. He quickly asserted, "Miss *Elizabeth* Bennet and Miss Lucas arrived with us last night and will be leaving tomorrow for Longbourn. I am to accompany them again..." His voice drifted off.

"I see."

Darcy groaned as he turned to his cousin and asked, "Richard, would you please excuse us? I find I have some business with Bingley."

The colonel, assessing the brewing tempers and determining he wanted no part of what was about to transpire, acquiesced.

As soon as the door closed, Bingley rounded on his friend, seething. "Pardon my impertinence, Darcy, but were you going to tell me that Miss Bennet was a guest in your home?"

Darcy ran his hands through his hair. "Bingley, will you not have a seat? I can explain."

"I thank you, no! What have you to explain, *friend*?" he spat. "I can see you wished to keep her visit a secret. I suppose you thought I ought not to see her; perhaps seeing *her* would make me think of Jane, right? Blast and damn you, Darcy! I think I can manage seeing the sister!"

Darcy declared, "It is not what you think," although he knew it was exactly as Bingley thought. The small falsehood tasted bitter in his mouth and reminded him of the other deception: he had hidden Miss Jane Bennet's presence in town from Bingley the past few months. He hated deceit of any kind. *Have I always been so conceited?* He groaned at his own hypocrisy.

Bingley laughed sardonically. "You think I am so weak as to need further protection? I have resigned myself to the fact that she does not love me. You can at least give me the honor of trusting me with her relations."

Darcy lost all composure then and bellowed, "For God's sake, Bingley! She is here because her sister died! She received the news in Kent, and I transported her here yesterday. She was barely well enough to leave her room this morning—so stricken with grief." He regretted his brashness immediately as Bingley stuttered incoherently and stumbled backwards onto the sofa. His face went white and he murmured, "Her sister died..."

Darcy was horrified when he realized Bingley's misunderstanding. Recovering himself, he quickly clarified. "Bingley! Miss Lydia was the sister who died." His voice was slow, deliberate and clear.

Bingley felt numb to a world where Jane Bennet did not exist and did not hear his friend. He loved her still, and he had subsisted these many months with the knowledge that, even though she did not return his love, at least she was alive and well. He could wish her well. But now she was gone. He felt broken all over again. How was he to live through it? *Oh, Jane!*

Darcy sat next to his friend and placed his hands on his shoulders, shaking him from his daze. Bingley had obviously not heard his last words. He shook him roughly until he made eye contact. "Bingley, it was Miss Lydia, *not* Miss Bennet!"

Slowly, recognition returned. Bingley whispered, "Not Jane." He sat up and turned to his friend, repeating louder, "Not Jane!" before falling back onto the seat. He rubbed his face vigorously and began in his relief to laugh, though it sounded closer to sobs.

Darcy, too, sat back on the sofa next to his friend. As Bingley's expressed relief buoyed his own spirits, Darcy's guilt intensified.

Coming to his senses, Bingley realized his joy and relief were inappropriate given that one sister had died. He was then acutely aware that *his* Jane and Miss Elizabeth must have surely been suffering from the loss of their sister. He turned to his friend and said, "I must pay my condolences to Miss Elizabeth!"

Darcy panicked. Until he could ascertain Miss Bennet's affections, he still did not think it was a good idea to press the acquaintance. Having seen his friend struggle through heartbreak, panic, anger and dread in one afternoon, he knew this was the right course. "I am afraid that is not possible, Bingley. She is resting now, and we depart tomorrow morning for Hertfordshire. Perhaps, you might write the Bennet family a note, and I will deliver it for you." It was the least he could allow under the circumstances.

Bingley eyed his friend. "I suppose you are right. Please convey my sincere condolences to Miss Elizabeth, and I will send a note later today for you to deliver to Longbourn."

"Certainly, Bingley."

The gentlemen stood, and Darcy walked his friend to the front door. When the door closed behind Bingley, Darcy sighed heavily. He thought that, if Jane did return Bingley's regard, he would have much to confess. He hoped he would be forgiven.

STILL A BIT MORTIFIED FROM the morning's events with Mr. Darcy, Elizabeth decided to have a tray brought to her sitting room for supper. She was not sure she could encounter him again with any degree of composure. She asked Mrs. Carroll whether Miss Lucas might wish to dine with her. Soon the girl was at her door, and another tray was brought in. Together they spoke in hushed tones as they dined alone.

After supper, Maria returned to her chambers, and Elizabeth found comfort in being alone with her thoughts. She indulged in a few tears as she stared blankly out the window. As the hour grew late, she decided to risk leaving her room. This time she knew where the library was. She prayed that she would not encounter Mr. Darcy there as she walked quietly through the corridors of the house.

The soft sounds of the piano drew her to the door of the music room instead.

The music was melodious and pleasing. Elizabeth quietly peeked inside the room to discover Miss Darcy playing the pianoforte to an audience of one. Mr. Darcy was sitting with his back to the door. Elizabeth was fascinated by the scene. It was the most beautiful rendering of that particular sonata she had ever heard. Miss Darcy was in every way as talented as portrayed. For a moment, Elizabeth leaned against the entryway and closed her eyes to listen.

When the final cords of the song no longer resonated in the air, Elizabeth opened her eyes and was surprised to feel her cheeks wet with tears. She wiped at them and looked into the room again. She froze as she watched Mr. Darcy stand, walk towards his sister, and place a kiss on her cheek. He whispered something tenderly into her ear and exited through a door behind the piano. The gesture was so sweet that Elizabeth had to wipe her eyes again. She was grateful that he had exited another way and had not come upon her. Another soothing piece of music began. She saw that Miss Darcy was in an almost trance-like state with the music. Elizabeth tiptoed into the room and took a seat at the back where she might not be noticed.

She had closed her eyes again and was enjoying the soothing melody when she realized the music had stopped; she heard a quiet gasp. Opening her eyes, she saw Miss Darcy covering her mouth and staring at her.

Elizabeth quickly stood and apologized for disturbing her performance. She bowed her head in embarrassment, and when Miss Darcy did not say anything, she chanced a look at the girl. It would appear Miss Darcy was nearly as embarrassed as she was!

Elizabeth walked closer to the instrument and said gently, "I hope you do not mind that I intruded upon you. The music was so beautiful, and I could not very well help myself." She smiled kindly at the girl.

Miss Darcy returned a weak smile and, without lifting her eyes off the keys, said, "You are perfectly welcome, Miss Bennet. I was merely surprised to see you."

Elizabeth moved a bit closer. "May I ask the name of that piece?"

Miss Darcy kept her eyes down still but answered, "It was Beethoven's N. 28, Miss Bennet."

Touched by Miss Darcy's obvious shyness and natural modesty, Elizabeth stepped yet closer. "It was very lovely. You play beautifully."

"Thank you." Miss Darcy demurred then raised her eyes for the first time towards Elizabeth.

Elizabeth walked around to the side of the piano and said, "May I see?"

When Miss Darcy nodded, Elizabeth surprised her by taking a seat next to her on the bench to look at the sheet music and then again when she began speaking of the music and asking after her favorite parts. Elizabeth was pleased to see that soon Miss Darcy seemed more at ease and their conversation came more readily. She liked Miss Darcy very much and ventured a brief thought for the complete mischaracterization that Mr. Wickham had described. *For someone who is so intimately acquainted with the family, he ought to have known her better,* she mused.

Miss Darcy gave Elizabeth a heartfelt smile and a look of compassion. "Miss Bennet, I am sorry to hear about your sister. It is difficult to lose a loved one."

Elizabeth could see what effort it took for Miss Darcy to put forth such a sentiment and reached for her hand to give it a little squeeze. "I appreciate your words, Miss Darcy. It has been very difficult."

She was astonished to hear the young lady continue. "If you would like to speak of her, I will listen."

When Elizabeth did not say anything for a moment, merely out of surprise and gratitude for the tender offer, Miss Darcy hastened to add, "Forgive me for my presumption. I know it can be helpful sometimes... When my father died..." Her voice broke off uneasily at her own lack of decorum. Apologizing again, she attempted to stand and leave the room.

Elizabeth reached for her hand and forestalled her quick departure. It still hurt too much to speak of Lydia, but she could see her silence had given Miss Darcy the impression that she had said the wrong thing. She was not sure what prompted her, but she said, "Please, Miss Darcy, if you are still willing, I think speaking of Lydia might be helpful."

As soon as the words were out, she regretted them. *What am I to say? I do not want to say anything.* But Miss Darcy sighed in relief as she resumed her seat at the piano. It made Elizabeth smile. Elizabeth found that she did not know where to begin; indeed, she did not want to begin at all.

"Why do you not tell me what Miss Lydia was like?"

What started as a stilted recital of her sister's likes and dislikes, general appearance and habits turned slowly into a tender narration of a few favorite memories. Before Elizabeth realized it, she was speaking freely of her sister and animatedly recalling past experiences. Miss Darcy sat silently, never speaking a word, though Elizabeth knew her to be listening attentively. One poignant memory of a kidnapped bonnet made Elizabeth laugh. She had even sent Lydia a ransom note for the article of clothing. Miss Darcy smiled kindly while she listened, allowing Elizabeth to relive the memory. Elizabeth was embarrassed when her laughter quickly turned to tears.

Miss Darcy pulled out her handkerchief and handed it to Elizabeth as she bravely extended an arm around her shoulder to rub her back. As Elizabeth's round of grief subsided, she looked up thankfully to Miss Darcy. Attempting a lightheartedness she did not really feel, she said, "You Darcys must have a vast number of handkerchiefs."

Miss Darcy's bemused expression made Elizabeth chuckle. "Thank you for listening, Miss Darcy. I believe it was helpful." Elizabeth was surprised that she did feel better. She smiled again at Miss Darcy.

"It was nothing, Miss Bennet."

"After all I have related to you this evening, I believe 'Miss Bennet' sounds a bit too severe. Would you mind very much using my Christian name?"

Miss Darcy smiled a wide, generous smile that struck Elizabeth as similar to the one her brother rarely displayed. It rendered her as beautiful as it did him handsome.

"I would like that, Elizabeth, if you will call me Georgiana."

"I am pleased to make your acquaintance, Georgiana."

Both girls giggled. Georgiana was gratified to have found a friend in the poised, lovely Miss Bennet. And Elizabeth was amazed to feel such a strong connection with Mr. Darcy's sister: the last girl in the world she ever could have expected to befriend! Georgiana, after much gentle persuasion, agreed to resume the Beethoven piece.

After it was finished, Georgiana asked, "Elizabeth, will you not play for me?"

"I am not sure that my performance would give you much pleasure, Georgiana. I play little and very poorly."

Georgiana looked astounded and exclaimed, "That cannot be true, for my brother has often said to me that you play so well."

Laughing and shaking her head, Elizabeth quipped, "Then he has perjured himself most abominably. I do not play well at all."

"I cannot believe that, Elizabeth, for my brother never exaggerates." When she saw that Elizabeth was still finding her assertions comical and responded only with a skeptically raised eyebrow, she went on to further state, "Elizabeth, he has told me many times that he has rarely heard anything that gave him more pleasure."

The serious tone in her voice made Elizabeth blush uncomfortably at the compliment—and its source. *Mr. Darcy could not have spoken so of me.* It was vain of her, she knew, but somehow hearing herself praised by Mr. Darcy seemed to make her think, perhaps, she did not hate him so very much after all. *I simply dislike him,* she thought resolutely. Almost as soon as she had decided that dislike was what she felt, her heart rudely reminded her brain of all the kindness he had bestowed on her those last days, of all the compassion and understanding, and most traitorously indeed, of the beguiling way he looked in his shirtsleeves *sans* cravat that morning. *Perhaps, I do not 'dislike' him per say,* she thought. *Perhaps, I am merely indifferent. That is it; I do not like or dislike the man.*

She was thankful, then, when her mind reasserted itself in the matter and reminded her of his actions towards Jane and Bingley and, of course, Mr. Wickham. She could remain angry with him for Jane's sake, but oddly enough, she began to wonder whether her beloved sister was correct in assuming there might be a misunderstanding about the latter. *No, I am safer with dislike for now.*

She was summoned from her reverie by Georgiana's insistence. "Will you then play for me, Elizabeth?"

Thankful for the distraction, Elizabeth readily agreed and played a simple piece she knew by heart. Georgiana was profuse with her praise, and Elizabeth laughed humbly at her friend's enthusiasm over her mediocre performance. They played a few duets together, and the hour grew quite late, so Elizabeth felt she should retire.

She thanked her new friend for the lovely evening and stood to go. A movement caught her eye at the door, and she turned, only to see the doorway empty.

"Good night, Georgiana. It has been a pleasure and a blessing to spend the evening with you."

"Indeed, Elizabeth, good night."

Elizabeth turned down the corridor towards her room just as a figure disappeared around another corner. She recognized his shape immediately.

Chapter 5

Impatient to be in the bosom of her family and on the road to Longbourn, Elizabeth waited for Miss Lucas as she descended the stairs of Darcy House. She woke earlier than necessary, determined to be off as soon as possible. Her heavy heart longed to be amongst loved ones, and she hurried her toilette, making her ready for departure a full half-hour before Miss Lucas and even Mr. Darcy. That gentleman had joined her in the vestibule just moments before, and apart from the briefest of civilities, she avoided his gaze. Elizabeth sighed with relief as Miss Lucas's arrival signaled their journey could begin at last.

After the embarrassing experience the day before, Elizabeth was grateful Mr. Darcy opted to ride on horseback alongside the carriage. It would have been a torment to spend the entire journey opposite his handsome face. Added to that was the confusing phenomenon of finding herself longing for his comforting embrace, a complication she need not consider as she neared her home.

After handing Maria into the carriage, Mr. Darcy turned to assist Elizabeth when his actions were interrupted at the sound of Georgiana calling from the entrance. The young lady rushed down the steps and pressed a letter into Elizabeth's gloved hand before giving her an enthusiastic hug.

Elizabeth gasped as Georgiana's sudden affection seemed to expel the air from her lungs. Chuckling, she returned the embrace and smiled warmly at her new friend even as her eyes began to glisten at the thoughtful gesture.

"I have been hurrying myself in the hope of not missing you. Will you do me the honor of reading that letter?"

"Of course." She pulled her friend aside and squeezed the young girl's hand. "I had hoped to have the chance to thank you again for your kindness last night. You are a dear girl."

With adoration, Georgiana said, "I hope that I can count you a friend, Elizabeth."

Elizabeth was touched and yet looked swiftly to her brother standing near the carriage. Should he not approve of her acquaintance with his sister, he need only tell her. When Darcy's eyes met hers, she turned back to his sister quickly. "Of course you may call me friend. I already consider you one."

After effusive good-byes, she could already see Mr. Darcy was displeased with her sudden familiarity with his sister, noting his stony countenance as he assisted her into the equipage.

She would be surprised to know he was far from feeling displeasure at seeing his sister and the woman he loved display such open affection for each other. The scene had thrown his emotions into such disarray that he was barely able to command his hand merely to assist Elizabeth into the carriage and not bring it to his lips to kiss it affectionately and repeatedly.

Earlier that morning he thought Elizabeth and Miss Lucas might prefer the privacy of the carriage and arranged to ride alongside on horseback. After that remarkable farewell, he decided a ride might be good for him as well. And so it was that, for the majority of the next three hours, Mr. Darcy attempted to regulate his feelings. He was beginning to think three months would be a terribly long time to wait to declare himself. His task was not an easy one given what he witnessed both that morning and the previous evening.

While he had enjoyed listening to his sister play one of his favorite pieces on the piano, he sensed Elizabeth. He dismissed the feeling, having spent much of the evening meditating on the very great pleasure which a pair of fine eyes in the face of a pretty woman — as his wife — could bestow, even imagining her next to him as Georgiana played. It was a happy fantasy and one that surprised him at how authentic it could feel. When Darcy opened his eyes and looked around the room as Georgiana neared the end of the song, to his utter enchantment, he spied Elizabeth in the doorway of the room with her eyes closed and her cheeks shiny. Hoping to avoid the embarrassment of having discovered her thus, he schemed that he would exit the room only to return again a few minutes later. Then it might appear as if he were simply rejoining his sister.

Whispering his praise to Georgiana and promising to return shortly after attending to some business, he purposely left the music room from another door. As he exited, his butler handed him Bingley's letter. How fortuitous that he had intercepted its delivery to the music room.

Now riding next to the carriage, Darcy swallowed and pulled at his neck cloth as he noticed that Elizabeth had removed her gloves and bonnet due to the unseasonably warm spring day. Her hair was in a thick plait that ran nearly the entire length of her back. He could see she was in the process of re-pinning the braid in a simple coiffure at the base of her neck. He found the vision too intoxicating, and he urged his mount forward a pace ahead of the carriage.

Forcing his thoughts down more gentlemanly avenues, he recalled returning to the music room the night before. By design, he appeared at the same door at which he first saw her, judging that if she had not yet entered the room he would encounter her there and invite her to join them. If she had entered, it could make his own entrance less abrupt. But as he reached the doorway, he had watched in stunned appeal as Elizabeth and his sister spoke comfortably with each other. In the end, he had not intruded on their interlude and had left to assure that his valet would be ready for their early departure the next morning.

Later that evening, when he was on his way to his study to retrieve a book, he had been surprised to hear music as he had assumed the ladies had retired long before. Expecting only Georgiana, perhaps still waiting for his return, he had walked right into the room. Discovering that neither lady had retired but were instead engaged in a rather silly duet, he backed to the edge of the doorway and left again soon after the piece was over. He made his way slowly to his study, thinking that the day could not have gone better and then hastily regretting his tactlessness as he remembered the loss of her sister.

It was with these dark thoughts of self-reproach that he spent the remainder of the journey to the last posting inn where they would change horses before reaching Longbourn. Those few days with Elizabeth had taught him a lesson, hard indeed at first, but most advantageous. He was beginning to learn his own insufficiencies. Worst of all, he was beginning to realize that Elizabeth may not be aware of his regard for her if the shock and surprise on her face at his boldness in the library the day before were any indication.

He was beginning to wonder whether he knew how to please a woman worthy of being pleased.

AFTER THEIR LAST STOP, ELIZABETH was startled when Darcy entered the carriage. She had thought he would continue on horseback for the last leg of their journey. She carefully observed his darkened brow and wondered at its cause. She rationalized he was ill tempered upon returning to a part of the country that he had so quickly abandoned for fashionable London not six months before. A familiar disapproval of him returned to her heart, aggravated by how little he esteemed her friends and neighbors. Having determined that Mr. Darcy might also disapprove of her friendship with his sister, Elizabeth decided to speak. Coldly, she stated, "I would speak to you about something, Mr. Darcy." Georgiana should not have to suffer the consequence of her brother's disapproval of her friendship with Elizabeth.

Mr. Darcy looked up from his hands; Elizabeth's frosty demeanor was not lost on him. Considering his own self-censuring thoughts, it seemed oddly deserved. He nodded for her to continue.

Observing Maria still asleep, Elizabeth thrust Georgiana's note at Mr. Darcy.

Puzzled, he reluctantly accepted the missive and raised his brows for explanation.

"Your sister made a request of me that I thought you ought to be aware of, sir."

"And will you not tell me the manner of this request, Miss Elizabeth?" Darcy held the letter in his hands, preferring not to read the private letter of his sister.

"If you will not read the letter yourself, then I will tell you. She requested permission to further our acquaintance through correspondence."

Mr. Darcy was well pleased with the prospect of his sister and Elizabeth furthering their friendship through letters. *I wish I had thought of that.* His joy was open until he realized her tone was anything but happy. His visage became grim.

Hiding his disappointment, he said, "Am I to assume the prospect is distasteful to you?"

Elizabeth narrowed her eyes in confusion. "On the contrary, sir. I like your sister very much, and I would be happy to further our friendship in this manner. However, I am conscious of the fact that you are her brother and guardian and therefore have the power to choose her acquaintances. I simply made you aware of her request, so that you could inform her of your disapproval in a manner best suited for her temperament. I am sure when you explain your reasons, she will not see my reluctance to accept as hurtful—"

"Miss Bennet"—Darcy's voice was grave as he interrupted her—"do you think that I would disapprove of her writing to you?"

"Indeed, I do, sir!" Elizabeth was skeptical of his performance and filled with exasperation as she exclaimed, "You made your opinion quite clear last autumn when you found the inhabitants of Hertfordshire, and indeed those in residence at Longbourn, to be quite below your notice. I should think you would not approve of your sister corresponding with someone from that district." Elizabeth paused to draw breath, attempting to remain in control of herself. "Do you deny it?"

Darcy remained silent as he considered his response. He knew now his behavior while in her neighborhood left much to be desired. He felt the beginnings of shame as he knew there was some truth to the sentiments she was attributing to him. *No wonder she detects nothing of my regard!*

"I will not deny that I felt…uncomfortable for much of my stay in Hertfordshire last autumn." He cleared his throat, trying to ignore the raised brow of his companion. "There were reasons for my reticence though."

"I suppose the behavior of my younger sisters and mother was your reason. Their behavior at the Netherfield ball, I admit, was lacking in propriety." Elizabeth was loath to admit that their behavior was ill mannered, but she knew it to be true and wished to show she was fair-minded.

"I will not comment on that, not after you have met and been subjected many times to the abominable manners of my aunt in Kent. Indeed, compared to me, you have no reason to be embarrassed by your relations."

Elizabeth turned to look out the window for a few minutes as she considered his response. His exoneration of her family derailed her righteous indignation. He had not denied the truth regarding her family's behavior nor his opinion of it but instead graciously redeemed them by his confession regarding his own relations.

With more charity, she acknowledged, "It seems we, neither of us, can acquit our relations."

Mr. Darcy offered a half smile. "Miss Elizabeth, regarding your writing to my sister, if you will allow me to explain to you something of our past, you will understand better my mood last September as well as my fervent *approval* of your acquaintance with her."

Elizabeth was startled by the evident conviction in his voice and discomposed when he leaned towards her as he spoke, his scent enveloping her senses in the process. She nodded, indicating he should continue.

He looked towards the sleeping passenger before dropping his voice yet lower and leaning in further. "Last summer, an old friend of some standing with my family, whose acquaintance with us I had reason to believe was at an end, intruded upon our lives in a most grievous way. A *young* lady I am very close to was hurt sadly by this acquaintance in a manner I am not capable of speaking about without much pain..." Darcy cleared his throat, glanced hastily towards Miss Lucas and then continued. "This young lady was not yet sixteen at the time."

Elizabeth paled, recognizing the pain evident in his voice as he spoke. She mouthed silently, "Georgiana?"

Darcy nodded solemnly. "I was not yet recovered completely from those events when I accompanied Bingley to your county last autumn. I am afraid that my reluctance to socialize may have given the wrong impression, and by the time I had realized it, I was not willing to change that assumption as it suited my mood quite well to be left alone. I only see now how it has damaged opportunities for myself that I would rather not have had stunted."

She was not too naïve to recognize that he was speaking of her and her opinion of him. And yet, she was still reeling from his earlier revelation and too overwhelmed with sympathy for his sister, her new friend, to truly give value to his statement.

"Sir, you said that you would not object to my correspondence with your sister?"

Unbelievably, Mr. Darcy leaned even closer to her. She found herself leaning forward as well to catch his whispered words.

"Miss Elizabeth, I have long thought you would be exactly the type of friend I would want for my sister. Indeed, I wish you might be more." He looked down as he said this and traced his finger lightly across the back of her hand, "I would be more than happy to have you correspond with my sister if it is your wish to do so."

Elizabeth gently moved her hands out from under the exquisite pressure of his fingers and simply nodded as she sat back and turned her face towards the window. *Certainly, he could not have meant what he said! Surely, he does not know what his words imply,* she thought repeatedly. She had much to think on. However, she could not consider his words now, not with her homecoming just minutes away. The news of her new friend's painful experience last year still pressed upon her as well. She sensed there was much to the story that he had not shared and that the event had affected them exceedingly.

It was fortunate that Elizabeth could not find the words to respond to his speech as Maria chose that moment to stir. Upon noticing their location, Maria declared with evident relief, "How glad I shall be to be home." Neither of the other two occupants said anything in response as they were both locked in their own thoughts until the carriage rolled to a stop.

Chapter 6

Mr. Darcy assisted Maria from the coach and was conscious of the surprised, questioning glances from her family when he took Elizabeth's hand. His eyes darted to her face as he felt her hand give his a gentle squeeze before he released it. *Did I just imagine that?* The idea was highly agreeable to him, but as her face betrayed nothing, he wondered whether it was his imagination after all.

He felt acutely out of place as he witnessed her family gather around the two ladies and embrace through murmured words and tears. He had thought to stay for a short visit, as was only polite, before venturing to the inn in Meryton to stay until the funeral. He had not spoken to Elizabeth about his intentions. He was fully aware that, although being perfectly fitting as he was an acquaintance of Miss Lydia, it might still be considered presumptuous on his part to assume more intimacy with the family. After beholding the raw emotion upon her reunion with her family, he wondered whether he ought to just take his leave quietly and go directly to the inn.

He had nearly decided to depart when Mr. Bennet approached him. The older man was stoic, but Darcy saw the strain in his eyes. He held his posture rigid in anticipation of the greeting.

"Mr. Darcy, please allow me to thank you for delivering my dear Lizzy back to us. We are greatly in your debt, sir."

Mr. Darcy bowed to the older man, uncomfortable that this was the first conversation he had ever shared with Elizabeth's father, despite living in the same neighborhood for nearly two months.

"Think nothing of it, sir. I could do no less under the circumstances."

Darcy discretely cleared his throat before he continued, "Please allow me to offer my sincere condolences for your loss, sir."

"Thank you, Mr. Darcy."

The two gentlemen stood quietly, watching the ladies cease their embraces and begin to enter the house. Mr. Darcy reached into his coat pocket to retrieve Bingley's missive and take his leave when the older gentleman surprised him by addressing him once more.

"Mr. Darcy, I recognize this request may cause some confusion on your part, but would you please join me in my study? I have a matter I wish to discuss with you."

"Of course, sir." Darcy was exceedingly thankful for the few extra moments to collect himself as he gave instructions to his coachman for acquiring accommodations in the village. It allowed him the opportunity to hide his nervousness regarding the nature of the business Mr. Bennet felt he had with him.

Upon entering the home, Darcy took in his surroundings as he divested his outerwear to a servant. The home was provincial, on a scale smaller then Netherfield, but with a comfortable, hospitable appeal. He could hear the ladies already in one of the parlors. He nodded when Mr. Bennet indicated he should follow him.

Closing the library door behind them, the older gentleman offered Mr. Darcy a drink. He could not politely refuse, so he accepted a finger of brandy, though with no intention of partaking.

Mr. Bennet finished his own glass before refilling it and sighing heavily. "One does not think to bury his own children in his lifetime." He seemed to be speaking more to himself, so Darcy did not respond. Although a distracted Mr. Bennet failed to offer him a seat, Darcy presumed it would not be offensive to the older gentleman if he simply took one anyway.

Finally, after what seemed like an interminable amount of time, Elizabeth's father began his address.

"Mr. Darcy, I recognize that my request to speak to you was unexpected. Firstly, please allow me to thank you again for bringing Elizabeth home. I cannot find your being in Kent at the time of her receiving the news of Lydia's...well...anyway, I found it fortuitous that you should be there to bring her home. I received an express from Mr. Collins at the request of his wife, informing me of her travel arrangements. I will not trouble you with his abundant words of consolation or the unctuous expression of advice regarding the proper outdoor activities for young ladies…"

Mr. Darcy shook his head. "Pardon me, sir. But do you mean to tell me that Mr. Collins had the gall to suggest that Lydia's accident was a result of improper outdoor comportment?"

Mr. Bennet snorted and raised his glass to the younger gentleman in confirmation. "I believe it was at the request of his patroness."

Darcy understood that Mr. Bennet was not attempting to shift the blame nor offend him by including his Aunt Catherine in his censure regarding the ill-mannered advice from the parson. Nevertheless, he felt compelled to apologize for the inconsiderate words of both his aunt and his aunt's parson.

"Forgive me, Mr. Bennet, for their unkind words at this time; I had not thought my aunt so unfeeling."

"Think nothing of it, sir. If this were not such a sad business, I would find great amusement in their combined solicitousness. However, I did not ask you to join me here to discuss your aunt or Mr. Collins. I wished to speak to you about Mr. Wickham."

Darcy stiffened at the name of the man who caused him profound pain his whole adult life and immediately changed his mind regarding the drink he held in his hand. He finished it nearly in one gulp before nodding for Mr. Bennet to continue, his face stern.

"I do not wish to delve into your private business, sir. Indeed, the whole story simply exhausts me. The entire neighborhood is aware of your past dealings with the man and his tale of 'mistreatment.'"

Darcy huffed. "Mistreatment, indeed!"

"I found his account rather fanciful myself, but that is neither here nor there. As I said, I care little for your past with the gentleman." At this point Mr. Bennet paused as his guest let out an oath regarding the appellation of 'gentleman' and smirked in amusement. "I wished to speak to you because, despite your falling out, I believe you may be the person best acquainted with Mr. Wickham."

"Unfortunately, I am well acquainted with the character of that man. I do not understand, though, what it is you wish to know if you are not asking for my history with him?"

"I will speak plainly with you then. I am not sure with what details regarding my daughter's death you are familiar, so I will relate to you all we know."

Mr. Darcy accepted another glass of brandy before Mr. Bennet continued.

"Mr. Wickham has been blessed with such happy manners as may insure his becoming a favorite of my daughters for some time now. He was out walking with my two youngest daughters and Mr. Denny when Lydia fell. What I find odd is that, upon returning her to Longbourn, Mr. Wickham seemed agitated and nervous, especially before the apothecary could come and administer a calming draught. Despite the turmoil of the moment, you see, I took notice of his behavior. At the time, I confess, I believed him to be acting the concerned suitor. It has been his later actions that have made me wonder whether perhaps his behavior was more suspicious."

"Suspicious, sir?" Mr. Darcy was beginning to feel unwell.

"He has not returned to our home once since the day of the accident— not when she was ill nor when the news of her death was generally known. Indeed, nobody has seen him in Meryton at all since the day of her fall. From what you know of the man, do you find this behavior odd?"

Darcy pondered this discourse. *Damn you, Wickham!* He was beginning to worry that his old friend was involved beyond what was known. Hoping to shield Mr. Bennet from further grief, Darcy decided that, until he could discover more of Wickham's motives and disappearance, he would not share his conjectures.

"I cannot say for certain, sir. I understand what you are hinting at, and although I know Wickham capable of the worst kind of deceit, selfishness and mercenary behaviors, I cannot confirm your suspicions. Please do not allow his disappearance to distress you further. It would not surprise me if he simply left to avoid an uncomfortable situation."

"Do you know where he might have gone? I should like to ask him some questions. The accident occurred around a bend in the path, therefore Mr. Denny and Kitty did not see it happen as they were a few paces behind." The frustration was evident in his voice.

Darcy stood and returned his glass to the sideboard. "Unfortunately, I do not. I will see whether I might learn more. For now, if you will forgive my presumption, you should forget about Wickham and focus more on the needs of your family at this sad time."

Mr. Bennet nodded solemnly. "I appreciate your understanding regarding the altogether untoward manner of this conference. Although we were formally introduced last autumn, I do not believe we have had the pleasure of any kind of conversation before this. I recognize my familiarity in addressing you is rather unprecedented."

Darcy gave a wry, half smile as his own thoughts echoed those sentiments.

"For whatever it is worth, I never believed Wickham's stories of maltreatment at your hands. Other than being a rather boring, disagreeable fellow, I did not think you so dishonorable that you would go against your father's wishes."

Darcy ignored the unflattering description of his person as not intentionally insulting and recognized Mr. Bennet's words acquitting him of his cruelty towards Mr. Wickham. He did begin, however, to understand the manner of falsehood Wickham had blandished about regarding their past, but he was grateful to hear nothing about his sister.

A moment or two passed in which both gentlemen were occupied with their own thoughts before Mr. Bennet recalled himself and suggested they join the ladies.

ELIZABETH HAD NOT REALIZED MR. Darcy was still at Longbourn until he entered the parlor with her father. She mulled over their delay until Jane stood and said, "Mr. Darcy, thank you for returning our sister to us. It was very kind of you to go to so much trouble." Her voice faltered only briefly, and Mr. Darcy saw the manifold effort it took for her to hide her feelings. Seeing her struggle for composure brought Elizabeth's words forcibly to his mind once again. *"Her emotions, though little displayed, are fervent and tender." How could I have thought her heart untouched?* He recognized they shared a character trait: neither of them performed to strangers by displaying their feelings openly. This new understanding only caused him greater discomfort.

"You need not thank me. As much as I respect your family, I thought only of Miss Elizabeth and yourself and how you might be of comfort to one another."

Mr. Darcy's kind words struck both ladies powerfully—one lady decidedly more than the other. Jane, unable to hide her feelings any longer, thanked him again profusely and turned her head into the shoulder of her sister. A tearful Elizabeth looked at him over her sister's shoulder as she tried to make sense of his tender, warm consolation. *That he could do this for me…?* It was something she could not understand. She stared deeply into his eyes, and she was greatly moved by the tenderness she saw there. *Who is this man?*

Their gaze held until the sounds of a carriage on the gravel caused Mr. Darcy to look out the window, expecting to see his own coach returning. He was momentarily relieved to see that it did not belong to him as he found himself suddenly wishing to stay longer. His relief was fleeting when, with alarm, he recognized the conveyance.

"Mr. Bingley?" Mrs. Bennet was all astonishment. Darcy's head turned abruptly towards the woman, having only just noticed her in the room. It surprised him that he had not seen or, more amazingly, *heard* the woman before then. Looking at her now, he could see that she was noticeably restrained from her customary behavior, and the transformation was vast. Even her abrupt notice of Mr. Bingley was comported in a genteel fashion, conveying surprise more than impropriety. She was sitting next to a fashionably dressed, younger lady. He wondered briefly at the lady's identity before he again remembered the situation and turned towards his friend with a face of obvious confusion.

Mr. Bingley studiously ignored the eyes of his friend as he walked directly to Mrs. Bennet and offered his sincere condolences before explaining to the assembled group at large that, as soon as he had heard about their tragic loss, he set out to offer his services and sympathy in person.

Mr. Darcy considered briefly whether he was imagining the scene before him as he watched Mrs. Bennet thank him politely and offer none of her usual matchmaking vocalizations that Mr. Bingley attend her eldest daughter. It was Bingley, himself, who ventured over to Miss Bennet to speak discretely to her.

Darcy turned towards his friend and said with veiled significance, "Bingley, I did not know you were planning on coming to Hertfordshire."

Bingley barely acknowledged his friend's words but responded with a terse, "Yes." Evidently wishing to say no more to Darcy, he again turned towards Miss Bennet to reaffirm his sympathies, effectively cutting him from further enquiry and soundly warning the gentleman that he was less than pleased.

A moment later, the fashionably dressed lady who had been seated by Mrs. Bennet, crossed the room on the arm of an equally well-appointed gentleman towards where Darcy sat next to Elizabeth.

He listened as the gentleman addressed her. "Elizabeth, would you do me the honor of introducing your friend?"

Elizabeth hid a small smile that Darcy did not comprehend as she turned and said, "Mr. Darcy, it is my pleasure to introduce to you my aunt and uncle, Mr. and Mrs. Edward Gardiner from Town. Aunt, Uncle, may I present Mr. Darcy of Pemberley in Derbyshire."

Darcy stood to bow properly over Mrs. Gardiner's hand and to shake Mr. Gardiner's. He was able to conceal his surprise that these were relations of hers and realized once again another aspect of his ill-judged perception.

"It is a pleasure, though I would wish it were under more happy circumstances, Mr. Darcy."

"Thank you, Mrs. Gardiner. I would wish that as well."

"Thank you for bringing Lizzy home to us. When we left town with Jane a few days ago we did not anticipate such a sad conclusion to Lydia's injuries nor anticipate the need for Lizzy to come so quickly."

Darcy was about to respond when he heard Bingley distinctly clear his throat. He speculated that Bingley must have just learned that Jane was in town not many days before. He groaned to himself as he returned his attention back to Mrs. Gardiner to address her once again.

"I would hope that your niece would know she could ask such a trifling thing of a friend." Darcy glanced at Elizabeth and detected her polite smile.

WHEN THE TIME CAME FOR the gentlemen to take their leave, Mr. Darcy was apprehensive about Bingley's mood, even musing that, if he were not such a great, tall fellow in comparison to Bingley, he might worry for his person. He was even a little perturbed by Bingley's abrupt presence in Hertfordshire. When they exited the house, Darcy saw that Bingley had sent his carriage on to Netherfield, leaving his mount. Although irritated, Darcy invited Bingley to ride with him in his carriage as he wished to speak to him.

"That suits me just fine, Darcy, as I have a few matters to discuss with you as well." Bingley threw the reins back to the groom, instructing him to attach his mount to the back of Darcy's carriage. Then he climbed in after Darcy and sat opposite him. He sat glaring at his friend for a few minutes, neither man wishing to speak within view of Longbourn.

"Well?" they both said at once.

Darcy clenched his jaw before speaking again. "What are you doing here, Bingley?"

Bingley allowed one irritated huff before replying. "What am I doing here? Offering my sympathies to a family of my acquaintance, of course."

"I thought we had agreed that I would convey your sentiments for you." He pulled out the note he had not delivered after seeing Bingley enter the home and tossed it back to his friend.

"Do you really think I could leave the Bennets with a few polite words of comfort when I could have attended them myself? *You* may think them below you; however, *I* respect them and wish to be of whatever service I can."

Darcy ignored the cutting remark. "I do not think this is a good idea, Bingley."

"In what way, my friend? Do you mean it is not a good idea that I venture to show my concern for a friend's loss in person, or is it the identity of that friend that you find distasteful?"

Darcy rubbed his eyes. "Bingley, I was wrong about the Bennets. And although I am beginning to believe that I might have been wrong about Miss Bennet's affection for you as well, I had not wished to better inform you until I was certain. That is why I am not sure this is such a good idea. I do not want you to get hurt."

"A fine speech, Darcy. Do you not think that I am old enough to make that decision for myself?" Bingley huffed again as he quoted him in a frightfully good impression. "'I might have been wrong about Miss Bennet's affection for you...'" In disbelief, he continued, "Do you really think you might have been wrong in that respect?"

Bingley was struggling against the hope building in his chest. Although still wishing to protect his friend, Darcy realized that Bingley was right; it was not his decision to make. "I now believe that Miss Bennet may have returned your feelings, Bingley."

Bingley sat against the back of the carriage in wide-eyed astonishment before a slow smile began to curl his lips.

"Do you know what this means, Darcy? My angel did love me!"

"Yes, and for your sake, I hope she still does."

Bingley's brow furrowed. "Do you suspect her feelings to have changed?"

Darcy expelled a deep breath before deciding to reveal all. "Bingley, I have something to say to you, and I hope after I confess it that you will still count me your friend, though I understand completely if you should not."

Darcy then began to relate to his astounded friend his actions last autumn in separating Miss Bennet from him. Darcy admitted that, although he thought he was doing his friend a service in his appraisal of Miss Bennet's feelings, he had purposely concealed her being in town all winter. He confessed that Miss Elizabeth had hinted that Miss Bennet had suffered another loss this year, leading him to believe that that loss was Bingley. He ended with his growing suspicion that Miss Bennet did not seem to show her feelings openly in company as his only excuse for his gross misjudgment of her character.

He watched Bingley during the entirety of his admission, as he changed from astonishment to renewed ire. Darcy ended his speech and looked out the window to avoid Bingley's last reaction, that of displeasure and despair.

He barely heard his friend whisper, "What must she think of me?" before leaning forward and allowing his head to fall into his hands.

"I am sincerely sorry for my interference, Bingley. Would that I could undo my actions..." For more reasons than his friend knew, he wished he had not acted in such an insolent manner. If he had not, perhaps Elizabeth would not have taken such an affront to him.

Bingley looked up at his friend when he detected the sincere tone of his apology. He could not be angry with him anymore, accepting that Darcy, in his own way, had tried to protect him. Likewise, he could not hold himself blameless. He had allowed himself to be persuaded. He had allowed himself to trust the words of his sisters and friend over the truth and love he saw in Jane's eyes last autumn. If he was to be completely honest, he knew that he allowed himself to be persuaded because he had been afraid. He had often 'been in love,' as his friend might say, but never had he been so completely bowled over by a woman.

After having experienced the torment of the past couple of months without her, not to mention the regret, he knew what must be done. He could not live without her; the only thing that made it possible to leave her before was the thought that she did not return his feelings. Now with renewed hope building in his breast, perhaps he could convince her to love again; he was determined to stay in Hertfordshire as long as necessary.

"I forgive you, Darcy." Seeing that they were arriving at the inn, he continued, "You must stay with me at Netherfield."

Solicitous of his friend's charitable forgiveness, Darcy said, "I thank you for your kind offer, but I think I will be less in the way as you open up Netherfield if I stay at the inn."

Sheepishly Bingley owned, "I may have sent an express to Mrs. Nicholls at Netherfield immediately after leaving you yesterday afternoon, instructing her to open up the house and to prepare for my arrival today."

Darcy could not help but laugh at his friend's impulsiveness. "You wasted little time at all, sir. Tell me, when did you decide to return? Were you even out of my house?"

Bingley beamed. "I confess I had no intentions of letting you go to Hertfordshire without me, though I knew it unlikely I could convince you to allow me. Hence I left town not long after you this morning, ensuring you would not hear of my plans."

"I see." Darcy was amused and a little proud of his friend's decision. He had acted in the determined manner of a gentleman.

"So will you not stay with me? You do plan to stay through the funeral services in a few days, do you not?"

"I had planned on attending the funeral. I also have a few things I want to look into here in Meryton." Darcy's jaw flexed as he thought about Wickham and wondered at his duplicity once again.

"Splendid! Inform your man to pack your trunks again and return with them to Netherfield. Then we shall be off."

Darcy's lips twitched at his friend's enthusiastic command and did as he was told. Before long, they were on the familiar road to Netherfield Park.

Chapter 7

lizabeth slid a hand down over the ebony fabric of her mourning dress. Until they had time to order mourning clothes, each lady in the house had dyed one of her day dresses black. Her eyes rose to meet Jane's in the mirror in front of them as her sister tied the black ribbon around her bodice. They shared a sad smile with each other in the mirror before changing places, so Elizabeth could button Jane's dress.

She could see Jane had been relieved to have her home, but she knew that Bingley's return added to her strain. Over the last few days, he had come to call nearly every day. Sometimes he came with his friend, sometimes alone. She knew Jane was carrying not only the burden of grief but also a further tumult of emotions over his return. She was more guarded around him as well. Elizabeth was sure that Jane's solemnity was more pronounced during his visits — not wishing to attribute too much meaning into his return if he were simply to leave again. She hated that her sister had reason to guard her heart so closely.

The presence of his friend was distracting enough for Elizabeth. She could not make out why he remained in the area. He had safely delivered her home; his duty was fulfilled. Yet he remained. When he called with Mr. Bingley, although his manners remained solicitous of her comfort and he was indeed polite to everyone else, his expression was unreadable, and like before, she was still the recipient of his stern looks. *Why does he still look for flaws in me?*

"Well, Lizzy" — Jane looked at her sister in the mirror — "I cannot say that I am sorry that women are not allowed to attend funerals. It shall be difficult enough for our mother to host the visitors for the mourning hours."

Elizabeth could not agree. She wished she could be there, albeit she knew that seeing Lydia's casket lowered into the ground—to rest there forevermore—would be an image she could never forget.

"Mother is much changed, is she not, Jane?"

Jane sighed as she sat on their shared bed. "I cannot fathom it. She is so subdued and brought low. I never thought that I would say it, but I would wish to see her more intemperate self than this sad demeanor. It makes me worry for the state of her suffering."

Elizabeth nodded thoughtfully as she sat next to her sister and took her hand. "Aye, sister. Both of our parents seem to be very much shaken." She thought of her father's altered behavior as well. He was spending more time with her mother. Lydia's death had prompted one thing that nothing else had previously been able to do: her parents were united in their sentiments.

"I hope with time and careful care, we shall see them through this," Jane murmured sadly.

Elizabeth nodded her head. "I am glad our aunt and uncle are here."

"Yes, they have been invaluable."

Both sisters elapsed into their private reverie about poor Lydia, then to their parents and back again.

Elizabeth sighed and patted her sister's leg. "Come, Jane. It is time to join the ladies in the parlor."

Standing, she took her sister's hand, and they both drew a bracing breath. Then they left their chambers to sit with the other mourning ladies, awaiting the gentlemen's return from the funeral.

Upon entering the parlor, Darcy could not help scanning the room, his gaze finally resting upon Elizabeth. She had her head lowered and her hand intertwined with her mother's. He could not find her anything but beautiful despite her black attire. Indeed, he was sure there was not a color in which she would not look lovely. Her usual, bright and cheery disposition was more suited to a pretty yellow or mint hue. However, her warm, rich brown tresses, combined with the dark fabric only made her ivory skin seem to glow in contrast.

He patted the item in his breast pocket to assure its presence. He hoped she would find comfort in his offering as a similar gift had done for him in years past when he buried his own father and mother.

Walking over to the ladies, he bowed and murmured the customary phrases for such an occasion. He noticed Elizabeth was, indeed, surprised to see him there. He had thought his continued presence in the neighborhood for the last few days would have indicated his intentions to attend the services.

Uncomfortable with the occasion, as well as the growing number of visitors come to pay their respects, Darcy excused himself to the edge of the room where he might find some solitude.

He spoke to nobody and soon became lost in his thoughts. The funeral had been much like any other he had attended—solemn, quiet and formal. The men had gathered around the grave and listened to the parson utter the final prayers on behalf of the deceased, and then the box was lowered into the ground. Mr. Bennet had tossed the first shovel of earth onto the casket, followed by Mr. Gardiner as was the custom. All the men took turns before the job was handed over to the grave diggers. The walk back to Longbourn was silent.

Mr. Denny had attended along with several of the officers from the regiment. They were to depart for the summer to Brighton in a fortnight. Seeing the officers had brought Darcy's mind to the situation with Wickham. He was frustrated that he had not gained any valuable information. The tradesmen and shopkeepers of Meryton had been willing—he assumed because of his wealth and the hope of remuneration—to divulge that Wickham held debts with them.

But Mr. Denny and some of the other officers were tight-lipped with Darcy and would not offer any clues as to Wickham's whereabouts. He had questioned them, but they were less forthcoming due to their prejudice against him because of Wickham's tales. Darcy cared little for their approbation but was irritated that he could not learn anything useful. However, a few disgruntled officers admitted Wickham had debts of honor in the regiment, and like the tradesmen in Meryton, they feared they had been cheated, and they wanted retribution.

The only valuable information came from Colonel Forster who had said that Wickham asked and had been granted a short, three-week leave of absence from his commission to attend his sister's wedding. He was told to report to Brighton at the end of his leave. To his dismay at this intelligence, Darcy knew Mr. Bennet's suspicions garnered real merit. Firstly, the leave was requested a few days prior to Miss Lydia's accident and granted the next day. Secondly, he knew Wickham had no sister.

Tormented in his private fury, Darcy was unaware he was being observed. Elizabeth watched his scowl grow and deepen the longer he was in the room. It was too much for her to think that he could harbor such uncharitable thoughts regarding present company while her family grieved. It was for this purpose she charged herself with the task of taking Mr. Darcy his tea.

Darcy was deep in his taciturn speculations when Elizabeth approached with a cup for him. He looked about and realized that, in his distraction, the refreshments had been served, and all the ladies of the house were bringing cups to their guests. He was gratified that Elizabeth had chosen to bring his herself. He had to press his lips together in an effort not to smile.

"Mr. Darcy, your tea."

He could not help the slight upturn of his lips when he heard her voice while accepting the cup and saucer as he looked down at her. "Thank you, Miss Elizabeth."

He raised the cup to his lips to hide the smile that pulled at his mouth as he recognized she intended to stay near him instead of returning to the tea table to prepare another's cup. His eyebrows rose only slightly upon tasting the tea and confirming it was prepared exactly as he liked it—with honey instead of sugar.

Was she indicating a preference for him by her continued presence and by her special preparation of his tea? *She must be!* And the idea thrilled him. Since leaving Hunsford, he had begun to suspect that she was indifferent, or worse, disinclined towards him. It had been a startling revelation that she might not have been expecting, with delighted anticipation, his addresses! This show of preference with the tea was highly gratifying—hopeful even—indicating a possible alteration of her affections.

He acknowledged her coy attentions to him by lowering his voice so others nearby would not hear. "Thank you for preparing my tea as I like it, Miss Elizabeth."

The turn of her countenance from the blank expression she held to the steely set of her jaw was not what he had anticipated. He was slightly embarrassed and indeed disappointed when he heard her next words.

"Surely, you know that it is the responsibility of a lady to notice the preferences of her guests, Mr. Darcy." Her tone was harsher perhaps than she intended, but Elizabeth was confused by his benign talk of tea. Moreover, she was still fuming at him for behaving so disagreeably on such a somber day.

She breathed slowly, realizing that if she allowed her anger to be noticed then she would not be able to manage what she wished. It still did not seem possible to her that Mr. Darcy might feel anything more than indifference for her despite some of his rather unsettling statements since leaving Hunsford. And he disdained her family and neighbors. It only pricked at her already volatile emotions that he could mock her accomplishments as a lady. Of course she knew how to entertain her guests!

Darcy hid his disappointment well and chastised himself for presuming more. Still he commiserated with her as she was obviously distressed. "Of course, Miss Elizabeth, you are the consummate hostess. It is especially meritorious in light of the difficult situation."

Elizabeth closed her eyes for a few seconds as her heightened emotions abated. His gentle tone had diffused some of her frustration, and she remembered his benevolent and gracious manner towards her since encountering her at Hunsford. Her motive for bringing his tea had not changed; however, she believed she was under better regulation to go through with it now.

Darcy watched her eyes open and look up at him. He saw a fire in them and wondered at its source. Whatever it was, it made her eyes brilliant with passion. A single curl drew his attention. It was nearly escaping a pin at her temple and he yearned to pull it out and wrap it around his finger. He was so consumed in this delicious thought that he had not heard a word she had whispered.

When he had looked away from her eyes, she had gained the courage to whisper, "Mr. Darcy, I need to speak to you in private. If you are willing, I can meet you in the garden." When he did not respond, she looked directly at him. His familiar stern gaze was boring into her. Elizabeth seethed as Mr. Darcy deliberated over her improper request with what looked like marked disapproval.

When his eyes returned to hers she cleared her throat and hissed through clenched teeth, "I can see that you disapprove, but I thought that under the unique circumstance… But indeed, it seems I am wrong. Forgive me for my presumption."

Mr. Darcy furrowed his brow. *What is she talking about? We were just discussing the tea.* He hastened to correct her. "No, indeed, Miss Elizabeth, the tea is perfectly acceptable." He said in confusion, and as if to prove it to her, he emptied his cup.

Fatigued by this frustrating man, Elizabeth dispassionately looked about the room, feigning the impression to anyone observing them, that their conversation was inconsequential. She spoke to him as her eyes wandered, "Mr. Darcy, sir, you do not need to dissemble. A simple decline of my request would have sufficed. I will trouble you no more then."

Darcy was alarmed with her insolence and confused at her words. *Request?* He hastened to stop her and placed a gentle hand on her arm, just above her elbow. A current shot through his fingers at the feel of her bare arm. He swallowed.

Elizabeth tried to remain unaffected by the feel of his hand and the sensations running up and down her spine as a result of his touch. As she turned back to him, he released her.

He bent his head to her. "Request? Forgive me, but I heard no request. I confess I was woolgathering a moment ago..." Darcy could see the skepticism in her face, and so he continued in a lower voice, "Please, Miss Elizabeth, will you not ask again? I assure you I have never been able to deny you anything you ventured to ask if it was in my power to grant it."

Despite her frustration with him, or perhaps adding to it, she blushed. She absently rubbed the spot on her arm where he had touched her to dispel the heat still there. After a moment, she braved a look at him and nodded. "Sir, I wished to speak to you about a matter that cannot be discussed amongst so many people. I had asked if you might be willing to meet me in the garden for a moment."

Breathe, man. Do not read too much into it. He was desperate to appear unaffected even as his heart raced. *The garden. Alone with Elizabeth.* Darcy took a deep breath as he returned her look. It was but a moment before he replied, "It will be as you wish, Miss Elizabeth. I will leave first if you like."

With much relief, she said, "There is a set of stone benches behind the arbor on the north side of the house. I will meet you."

He discretely nodded his head. Modulating her voice to a conversational level she said, "Mr. Darcy, sir, if you are finished with your tea, I will take that from you now."

Mr. Darcy gave her a half smile. "I thank you, Miss Elizabeth." He handed her his saucer, careful not to brush his fingers with hers in the process.

She curtsied before she left him to deposit his cup. He spent a few minutes walking nonchalantly around the room, stopping briefly even to speak with Sir William Lucas. When he decided that enough time had elapsed, he excused himself from his present company and casually made his way towards the parlor door and out to the gardens.

HE HAD VERY LITTLE TROUBLE finding the benches she had indicated, and he was pleased to note that, although it was a small distance from the house, a large hedge obstructed its view of any windows. It was only after he had arrived at the bench and assessed its relative privacy that he allowed himself to imagine all kinds of contexts under which Elizabeth might plan this assignation. He knew from the tone of her voice during their exchange that she was not altogether pleased with him. Despite this knowledge, he could not help himself from dreaming more than believing that she wanted to acknowledge her awareness of his feelings and declare hers for him.

That happy fantasy was interrupted by the lady's arrival a moment later.

Elizabeth was beginning to doubt the wisdom of such a venture. She knew it was one thing to encounter a gentleman by accident somewhere as happened in his study or the many walks at Rosings Park. It was quite another thing to seek out a private meeting. It was not like her to dispense with propriety, and if it were not for the importance of the topic she wished to discuss, she never would have considered it. Out of nervousness and habit, Elizabeth offered a curtsy, after which Darcy bowed.

Mr. Darcy cleared his throat when she began pacing. *Well, this breech of propriety can only be added to the many things of which he disapproves about me.* She sighed. The previous kindness he showed her at his home and his polite behavior throughout the week had made her want to esteem him. It bothered her that he might think ill of her, especially if caused by her own actions. And it bothered her that she was bothered by it! *Add this to my book of sins, Mr. Darcy*, she thought sadly.

"Miss Elizabeth, you wished to speak to me?"

"Yes, Mr. Darcy. Please, do be seated."

He nodded and sat on one of the benches when she sat on the other. "Mr. Darcy, I recognize the impropriety of asking you to meet me here. No, please, do not argue. It is not proper for us to be here, and we both know it."

Darcy wished to object again but instead nodded his head.

"If I thought we might have an opportunity to talk privately within company, then I certainly would have done so. As it is, with all the guests, I could not foresee such a possibility, and I did not know when you intended to return to Town. Indeed, I did not think you would have remained thus far."

Darcy looked at her with an unreadable expression. "I wished to show my support for you... err... your family, by attending the funeral. I return to Town tomorrow."

Elizabeth took in a deep breath. "Thank you for attending, though I do not know why you persist in putting yourself amongst company so disagreeable to you."

Mr. Darcy closed his eyes and groaned. He pinched the bridge of his nose and said in exasperation, "I do not find the company disagreeable."

Elizabeth mistook that his frustration was for her speaking so bluntly, not with himself for understanding her accusation. As such, she spoke heatedly. "Oh, please, sir. Despite your kind manners this week, we both know how you find the society in Hertfordshire. We are already breaking with propriety by meeting together; you might as well drop the pretense and speak plainly. I certainly intend to."

"Miss Elizabeth"—Darcy waited until she met his eyes—"I...I do not find the company here disagreeable...anymore. Is that plain enough for you?"

Elizabeth looked away, embarrassed to see that he spoke the truth and sorry to have made him admit his fault, especially considering the remorse clearly written on his face.

"But you stood just moments ago with a scowl on your face as you looked around at my friends and family," she said softly without understanding the discord between his recent words and earlier behavior in the parlor.

"Did it not occur to you that a funeral would not bring to mind memories most unpleasant to me?" he answered with some truth. It had reminded him of his parents' funerals; also, he did not want to discuss Wickham with her at that moment.

Elizabeth moaned. "Oh, Mr. Darcy, forgive me; I did not think." She slipped to the edge of her bench and closer to where he sat on his and, without forethought, took his hand in hers. "I am sorry, indeed, truly repentant for presuming..."

As much as Darcy relished his sudden possession of her hand and as much as he wished to keep it, he suspected she seized his hand without any intention of intimacy. Knowing she would be mortified as soon as she became aware of her actions, he gently removed her hand from his and placed it tenderly back on her lap.

"Please, Miss Elizabeth. It is of no consequence." After a few awkward moments, he continued. "Is my behavior the matter you wished to discuss with me?"

"No...well, yes...but not entirely." She stood up, causing him to stand. She could not prevent a small smile at his gentlemanly manners and sat down again so he could sit. She tried to formulate her thoughts. For her sister's sake, she had risked his censure, breaching all propriety to discuss what he knew of Mr. Bingley's intentions. She wanted to be prepared to care for Jane in the eventuality that he may abandon her again.

She looked at him and saw that he was standing again. "Mr. Darcy, please. You may sit, sir."

He smirked a little. "I cannot if you will not, Miss Elizabeth."

It was then she realized that she had stood again and had resumed pacing. She laughed a little and acknowledged he was correct. She returned to her seat, chuckling with him as he took his once again.

She bit her bottom lip as she hesitated. "Mr. Darcy, could you please tell me what Mr. Bingley is about in returning to the neighborhood?"

Darcy raised his eyebrows in surprise. "What Mr. Bingley is about? He has come to show his support to your family."

Elizabeth shook her head. "I know that, sir. What I mean is, do you know whether he plans to stay in the neighborhood afterwards?"

Darcy was unsure what he ought to reveal about his friend's private business regarding his affection for Miss Bennet and therefore was silent.

"Forgive me if I speak plainly of matters unpleasant to you, but I know about your actions last autumn regarding my sister and Mr. Bingley, and I wished to know whether I will have to guard her heart again from your friend."

There was steel in her voice again that stabbed at his heart. *How will she ever love me when I have hurt her so already?* "Miss Elizabeth..."

"No, Mr. Darcy, you may not deflect my question." Impassioned, she continued. "For the sake of giving relief to my sister's feelings, I care not how much I may be wounding yours. Is your friend a danger to my sister?" Although Elizabeth was filled with righteous anger, she finally felt relieved to be confronting him.

Darcy sighed. "I will tell you what I know if you will allow me to apologize for my hurtful and presumptuous actions last autumn."

That he wished to apologize and appeared to regret his actions rendered her speechless, and she could only manage a weak nod.

"I was wrong, I admit, in acting to separate your sister from my friend. At the time, I did not think she had feelings for him, and I did not wish him to connect himself with someone who did not love him. I thought that your mother—forgive me, I can see that it pains you to hear it—had mercenary motives in the match. That I also wished to remove myself from Hertfordshire, I shall not deny, but not for the reasons you may assume."

"What other reason could you have?" She was all curiosity. In the past few days, she found herself intrigued about the man who seemed so changed from before. *I am only curious,* she tried to convince herself.

His steady gaze caused her heart to beat rapidly, and a sensation she could not explain reminded her of similar feelings during her stay at his house in Town.

When he finally spoke, his voice was hoarse. "Can you not guess, Elizabeth?"

She barely managed to look away at his use of her Christian name. She felt discomfited and still could not fathom what he could mean by it. Recognizing her discomfort, he cleared his throat to address her with some composure.

"As for Bingley, I believe your sister is quite safe from him unless of course she would not welcome his attentions now...after both our actions last autumn."

Elizabeth looked up. "I will not betray my sister's confidence, but I believe that, if he is in earnest, then he will be most welcome in the neighborhood."

"He is devoted to his mission, I assure you, and has only the most honorable of intentions," he said with significance.

Elizabeth's smile was bright and beautiful. It was the biggest smile he had seen grace her features since before Lydia's death. His heart beat wildly, and he was lost to her all over again.

"I am pleased to hear it, sir." Her smile faded. "He will have to wait, you know, as we are all in mourning. It would not be proper."

"I know." *More than you know, Elizabeth!*

Then a thought came to her, and she looked at him in horror. "Please do not think that any of us, that Jane, could ever forgo propriety in lieu of a chance for happiness!"

Darcy shook his head. "I could not think any of you capable of that. It would not be honorable for any man to be so indelicate as to ask that of a lady in mourning." He paused, feeling his own conviction behind the words. "Bingley will wait until it is proper and pay his addresses to your sister then — if it pleases her."

Elizabeth was relieved at his assurances. Oddly, she felt more relieved that he did not think so ill of her family. Loath to interrupt their companionable silence, he was conscious they might be missed. "Have I satisfied you, Miss Elizabeth?"

Elizabeth startled but turned to him with a half smile. "Not quite; I have one more thing." She reached below the bench to retrieve a small package wrapped in paper she had hidden earlier in the day. She handed it to him.

At the look of confusion on his face, she teased, "Oh do not be so missish, Mr. Darcy. I am only returning what is yours."

He chuckled softly. "I shall not swoon at your gift, I assure you..." *my dear.* "I was only... confused. And now a bit curious." He raised an eyebrow at her as he turned the package in his hands.

She covered her mouth to hide her mirth. "Then you may as well open it." *Who knew Mr. Darcy had a sense of humor?*

As he pulled at the hemp cords of the packaging, the paper fell away to reveal four freshly laundered and starched handkerchiefs with his initials on them and one with his sister's. He laughed at the sight.

"I told you I was accumulating quite a pile. For the sake of our housekeeper and our linen closet, I found it imperative that I return them right away, sir."

Darcy smiled at the mischief in her eyes. "Thank you, Miss Elizabeth. I would not want to overwhelm your linen closet." He found himself slightly disappointed that she had not kept even one. He had wanted to give her so much more than a few scraps of cloth — say, perhaps all his worldly goods.

"You can understand why I could not return them in front of my family."

"I do." He paused, considering for a moment. "I have a gift for you, too, Miss Elizabeth."

She looked up sharply and shook her head even as he placed a small book in her hands. It was a beautifully bound journal, obviously expensive and of the highest quality. She brushed her fingers along the spine and then flipped through the blank pages.

"It is so you can write down your feelings regarding your sister. My aunt gave me a mourning book like this when my parents passed, and I found it quite therapeutic."

A tear escaped her eye as she pushed the book back into his hands. "I cannot accept it, Mr. Darcy. You know it is not proper for me to accept a gift from you. We are not... We do not have an understanding." She swallowed, attempting to quench the emotions swelling in her breast for such a thoughtful gift.

With disappointment, he replied, "You gave me a gift; can I not give you one?"

"Mr. Darcy..." She drew a steadying breath. "I cannot. I am sorry. I thank you for your consideration, but indeed, you know it would not be proper for me to accept it."

He knew she would not be persuaded but endeavored once more. "I thought we had decided to discard propriety for this meeting."

His voice was kind, but she shook her head. He acquiesced and returned the book to his breast pocket.

She smiled with unshed tears. "And I must also thank you for your hospitality earlier this week as well." She paused with indecision and then straightened her shoulders as she continued. "I am lucky to count you among my friends, sir." She was surprised how much she meant it too. Despite the way he frequently infuriated her, she did indeed count him a friend. As she tended so frequently to misinterpret his actions, she wondered whether her previous assumptions about him had been in error.

What joy her words brought him! He could kiss her for them. When she said such things with such sweetness to her tone, he wondered how he had ever thought she was anticipating his proposal back in Kent. He could see the difference now.

"Anyone admitted to the privilege of your presence, Miss Elizabeth, could not wish to be called less," he said tenderly. Seeing her wet eyes, he instinctively reached in his pocket for his handkerchief and held it out to her.

She began to laugh as she shook her head, pushing his hand away. Elizabeth pulled out her own from her pocket, waving it, and cried with mock indignation, "That will not do, Mr. Darcy! How am I ever to keep out of your debt if you persist in throwing your linens at my person?"

Darcy threw his head back and laughed openly at her words. When he looked at her again, he wanted nothing more than to kiss her sweet, impertinent lips. "You found me out, madam. I wished to enslave you through twelve inch-square pieces of cloth."

"It will not work, sir. I am keen to your plan now." She laughed, feeling the natural release of her weary emotions. "I think we had better go in. We will be missed soon."

"Of course. I will go first." He stood, bowed to her and walked around the side of the hedge towards the house.

She left a few minutes later after a quiet cry, reflecting on the tumult of her mind regarding Lydia's death, Mr. Bingley's intentions and, of course, Mr. Darcy's most solicitous almost-gift. Upon entering the parlor, she noted that everyone seemed occupied and her absence had gone unnoticed. She found Mr. Darcy standing in a corner speaking to one of her neighbors. Their eyes met briefly before she joined Jane and Mr. Bingley on the other side of the room.

When the gentlemen from Netherfield took their leave, she could not meet his eyes when he murmured his good-byes and bowed over her hand. With regret, she watched his broad shoulders as he left Longbourn and wondered when she might see or hear from him again.

It was then, with no small amount of surprise and curiosity that, upon returning from her afternoon walk two days later, she spied Mr. Hill receive a large package from a delivery boy, addressed from Mr. Darcy to her father.

Chapter 8

Elizabeth could not constrain her eyes from wandering repeatedly to the package on the side table of her father's library. Unopened, it glared at her, and she was wild to know its contents. She brought a cup of tea to her mouth in another attempt to distract herself. She sat with her father in the early morning hours as she had often done over the years. They would share a cup of tea, read and visit together. This morning was no different—except for that blasted box!

Her eyes betrayed her again as they moved to the side table. *What could it be?* It was driving her mad that her father had not yet opened the package, and it had been delivered more than a week earlier! It was none of her business; she was sure. And she kept telling herself that. Once again dragging her eyes away from the package, she sighed into her cup.

Asking her father about it would surely arouse his suspicion. Frustrated and unable to do anything but think and look at the package, she politely excused herself from her father's company and left for a walk.

The expectation of the pleasant exercise her walk would bring was essential if she were to accomplish the job she had set for herself that day. Indeed, she needed the exercise to help her forget about that box, too—*and the man who sent it!* if she was being honest with herself. He had intruded upon her thoughts far more than was comfortable. It was all because of that mysterious package; she was sure of it. *Why else would my mind choose to think on him?*

But that day she could not dwell on Mr. Darcy and his peculiar behaviors or his disturbing words while he was lately with her. It had been almost a fortnight since her sister's death, and she had determined that she alone would take up the task of cleaning Lydia's room. Nobody had ventured into that room since the day of the accident as Lydia had remained in the sickroom on the main floor. It was too painful for any of her sisters, and especially her mother, to consider entering the room. Elizabeth knew it to be a taxing undertaking, considering her own emotional stores; nevertheless, it must be done.

She set out at a brisk pace, hoping to bring peace to her mind and strength to her heart for the grim day ahead.

HE WAS DISGUSTED WITH HIS surroundings—and even more so with the lack of punctuality of the person whom he was to meet—and Darcy's mood was taking a decided turn south. He dared not touch the soiled tablecloth covering the wobbly table in front of him. He had barely summoned the courage to order a glass of brandy from the grubby looking bar maid; her suggestive propositions and unwashed odors were making him ill. *Where is that blasted man?*

After eyeing the glass suspiciously and reminding himself why he must bear these mortifications, he tentatively took a sip of his drink. Upon his arrival at Netherfield, Darcy had sent his valet to gather information about Wickham or his whereabouts from within the exclusive, secretive world of the servant class. Some hard-earned confidences led Darcy to this fetid part of London.

It was not much of a surprise, considering there was no other place Darcy thought the man could be so well hidden. His man also discovered that the scoundrel, instead of simply disappearing to London, had slipped away with bit of muslin; the now-missing servant girl from the Meryton Inn had boasted that Wickham wished to marry her. Darcy knew better.

He took out his watch and looked at the time again. Regretting the action almost immediately, he groaned and then returned it to his pocket. He felt several eyes upon him, eyeing the gold chain of his watch fob still visible. He should have known better than to draw attention to himself in such a way. His valet had taken careful measures to dress him in less than auspicious clothing in an attempt not to stand out. He sat up, straightened his shoulders to show their broad, sheer strength, and glowered at a few patrons, intimating they should reconsider their interest in him.

Darcy was yet hopeful that Wickham had merely left Hertfordshire to avoid his mounting debts. There had been no evidence Wickham was responsible for Miss Lydia's death. It was only a sinking feeling in his gut that told him otherwise. He wanted to believe his instincts were wrong because, if his former friend had a hand in Lydia's death, Darcy's own hopes for a particular member of that family would surely be lost. For who would connect themselves with someone who could have prevented her sister's death when he had the chance simply by revealing the character of the man responsible?

He was investigating for Elizabeth's family as much as he was for his own hope of happiness. His valet's work had taken him thus far to meet a man who claimed to know Wickham's whereabouts. Darcy was there instead of his man because the informant was at least clever enough to recognize when he might get some blunt for his knowledge, refusing to meet with anyone other than the gentleman wishing for the information. At least his identity was concealed. The last thing Darcy needed was for Wickham to hear that he was looking for him. That would only cause Wickham to burrow himself deeper.

Darcy wished he were back at Netherfield attending to Elizabeth. He wondered what she thought of the package he sent to her father. He hoped she would not be angry with him for his presumption. Bingley had invited him to come back at any time; however, he could not go back until he had some answers.

But first he had to find the reprobate.

ELIZABETH STOOD BEFORE HER SISTER'S door, her hand on the knob. She turned the handle and entered, bracing herself for the feelings she was sure would overwhelm her. Standing just inside the room and looking around at the treasures and baubles belonging to her late sister, instead of being overwhelmed with grief, her heart filled with longing. Lydia's disorganized writing desk was covered with ribbons, bonnets and adornments. Her closet hung open where she must have pulled out her spencer with haste when she left for her walk.

Elizabeth walked around the room and lightly touched the furniture where dust had begun to accumulate. The dust saddened Elizabeth with the knowledge of how much the world kept turning even when one was gone. She indulged in a few tears before she set about her work. She had to get through this.

A noise at the door alerted Elizabeth to Mr. Hill bringing in a trunk to consign her sister's treasures. Sue, an upstairs maid, was behind him, waiting to help Elizabeth with the task. She was grateful for the presence of the maid as it helped her to hold her emotions in check.

Together they placed items in the trunk as they worked through the room. Elizabeth came to a table next to the bed. There was a small traveling box meant for perfumes and hairbrushes sitting underneath the table. She sat down on the floor to open it, intending to save anything her sisters might find as comforting keepsakes. Inside, she found a small book, bound with worn leather and strapped to a pencil.

Leaning back against the side of the bed, Elizabeth carefully removed the strap with the pencil and opened the book. Her heart tore and her hands stilled as she realized she held Lydia's journal — her dear sister's heart's desires, thoughts and wishes. Tears rolled down Elizabeth's cheeks as she closed the book and hugged it to her chest. *Oh, poor, poor Lydia.*

When her tears had ceased, Elizabeth stood to place the journal in Lydia's trunk. She kissed it tenderly before placing it under some lace, out of sight. She excused the maid and closed the door to her sister's room after she left. She had managed all she could that day.

WHEN DARCY FINALLY REACHED HIS home, he wished for nothing but a hot bath — maybe two. Never before had he been as discomfited by a place as he had been in the pub that day. After waiting nearly an hour past the scheduled time, he yielded. Peeved, he stood and tossed a few coins on the table. It was then that a man who had been sitting at the table next to him the whole time stood and addressed him by the alias surname he had given himself.

Darcy wanted to rage at the scamp for having been there the whole time, toying with him in such an establishment! Instead, he clenched his jaw and acknowledged the man.

"I had'a see for m'self how much a bloke like y'self wanted to know whats I know, see?" he explained. Darcy grumbled to himself but got to his purpose directly.

The man vouched for the whereabouts of Wickham as of four days earlier. He said they had been in the same gaming hell when Wickham had won a hefty purse. The grungy fellow sitting before Darcy had secreted himself in a corner of the room and then followed Wickham to a boarding house not far away. This Perkins, as he referred to himself—and which Darcy was sure was not *his* real name either—made his living skulking about, detecting the interests of others. He had been hired by another gentleman to follow Wickham; it would seem Wickham owed the other gentleman a significant amount of money, and Perkins was to inform him when Wickham's luck turned, so he might reclaim his debts.

Somehow, Perkins heard that another gentleman by the name of Burns—in truth, Darcy—was looking for Wickham too. That was how Darcy's man had been introduced to the informant who wanted to meet this fellow Burns. And so Darcy went as 'Burns' to meet this carrier regarding Wickham.

He pulled at his cravat and wrestled out of his now filthy greatcoat as he shook his head in aggravation. Perkins had found himself ten pounds richer for the information he had gathered. He demanded that price from Darcy before he would reveal what he knew. It was not a wasted investment in Darcy's mind if it brought him another step closer to Wickham. But it left him needing to investigate an even seedier part of town. Even more disagreeable to Darcy, it required 'Burns' to have to employ Perkins again as a go-between. And worse, it meant Darcy would have to go back to the same disgusting haunt to meet with his new employee.

The only comfort Darcy gained from the day's events was that there was still no further evidence that Wickham had anything to do with Lydia's death other than his presence. Nothing was unusual in Wickham's behavior since coming to town; he gambled as was his wont. Unfortunately, Perkins did not have any information as to the whereabouts of the servant girl from the Meryton Inn. It would seem Wickham had dispensed with her, and alas, she was now lost in London's underworld, not likely to be found again.

Blast and hell, Wickham! Must you always cause me trouble? He sank into his hot bath and hoped it would serve to wash his mind clean of all this business. As had become his habit since he had met Elizabeth, whenever Darcy was troubled, he turned his thoughts to her. It was the only thing that would truly bring him peace. He pictured her back home in Hertfordshire, gaining strength in the face of her loss.

ELIZABETH CROSSED THE LAST 'T' of her name with her quill and blew on it to dry the ink. While she blew, she looked towards that irksome package on the side table again. Her father still had not opened it, and it had been another week. *Two weeks and he has not opened it! What could he be about?* The whole situation was maddening. She had turned to her only hope for information: Miss Darcy.

They had written each other only once since Elizabeth left London with Georgiana's brother. Georgiana empathized with coping with the loss while Elizabeth had shared an accounting of the mourning hours—minus, of course, her meeting with Mr. Darcy—and the emotional trial of sorting out Lydia's room. She did not know whether it was the profound connection she felt after having wept with her at the piano in London or Georgiana's sincere kindness and understanding expressed in her letters that caused Elizabeth to be so open after such a short acquaintance. Whatever the reason, Elizabeth was growing to love Georgiana dearly.

In the letter she had just signed, she hinted to the package her father received. She contrived to sound as if she knew its contents, thus possibly encouraging her friend to expand upon what she knew of it. *For surely, she knows what her brother sent.* Elizabeth certainly hoped it was so.

She stood and placed her letter on the mail tray. Looking to where her father sat near the hearth, she thought about his changed demeanor. He had been a bit more subdued than usual, and oddly enough, so had her mother. She had heard them talking late at night and felt encouraged by the behavior. She had never seen her parents interact so frequently. It caused her to wonder whether there was some good to have come out of the whole, sad affair. For the first time in her nearly one and twenty years, Elizabeth had parents who acted as if they cared about one another.

Her eyes, for probably the tenth time, returned to the box. Looking down at the letter on the tray, she thought how Miss Darcy's reply could not come for another week at least, and a week was certainly a long time to wait for information that her friend might not even know.

"Papa?"

Mr. Bennet looked up from his book—a book so engrossing that he had ceased to turn the pages the past twenty minutes she noted—and smiled, though it did not quite reach his eyes.

Keeping her back to him so he would not see the flush of her cheeks, Elizabeth walked over to the beguiling package and inquired offhandedly, "What can Mr. Darcy have sent you, Papa?"

"I know not. To be honest, I had forgotten it was there, poppet."

Forgotten? The package was as prominent in the room as an elephant! She swallowed and continued with feigned indifference. "Do you not think you ought to find out?"

"I suppose so, though I cannot think what the man would wish to send me."

Elizabeth smiled and took the package in her hands, wondering at its weight. Her curiosity was at near boiling point as she paced herself to step leisurely to her father.

He shrugged when she reached him and waved her off. For a moment, she panicked and thought he might not wish to open it at all. To her relief he merely said, "You open it, dear. I find I care little to know its contents."

Elizabeth then sat, perhaps too eagerly, in the chair next to him. Her nervous fingers tried to open the strings of the package. She was finally able to fumble her way through the cords and to pull apart the paper. When it fell away, her breath caught in her throat and her heart began to beat faster. Her eyes could not believe what she saw, and not because they were now filled with new tears.

Mr. Bennet looked at his favorite daughter and saw the raw emotion on her face. Looking at her lap and the opened package, he nervously asked, "What did he send, dear?"

Elizabeth had to swallow a few times to gain control as she whispered, "He has sent us each a mourning book to remember Lydia by." She caressed the six spines of the gilded bindings. At the bottom a letter was enclosed. It had a strong, clear script in a decidedly masculine hand that read, *"Mr. Bennet."*

She handed the letter to her father and said weakly, "He included a letter."

While her father read the letter, Elizabeth returned her attention to the books. She could not find even a modicum of aversion at his presumptuous skirting of propriety to find a way to give her his gift. She felt only gratitude. She opened the first book and saw her father's name across the bookplate in the same elegant handwriting. She turned to the next book, seeing it labeled for her mother. She flipped through each book, labeled for every one of her sisters. Eagerly she searched for her own and found it to be the last. She gingerly opened the binding to the bookplate. Seeing her name in his elegant handwriting caused her heart to flip. She ran her finger across it: *"Miss Elizabeth Bennet."* Her eyes filled with tears again, but this time, she felt more than she could understand.

"That was kind of him," her father said as he removed his glasses from his face to pinch the bridge of his nose and lowered the letter to his lap.

Elizabeth drew in a shallow breath as she said, "May I read it, Papa?"

She reached for the letter as her father nodded his approval. She handed him the open parcel, minus her own book. The letter, she knew, was written more for her than for her father.

Mr. Bennet,

Please accept this gift from me to your family as a fervent wish for their future comfort. And please forgive me the liberty I have taken in getting it into your hands. If it were not for the comfort I derived from a similar item when my own dear father passed five years ago and a sincere wish to see your family healed from this tragedy, I would not have presumed upon you. I will only add,

God bless and keep you,
Fitzwilliam Darcy

Chapter 9

Elizabeth knocked on the door to her mother's bedchambers and waited for an answer. She had personally delivered Mr. Darcy's gift to each of her family members at the request of her father. Her mother's was last, and Elizabeth worried about her reaction. Her mother had been much subdued since Lydia's death, and every day since, the Bennet household anticipated her return to her previous disposition with some trepidation.

"Come in," she heard her mother say.

Elizabeth gingerly opened the door, holding her mother's new mourning book close to her chest. Her mother was sitting at her dressing table preparing herself for bed. Elizabeth was beset with emotion as she took in her mother's countenance, solemn and downcast, and yet quite a beautiful woman for her age. She was combing her long, dark hair and looking at her daughter through the mirror.

"What is it you need, Lizzy?"

Elizabeth stepped forward and placed the book in front of her mother. Stalling her mother's hand, she took up her brush for her. Brushing her mother's hair, she noticed for the first time the beautiful streaks of grey coming through. She swallowed as she observed through the mirror her mother slowly reach for the book.

"It is a mourning book, Mama. Mr. Darcy sent one for all of us, to remember Lydia."

Mrs. Bennet reverently turned the book over in her hands a few times, a single tear running down her cheek. Elizabeth put the brush down, wrapped her arms around her mother's neck and kissed her teary cheek.

"My poor, poor Lydie."

Elizabeth choked down her own emotion at hearing her mother whisper the endearment that only she had ever used. She was surprised then, when her mother sat up straighter, pulled Elizabeth's arms from about her shoulders and gave the book back to her.

"Take it away, Elizabeth; I do not deserve to have such a fine thing." Her voice was somber but resolved.

Elizabeth backed away from her mother when she stood and walked towards her bed. "Mama, of course you must have one. It is a lovely way to write down your memories and thoughts about my sister."

"No, Lizzy, take it away." Elizabeth stood gaping at her mother until her ears caught her mother's anguished voice mumble to herself, "It is my fault she is gone anyway."

Elizabeth rushed to her mother, and ignoring her mother's protests, she threw her arms once again around her shoulders. "Mother, do not say such things! It is not your fault that Lydia died. It was an accident, Mama!" Her eyes were streaming as Elizabeth tried to convince her mother to listen to her.

Instead, her mother struggled to disentangle herself from her second daughter's embrace. She could not have guessed that her mother's dreadful state was compounded by guilt. The thought caused her to tighten her embrace.

"No, Lizzy, let me at once feel how much I have been to blame."

"But, Mama, you are not to blame!"

"Say nothing of that, my dear. Who should suffer but myself? It has been my own doing, and I ought to feel it."

Elizabeth sat herself on the bed next to her mother, whose face by now was also wet with tears. She grabbed her mother's hand and squeezed it. She knew her mother could not possibly be at fault and somehow needed to convince her of it. She harkened back to her time with the Darcys in London and to her letters with Georgiana. Sharing her grief had helped Elizabeth manage the pain of her loss. She knew the same would be a balm to her mother.

"Mama," she began with sincere feeling, "I cannot but disagree with you. How can it be your fault? You were not even with Lydia at the time."

Mrs. Bennet looked towards her least favorite daughter, and for the first time, she was struck with feelings of tenderness for Elizabeth. Her estrangement with Mr. Bennet had begun with Elizabeth's birth. He had doted on Elizabeth, loved her, and spent countless hours devoted to her care and education. Mrs. Bennet, a woman of mean understanding, little information, and uncertain temper felt ignored, and she resented her second daughter. She could love Jane, for who could not love such beauty. But Elizabeth was much like her father; she had his odd mixture of quick parts, sarcastic humor, reserve and caprice. Having failed to produce an heir for a second time, Fanny Bennet had begun to worry that she was a disappointment to her husband. Discontented, her nervous complaints began; with each subsequent pregnancy and birth of another daughter, she drew further into her insecurities. Furthermore, she believed he had not forgiven her for not producing an heir.

It was not as if Lydia were the first child she had lost. *Both were my fault*, she thought sadly. Shortly after Lydia's birth, she became with child again but delivered early in her confinement. The infant, small and weak, was the coveted heir but only lived a few hours. They had never mentioned his birth to any of the girls. Mrs. Bennet deemed that, if she had only taken greater care, she could have brought their son to birth safely. With his death on her hands, she withdrew completely from her husband's company. She spent the subsequent years doting on her youngest living child, her baby Lydia, and plotting and preparing to find suitable husbands for her daughters.

Looking towards Elizabeth again, Mrs. Bennet patted her daughter's hand. "It is my fault again, Lizzy. I have always tried to look out for you girls—to find you good husbands. I encouraged Lydia to go out walking that day with the officers. I should not have sent her."

Again? Lizzy wondered as she sank into the space next to her mother and rested her head on her shoulder. "Mama, you could not have known she would fall. You cannot blame yourself that it happened."

As her tears fell, Mrs. Bennet slowly lifted her arm and rested it around her second daughter's shoulders. It was the first time she could remember holding Elizabeth and she was sorry for it. Elizabeth was not unaware of the unprecedented gesture of affection and was equally moved.

"No, Lizzy. I have pushed you girls too much. I shall not orchestrate your futures anymore. I do not know what shall happen to us if your father should die, but I would rather starve with you girls by my side than to have my matchmaking ambitions push you towards unhappiness or worse…" Her voice faltered at the end, and they remained silent for a few minutes.

Elizabeth looked into her mother's eyes. "Mama, you must stop blaming yourself. Lydia's death was not your fault, and I will not hear it."

"Hush, child, I shall be all right. I have more children who need me, and Lydia will have Sammy, after all."

Sammy? Elizabeth returned to her mother's embrace. *Who is Sammy?* When her mother began to hum and comb her fingers through Elizabeth's hair, she forestalled asking aloud. For the first time, she held her mother's affection, and she could not bear to share it with anyone else.

Elizabeth fell asleep in her mother's bed next to her. When Mrs. Bennet ascertained her daughter was sleeping, she carefully tucked her in around the counterpane. She looked at the book on her dressing table that her daughter had delivered. Briefly, she wondered why Mr. Darcy would bestow such a gift on her family. As she looked down at Elizabeth's sleeping form, she smiled. Though Mrs. Bennet had sworn off matchmaking, she was not so daft as to sit idly if an honorable suitor came for one of her daughters. If Mr. Darcy were interested in one of them, she would not be the one to stand in his way. Returning her thoughts to the book, she even considered using the gift. Perhaps it would be comforting to have something by which to remember Lydie. She would place it in her keepsake chest next to the willow wood box with the lock of hair from Sammy.

Mrs. Bennet blew out the candle and slid into bed next to her daughter. She could not discharge her culpability in Lydia's death, but talking about it with Elizabeth had strengthened her resolve to be a better mother to her remaining daughters. Lydia's death had brought her closer to her husband at least. They talked more, and Mrs. Bennet determined to continue that as well. Sighing, Fanny felt another tear roll down her cheek and soak into the pillow.

SITTING AT HER WRITING DESK, Georgiana considered her reply to Elizabeth. She had written concerning a gift that, apparently, her brother had sent to the Bennets. Georgiana was not aware that William had sent anything and was intrigued. Her brother was most peculiar regarding Elizabeth. He would feign indifference when a letter would arrive from Elizabeth but then hover about while she read it. He would even inquire after the letter, although he had never taken such an interest in her correspondence before.

At first, she wondered whether it was merely a courtesy because Elizabeth had lost her sister. But Georgiana discarded that theory as soon as she came across a letter her brother had written her from Hertfordshire last autumn. She had not heeded it much at the time, but he had written at length about Miss Bennet. Georgiana had been too distracted by her own troubled feelings still reverberating in her mind after Ramsgate to discern that it was the only time he had ever written to her about a lady — other than to relate Miss Bingley's raptures, of course. She knew his feelings about Mr. Bingley's sister, and she had learned to skim over any part of his letters with her name in it. But he had written of Miss Bennet even back in October when he was at Netherfield!

This discovery had made Georgiana rush to her drawer and review all of his letters over the past few months. She noted that he wrote of Elizabeth again while at Kent, and Georgiana was stunned when she finally comprehended his strange behavior — *My brother is in love with Elizabeth!*

Georgiana secreted a smile as she drew forth a fresh sheet of paper to write to Elizabeth. Since their correspondence had not yet ventured beyond the Bennet's current situation, Georgiana was not sure of Elizabeth's feelings towards her brother. She believed that no one could help but fall in love with him, for he was the best of brothers and the best of men. She was certain that, if Elizabeth was not already in love with her brother, all she needed was time. *For who could not love him?* She spent a few minutes contemplating how she might contrive for her brother and Miss Bennet to be in each other's company again.

With a smile and a plan, Georgiana bent her head to write to her favorite friend.

ELIZABETH WAS JUST RETURNING FROM her walk with her mourning book in hand, as had become her custom, when the post arrived with a letter from Miss Darcy. She smiled as she tucked it into her book before ascending the stairs to her room to read. She knew that this letter would be the one in response to her own letter about Mr. Darcy's present. She looked down at her cherished book and smiled. She knew what had been in the box now, and thought about how superfluous Miss Darcy's letter was likely to be.

His gift of the mourning book had come to mean a great deal more to Elizabeth than a way to help formulate her thoughts and feelings regarding the loss of Lydia; in truth, it was because the book was from him.

It had now been several weeks since she received the news at the parsonage of Lydia's death. Her feelings and thoughts about Mr. Darcy were so different now. Mr. Darcy had left for town several weeks before, and Mr. Bingley had remained. While walking in the garden with Elizabeth and Jane, he had indicated his intention to stay in the area at least through the summer. His words had served as a way to soothe Jane's worries regarding his arrival in the area. Elizabeth turned her head to hide a smile when she realized her secret meeting with Mr. Darcy on the day of the funeral had been for naught as Mr. Bingley had revealed his intentions himself only a few days later.

Elizabeth chuckled as she retrieved Georgiana's letter from the cover of her mourning book, running her finger along her name written in his handwriting on the nameplate before closing the book again. Regardless of Mr. Bingley's pronouncement, Elizabeth could not repent her time alone with Mr. Darcy that day in the garden.

Sitting on her bed, she drew her feet up underneath her as she turned the letter over to break the now familiar Darcy seal.

Dear Elizabeth,

It was lovely to receive your most recent letter and to see that your spirits seem to be recovering. I often think of my dear friend and hope that you are improving. I hope my brother's gift was acceptable to you and your family. I wish I could say more about it, but unfortunately, I do not know what it was that he sent. I do know that your family has been in his thoughts since he left you a few weeks ago. He is always concerned and pays particular attention when I receive a letter from you, often staying nearby until I share with him how you fare.

Enough about that—tell me, dear Elizabeth, what are your plans for the summer? Do I dare hope that you might come to London soon, whereby I may see you?

Sincerely yours,
Georgiana Darcy

Elizabeth smiled to herself as she refolded the letter. If she had not convinced her father to open the package, she would have found her friend's letter quite vexing. Instead the letter made her heart leap at the reference to Mr. Darcy, and she reread several times the portion containing his name before allowing herself to move on to the rest. She wondered at what it meant that he was so attentive when Georgiana received a letter from her.

Smiling, she moved to her desk to reply to the letter. Having finally discovered what was in the box, she felt determined to thank Mr. Darcy for his thoughtfulness. She first wrote to Miss Darcy regarding her forthcoming trip with her aunt and uncle. She explained that, due to Lydia's death, her uncle had taken too much time away from his business; therefore, they had to cut short their original plans. They were obliged to give up the Lakes and substitute a more contracted tour. According to the present plan, they were to go no farther northward than Derbyshire; they would be leaving in three weeks' time. It was with mixed emotions that Elizabeth thought about how quickly time was passing since Lydia had died. By the time she left for her tour of Derbyshire with her aunt and uncle, it would have been nearly two months.

She finished her letter with a request to Georgiana to please pass the last page on to her brother, its containing her thanks for his kind gift. She then pulled an additional sheet of paper out and addressed a note to Mr. Darcy. When she completed the missive, she folded both together in one envelope. She hoped that, since her note to him was open and part of her letter to Georgiana, he might take less umbrage on her presumption to write him, seeing it was not really private correspondence.

DARCY SAT AT HIS DESK drumming his fingers on the arm of his chair. It had been nearly a month since his plans for the future had taken a detour after Elizabeth received the news of her sister's death. He felt every minute of the subsequent weeks. He was irritated that he had still found no news of Wickham's location. His informant, Perkins, was on Wickham's trail and had followed him from establishment to establishment. At least they believed he was still in London. *Damn, if we are not always two steps behind!*

Their latest lead had been the closest yet, having missed catching Wickham by mere hours. The only satisfaction gained thus far from the sordid business was that Wickham had likely left because of his debts as well as a wish to escape the militia. Darcy had just received a missive from Colonel Forster, now established in Brighton, reporting that Wickham had not returned from leave. Darcy knew he had not gone to Brighton; Perkins was on his trail, and it only led him in circles around the seamiest parts of London. No, Darcy knew that Wickham had not gone to the seaside.

His thoughts were interrupted by the opening of his study door to admit his cousin Colonel Fitzwilliam. He still wore his greatcoat, beaver and gloves, though the latter he was in the process of removing when he spoke.

"Darcy! I have something I wish to speak to you about."

Darcy inclined his head and stood waiting while his cousin removed his outerwear and handed it to the waiting butler.

"This matter of business of yours could not have waited until you removed your coat in the vestibule instead of dragging your road dust into my study?"

Colonel Fitzwilliam laughed as he handed his coat to Mr. Carroll, whose face indicated he agreed with his master. With a short bow to the gentlemen, the butler left, closing the study door behind him.

"Well, Richard?" His mood was still a bit foul from his earlier ruminations about Wickham, and they colored his patience.

"First, a glass of your fine port, if you will. The major general does not have your exquisite taste or appreciation for a good drink." Richard sighed dramatically. "But such is the sad life of a soldier."

Darcy huffed. "I do not believe the second son of an earl, regardless of his profession in the army, would know much about deprivation."

Richard laughed as he poured himself a drink, surprising his cousin when he said, "You know, you are not the first to make that observation to me."

"Indeed," Darcy said with little interest.

Richard made himself comfortable in a seat with his glass, taking a sip from it before continuing. "Yes, *indeed*. The lovely Miss Elizabeth Bennet said as much to me on one of our walks at Rosings."

Darcy's attention was captured, but he turned his back to his cousin to pour himself a drink. He tried to retain his air of dispassion. "Is that so? Miss Elizabeth is an acute lady."

Richard smiled at the remembered conversation, causing his cousin to swallow a greater quantity than he would have otherwise.

"Yes, she is. You know, if my situation were different or her marriage portion were better, I could be quite content with a lady like Miss Bennet."

Darcy choked on his drink.

His cousin raised his glass to his face to hide a smile at his cousin's reaction. "Miss Elizabeth is quite a lady; that is sure." He watched Darcy's red face merely nod and turn to look out the window. He had begun to suspect his cousin had feelings for Miss Bennet at Rosings. Darcy had never been such a nodcock around a woman before. Aloof? Usually. Rude? Most of the time. But a bumbling mute and a fidgety mooncalf? Never. He stared at the woman more than he had talked to her.

"How is the young lady, you know, with her sister's...?"

Richard was never good with uncomfortable details if they had anything to do with emotions. He was a good soldier and could handle serious situations as long as nobody showed their feelings.

"She is doing much better, I believe."

"Have you been to see her lately?"

"Not since the funeral. Bingley is still in Hertfordshire though." Let Richard think his friend was supplying Darcy with information on the Bennets; it would keep him from nosing about Georgiana's friendship with Elizabeth or his own vested interest. "You said you had business with me, Richard. Or was that business to drink all of my port?"

Richard laughed and raised his glass. "That was part of my business, I confess. The other part was to ask why you are looking for Wickham."

Darcy's face drew into a severe frown. "How did you know I was looking for him?"

"Oh, come on, man. Do you think that after Ramsgate I would not try to keep an eye on the rogue myself? And furthermore, do you not think that, after all these years, I would fail to recognize the alias you gave yourself when we played games as children? *Burns.* Yes, I can see from your face that I am correct in the true identity of that man."

Darcy's frown deepened. "I concede I am looking for Wickham, but I have my own reasons."

"And have you found him?"

"No," Darcy said with evident frustration.

"I suspected as much. Do you not suppose that Wickham is aware of those who are looking for him? How do you think he is able to disappear so easily? No—if I knew you were the *Mr. Burns* who was looking for Wickham, then our old childhood friend would know it too. He played the same games with us as children, or have you forgotten?"

Darcy groaned and ran his hand through his dark curls. "I had not thought of that."

"Why are you looking for him?"

"It is probably nothing, Richard," Darcy said with a wave of his hand.

Colonel Fitzwilliam raised his eyebrows slightly. Darcy never did anything for naught. "Why do you not enlighten me as to this 'nothing'?"

Leaning back in his chair, Darcy closed his eyes. "When Miss Elizabeth's sister fell down that ravine, she was accompanied on the walk by Wickham, then Lieutenant Wickham of the ——shire Militia, encamped in Hertfordshire."

"And?" Richard asked uneasily. "I had heard he had joined the militia from my own informants."

"And he left on leave from the militia the next day, and no one has seen him since."

"That does not explain why you are looking for him, Darcy."

Darcy rubbed his eyes and looked over at his cousin. "Mr. Bennet had reason to believe Wickham's behavior was suspicious after Miss Lydia's accident, and Colonel Forster, his commanding officer in the militia, said his leave was granted so Wickham could attend his sister's wedding."

"Wickham does not have a sister."

"I know," Darcy said gravely.

The colonel was silent as he pondered Darcy's words. The realization came just as he was taking another drink, causing him to spit it back into the glass and sputter, "Are you suggesting that Wickham *caused* Miss Lydia's accident and death?"

Darcy leveled blank eyes at his cousin as he nodded slowly.

Richard stood abruptly and muttered a few choice words as he began to pace around the room. "Well, you cannot keep looking for him Darcy; that is for sure."

Darcy sat up, anger clear in his eyes. "Why is that?"

"Because we will never find him if he knows you are looking for him, *Mr. Burns.* He will make damn sure of that."

"We?"

"Yes. If that man is responsible for murder, especially while dressed in His Majesty's regimentals, I will personally see to it that he is found and punished."

"Well, I am glad to have your assistance, of course."

"Tell me, Darcy—what information do you have other than your suspicions that Wickham might be involved in this girl's death?"

Darcy was about to speak when the door to his study was opened to reveal his sister. She happily skipped into the room, oblivious to the tension and stern faces of her cousin and brother.

"William, when can we leave for Pemberley?" Georgiana nearly laughed. "I am tired of London and long to be back home."

Darcy attempted a smile for his sister while glancing at his cousin. Her excited countenance was a welcome change as she usually was not so animated, but neither gentleman was in the mood for such jovial spirits, considering their previous conversation.

"I have had some business keeping me in London, Georgie. But if you wish to travel to Pemberley, I can arrange it. I had not known you wished to go."

Richard spoke too. "Yes, Georgiana, you should go to Pemberley. London in the summer has little attraction."

Georgiana frowned. She needed William to come with her to Pemberley if her new plan was ever to work. She had just received a letter from Elizabeth about her trip north to Derbyshire!

Exuding her best pout, she griped, "Can your business not wait for a few weeks, William? I would wish for you to come with me."

"It cannot, dear. I am sorry."

Georgiana's shoulders slumped visibly as she nodded and, full of disappointment, turned to leave the room.

Richard looked towards his cousin and, knowing that the business that kept him in town was likely the one they were discussing earlier, indicated to him that he should go. He whispered, "Go for a few weeks, Darcy. I will take care of things here."

Darcy thought for a minute and quickly accepted his cousin's advice. "Georgiana," he called after her as she reached the door. "If it is your wish that I come with you, then we shall go to Pemberley together."

Georgiana beamed and rushed into his arms. "Oh, Brother! Thank you! I promise you will be glad you came." Satisfied that her show of disappointment had worked on her brother's heart, Georgiana kissed him on the cheek.

Darcy patted his sister's hair, happy to spoil her. He watched her skip to the door with a pleased smile.

Georgiana turned abruptly and, with a convincing expression, exclaimed, "Oh, I almost forgot, I received a letter from Miss Bennet today, and she included a portion for you."

Darcy's heart quickened at the mention of Elizabeth and then did a decided flip when he heard Elizabeth had written to him! He stood quickly and shortened the space between himself and his sister in a few strides. His expectant face and slight twitch of his lips convinced Georgiana of her earlier suspicions regarding Elizabeth. Unbeknownst to Georgiana, her cousin was confirming similar suspicions in his mind as well.

She pulled the letter out of the pocket of her dress and made a show of flipping through the many pages of the missive, taking her time finding the page for him. His impatience was comical, but she hid her amusement as she handed him the last page. "Ah, here it is." Reaching to kiss him again, she said, "Thank you, William. Perhaps we could leave in two weeks?"

Darcy was oblivious to his sister or his cousin's presence as he held the letter in his hand and saw the delicate, feminine script. He mumbled his agreement to his sister without being aware of what he agreed to and walked back to his desk in a daze. Georgiana exited the room smirking. His eyes were only allowed to deliciously devour, *"Dear Mr. Darcy,"* in her beautiful handwriting before his cousin's words interrupted his perusal of the letter.

"A letter from Miss Bennet?" He was chuckling.

Darcy folded the letter petulantly and put it in his pocket. He was not about to read it in front of his cousin and was certainly not willing to endure whatever teasing he would receive. Therefore, he spoke tightly when he said, "I believe we were discussing Wickham earlier. You asked what proof I had of his possible guilt regarding Miss Lydia's death. The fact of the matter is that I have nothing at all. All I have gathered is that Wickham has many debts in Meryton and was likely escaping them. Any motives beyond that, I know not. I had hoped that finding the bastard would shed some more light there."

Richard dropped the matter of the letter from Miss Bennet and returned to the topic at hand. "Well, let us hope that her death was not at the hands of that scoundrel. You go to Pemberley, and I will keep looking. Besides, I am beginning to think that, if Wickham thinks 'Mr. Burns' has lost interest, it will be easier to find him."

"You will write if you find anything?"

"Yes, of course." Richard stood to leave and smiled wickedly at his cousin. "I will take my leave now and allow you to return to your little dream world of Miss Bennet and her letter."

Richard laughed at the severe frown his cousin leveled at him. He sent Darcy kissing faces, complete with the accompanying noises, as he backed all the way out of the study door. Darcy resolutely remained grave until the door closed, whereupon his face broke into a wide grin as he pulled out Elizabeth's letter and opened it.

His eyes lit, and his heart skipped a beat as he again began reading the elegant handwriting.

Dear Mr. Darcy,

Please forgive my liberty in writing this letter to you. I have enclosed it with my letter to your sister so that no improprieties may be perceived. Though we both have reason to suspect that I care little for propriety, in fact that is not the case.

Darcy smiled at her humor and reference to their decidedly improper private meeting when last they were together and with relish continued on.

I am a very selfish creature and, for the sake of giving relief to my own feelings, care not how much I may be offending yours by writing to you regarding your gift to my family. I can no longer help thanking you for your unexampled kindness to us in the gift of the mourning books. Ever since I have received mine, I have been most anxious to acknowledge to you how gratefully I have cherished it. Were it known to the rest of my family that I am writing to you about this, I should not have merely my own gratitude to express.

Most sincerely,
Miss Elizabeth Bennet

Darcy folded the letter carefully and reverently placed it in his waistcoat pocket. He was pleased that she was not affronted at his roundabout way of ensuring she received the gift. However, he wished he were going to Hertfordshire instead of Pemberley.

Chapter 10

It had taken Elizabeth a week to summon the courage to speak with her father about the revelation she experienced with her mother. She had always been close to him, and they shared an uncommon understanding of each other. While collecting her thoughts, she again examined her feelings from that evening.

It had troubled her greatly that her mother had blamed herself for Lydia's death. Although Elizabeth had grown to have a better understanding of her mother's altered behavior, to be sure, she worried this change was founded on erroneous sentiments. Since that evening, however, her mother had been warmer in expression to her second daughter, and in that Elizabeth discerned some satisfaction.

"Papa, may I speak with you about something?"

Lowering his book, Mr. Bennet took off his reading glasses and smiled at her. "Of course, my dear."

"Who is Sammy?"

The color drained from her father's face, and his hands closed the book on his lap with exaggerated slowness. It alarmed her to see him struggle with emotion, and she feared her question had upset him but knew not why.

"Samuel Thomas Bennet." He barely spoke above a whisper, and his voice trembled. "Your brother."

Elizabeth's mouth dropped open and her brows furrowed in confusion. *My brother? I do not have a brother.* She did not comprehend his meaning.

Mr. Bennet had never anticipated Elizabeth's question and was even less prepared for the onslaught of emotions and memories that overcame him.

However reluctant he might be to explore the feelings such a confession would elicit, he knew he was beyond avoiding the consequence now. He explained, "After, Lydia, your mother became with child again; it was a boy, but he was born too early and did not survive. We named him Samuel Thomas; your mother called him Sammy.

"But why did we not know? Why did you not tell us?" Elizabeth asked numbly as she tried to assimilate the startling information.

Mr. Bennet rubbed his face and leaned forward to rest his arms on his knees. "It was one of the summers that you and Jane went to visit the Gardiners, and as I said, the babe was born too early in your mother's confinement. It was hard on your mother; she asked me never to speak of it, and together we never told any of you girls she was even with child."

Elizabeth wiped her tears with a handkerchief. She never considered what losing a second child might mean to her mother, having by no means recovered from losing Samuel. *And to think that she had carried this burden for so long!* "Oh, my poor mother," Elizabeth whispered.

Confirming her thoughts, Mr. Bennet's frown deepened as he said, "She has not been the same Fanny since."

He had lost both his wife and his son that day fifteen years ago. Mr. Bennet had felt the loss of the babe keenly, not only for losing the son and heir he had wished for, but because from that day on, his wife had completely closed the doors to him, both in her heart and to his company. He blamed himself for having loved her so much that he could not stay away from her. With each pregnancy, she became more silly and nervous over the years, and he blamed himself for putting her in such a condition time and time again. It was his fault she became with child each time and his fault that, each time, he saw her decline. When she had closed her doors to him after Sammy, he accepted his lot, feeling his guilt acutely.

"She blames herself," Elizabeth mumbled as the realization of her mother's words settled in her mind.

Mr. Bennet looked up sharply at his daughter. "What did you say?"

Elizabeth was startled by his firm tone and repeated herself hesitantly, "Mama said to me that it was her fault that Lydia died and she referenced Sammy too."

"Of all the pea-brained… Where is that woman?" Mr. Bennet stood abruptly, left the room and called out for his wife. He had to disabuse her of such a ridiculous notion! The last couple of months had only made him miss her more, and he was not about to allow Lydia's death to be another wall between them. He finally was determined to do all he could to make her love him again.

With no little alarm, Elizabeth followed his resolute stride into the parlor where her sisters sat with their mother.

"Fanny Bennet!" her father commanded with a certain gruffness. She watched her mother stand immediately, apprehension and shock transforming her features. He had not called her Fanny in many years.

Mr. Bennet walked right up to his wife and took her face in his hands before placing an unyielding kiss on her startled lips.

Elizabeth's hand shot to her mouth to hide her amusement at her stunned, blushing mother. All the while, her father wore a self-satisfied, toothy grin as he looked at his wife with undisguised affection, amazing everyone else in the room.

"Mr. Bennet! What is the manner of this...this..." she sputtered and was cut off by her husband kissing her soundly once again.

"Enough woman! To your room with you; I have something about which I wish to speak to you!"

Blushing anew, Fanny Bennet complied with her husband's order and left the room. He followed behind her up the stairs, and the parlor erupted in laughter as they watched the scene dumbfounded. None could remember the last time their father showed such blatant affection for his wife, nor when their mother had ever blushed so readily at him. When Mr. Bennet had closed her chamber door behind them, he turned to her, leaning heavily against it, and said with a changed tone full of emotion and love, "Oh, Fan! How I have missed you!"

Mrs. Bennet stood before her husband as tears filled her eyes. She could not believe what she was experiencing and was unable to manage the thickness in her throat.

"We need to talk, my love. I cannot have you thinking Sammy or Lydia's death was your fault. Come here, wife; please do not push me away."

She stood there a moment considering his words. Could she do it? She did not know. But she, too, had missed her husband. Hearing endearments from his lips and kissing those lips—yes, she wanted his love back. Slowly, hesitantly, she stepped forward, buried her head in his chest and gave way to her tears.

Elizabeth turned towards her sisters after her parents left and, for the first time, noticed Mr. Bingley in attendance. The bizarre moment caused her to cover her face as she continued to laugh without restraint. She lowered herself to the sofa, holding her sides, tears coming to her eyes. Jane sat next to her, chuckling, while Kitty and Mary turned to each other in their own astonishment and giggles.

"Who were those people, Lizzy?" Jane asked in good humor.

"I know them not!" The girls gave way to their hilarity.

Mr. Bingley sat uncomfortably on the sofa amongst the young women trying to fathom what had just occurred. A smile came to his face when he rested his eyes upon Jane. She was so beautiful when she laughed. He was sure she loved him, and his impetuosity was rankled that he must wait at least one more month to ask for her hand. *One more month*, he thought. He imagined kissing Jane soundly, not unlike the way her parents had done minutes before. He was pulled from his sanguine thoughts when the parlor door opened and Jane's Aunt Phillips entered.

"Oh, girls, where is your mother! I must speak to her."

Kitty snickered while the older girls tried to regain some composure. It was Elizabeth who managed to squeak, "I am sorry, Aunt; she is unavailable at the moment." And the room was in an uproar once more.

"Unavailable! Nonsense, I must speak to her this instant. I have heard the most troubling news! Kitty, go and fetch your mother right away."

Sobering, Kitty stood obediently, but Jane shook her head. "I am sorry, Aunt, but my mother is otherwise occupied speaking with our father at the moment. Can we not be of service to you?"

The lady sighed dramatically and slumped herself on the settee next to Jane. "Oh, Jane dear, how you have grown. It will be a pleasure to see you happily married one of these days." Jane colored in embarrassment when her aunt looked poignantly towards Mr. Bingley. Elizabeth was amazed at her vulgarity and realized how quickly she had become accustomed to her mother's new deportment in the past two months. It seemed an age since her mother displayed such brash manners. She felt for her sister, though, and for Mr. Bingley, who was obviously ill at ease.

Diverting her aunt's attention, Elizabeth inquired, "You said you had news, Aunt?"

With great exaggeration she announced, "I have just had word from our dear sweet, Mrs. Forster, the kind colonel's wife. She writes from Brighton that our Mr. Wickham, a great favorite to us all, who was on leave you know since after your sister's fall—God bless her soul—has not returned to the regiment!"

Elizabeth, annoyed by her aunt's rambling speech, summarized. "So Mr. Wickham did not return to the regiment. I cannot see what this means to us, Aunt."

"Oh lud, child! He did not leave the regiment as in give up his commission. He has abandoned it!"

"Well I suppose that is a bit more shocking, but I suppose he wished to remain with his family. His sister, I have heard, was to be married," Elizabeth offered.

"Mr. Wickham does not have a sister," Bingley heard himself say before he could stop the words.

Everyone turned to him with surprise. Elizabeth found her voice first. "How do you know that, Mr. Bingley?" She was sure she knew his source even before he confirmed it.

"Mr. Darcy told me; as you know, they grew up together." Bingley looked nervously around the room at the ladies.

"Oh heavens, I shall go distracted, for it only confirms my other news," their aunt screeched. "I have just heard from Mrs. Long that there are rumors all over Meryton that Wickham has left debts with every tradesmen and merchant in the town! And that is not all, my dears; he has debts of honor too! A gambler of the worst kind in the bosom of our homes!"

There was silence in the room before Elizabeth hissed, "Then he left to avoid his debts. And abandoned my sister..." Reaching these conclusions, a tempest brewed within Elizabeth. "And failed to pay his respects by coming to the funeral or to address this family!"

Jane placed a calming hand on her sister's leg. "Lizzy, who can say why he left. Perhaps he had some pressing business of which we are unaware. I cannot think he would have left our family, especially after such a tragic accident, if he did not have a good reason. I am sure if he could explain, we all would see this in a different light."

Elizabeth's teeth were clenched, and she could not agree with such blind optimism. "No, Jane, I have to agree with Aunt Phillips this time. He is a degenerate and heartless spendthrift at best. Even if he had business elsewhere that could not be delayed, why could he not have written? No, I shall go on believing as I have concluded."

Why had I not realized his abandonment before? she wondered, and then she knew her answer. Ever since she had come to respect Mr. Darcy, she had avoided allowing herself to think of Mr. Wickham since it only made her thoughts uneasy regarding the true nature of their history together. Either Darcy was not the man she had begun to believe he was or she was seriously mistaken in her assessment of Wickham. Neither option was appealing to her, so she had soundly refused to think on it.

She was pulled from her unhappy thoughts by her aunt's continuing gossip. "Forget Mr. Wickham; he is nothing to us now, although I must say that I never liked the man. I do have another piece of news I have just learned, so put that man out of your heads and prepare yourself for something very shocking indeed." She lowered her voice to emphasize the lurid nature of what she was about to relate. "A girl from the Meryton Inn—a serving girl they say—is missing!"

"Missing?" Jane's voice raised in concern.

"Missing!" her aunt repeated dramatically. "She told her friends that she was off to Gretna Green to marry a gentleman but has not been heard from since."

Elizabeth nearly laughed at her aunt's theatrics, effectively pulling herself out of ill humor. "Well that is not so shocking, Aunt. She is likely still with her husband, and they have not returned. What makes you think that she is missing?"

"Well they say that she left a note to her sister, who also works at the inn. She said she would write in a week's time after they arrived in Scotland. That was almost two months ago, and nobody has heard from her."

Elizabeth admitted that would certainly be troubling to the girl's sister but dismissed the rest of the story without further thought. She was grateful for the arrival of the post with a letter from Georgiana that allowed her to excuse herself to read her mail for the remainder of her aunt's visit. Jane also excused herself to see Mr. Bingley out, as he seemed to welcome any excuse to escape the confines of the parlor as well.

AFTER SAYING GOODBYE TO MR. Bingley, Jane found her sister in their room with her letter, her face emitting a nervous excitement as she read through the missive.

"What does Miss Darcy have to say that has you biting your lip, Lizzy?" Jane laughed at her sister's flushed countenance.

Elizabeth folded the letter and tried to affect an air of indifference. "Miss Darcy has written that she and her brother would like to invite the Gardiners and me to stay at Pemberley for the few days we are to be in Lambton."

Jane sat back and raised an eyebrow. "That is very kind of them. I did not know they knew the Gardiners that well."

"Mr. Darcy met them at Lydia's funeral I believe," she said dismissively.

Jane pursed her lips in thought for a minute. "Do you think you will accept their invitation?"

Elizabeth allowed a small smile to escape. "It is not up to me, you know. I am merely a guest of our aunt and uncle."

"That is true. Would you like to stay there if our aunt and uncle agree to the plan?"

Elizabeth blushed before she could school her reaction. She peeked through her lashes at her sister and dissembled. "I admit that I would like to see Pemberley. Mr. Darcy spoke of it often while we were in Kent, and Miss Darcy praises it quite thoroughly in her letter." Elizabeth raised the folded sheet of paper.

"And is it simply the grounds and home you wish to see, Lizzy?"

Elizabeth smiled shyly at her sister. "I suppose I would like to see Miss Darcy again."

Jane laughed out then and hugged her sister. "I am so happy for you Lizzy! I am glad to see you have found your equal. You and Mr. Darcy will be very happy together; I am sure of it."

"Jane! I have said nothing of Mr. Darcy!"

Shaking her head, she teased, "Do not think for a moment, Sister, that I have not noticed your changed opinion of that man since you returned from Kent. You jump to read any letters from his sister, and you keep that book he gave you with you all the time."

"It is my keepsake of Lydia," Elizabeth defended.

"Yes I know that, Lizzy, and I am grateful for mine too. I have gained much solace writing my thoughts about our sister. But I do not carry my book around, nor does anyone else."

Elizabeth blushed. "I will confess that I like him and respect him, but as to love and matrimony, I have no further thoughts there."

"Perhaps seeing his beautiful home will secure your love...hmm?"

Elizabeth shook her head with amusement and tossed a pillow at her sister.

"So are you going to write to our aunt and uncle about the Darcys' invitation?"

"Oh, I suppose I must," Elizabeth said with a dramatic sigh.

Jane rolled her eyes and hugged her sister again with a little squeal. She knew her sister was very close to being in love with Mr. Darcy, though maybe she did not know it yet herself.

Elizabeth sat down at her desk to compose the letter to her aunt. What would it hurt if she led her aunt and uncle to believe that the invitation included a mention of a day or two of fishing for her uncle or a ride about the park for her aunt? Embellishing the invitation a little, none would be the wiser. She was sure that the Darcys would be most obliging regardless. She was gratified when, a few days later, she received a letter from her aunt accepting with pleasure the invitation to stay at Pemberley.

If the Gardiners suspected Darcy's interest in their niece to go beyond friendship and her own interest towards him to be the same, Elizabeth was none the wiser. They were sure they would know the truth as soon as they arrived at Pemberley.

Elizabeth eagerly penned an answer in the affirmative to Georgiana for their stay at Pemberley and thanked her for the kind invitation. Part of her hoped that the invitation was not just extended for Georgiana's pleasure but for her brother's as well.

TWO WEEKS LATER, EN ROUTE to Pemberley with her brother, Georgiana tried to remind herself that she had extended the invitation to Elizabeth and her family for her brother's pleasure and not just for her own. She had received their confirmation to stay at Pemberley several days prior and had not yet found the courage to approach him about her scheme.

Although she was sure he would not be angry, she did not know whether he would be displeased with her for not having asked. She was hoping his obvious regard for Elizabeth would help him beyond the initial shock of her secrecy.

Clearing her throat, she decided that was as good a time as ever, even though she disliked the idea of being trapped in a confined carriage with him if he were to prove angry.

"William, may I speak to you about something?"

Darcy lowered the book he had been pretending to read, carefully hiding the fact that Elizabeth's letter was secreted there.

"Yes, sweetling?"

Georgiana just managed not to cringe in her own anxiety when he spoke to her with such endearment. "I was wondering...that is to say that...I know that after last summer you may have reason to believe otherwise but..."

Darcy frowned. "What is it Georgiana?"

"I was wondering whether you thought I was mature enough to act as hostess while we are at Pemberley."

She breathed a sigh of relief when he smiled. "Firstly, you must forget about last summer. Secondly, I think you are perfectly capable of being hostess and have only to let Mrs. Reynolds know you wish to do so. I think it would be good practice for you besides. I am glad you asked, Georgie."

He was proud of his sister as she was growing in to such an accomplished, lovely young lady. Whatever he might do to give her any pleasure was sure to be done in a moment.

"I am glad you think so because I might have already invited some friends to visit us while we are at Pemberley." She gave him a tentative smile as she nervously studied his face.

It was true that Darcy was not in the mood to have houseguests even if it was a few of his sister's friends. However, he could not voice his displeasure at the idea of guests after just complimenting her in earnest.

He gave her a tentative smile. "That is fine, dear. I hope you and your friends will have an enjoyable time. When do they arrive?" *I hope I have at least a week to enjoy Pemberley before having guests underfoot.*

Georgiana brightened considerably at his words. "In just over a week's time I believe. They are touring Derbyshire. When I heard their tour would bring them to Lambton, I invited them to stay a few days with us at Pemberley. It will only be for about four days."

Darcy picked up his book and made to resume his reading as he nodded to her. *At least it is only a few days.* "And who are these friends of yours, Georgie?" he asked with little interest.

Georgiana smiled to herself as she looked coolly out the carriage window. They were nearly home now, just inside Pemberley Woods.

"Just an acquaintance of mine, and her aunt and uncle."

Darcy nodded his head. They were quiet until the carriage rolled to a stop. Darcy exited the carriage and turned to hand his sister down. He breathed in a deep breath of the clean, country air and exhaled with a satisfied smile. *It is good to be home.*

Brother and sister divested themselves of their traveling coats in the front entry and greeted Mrs. Reynolds, who always welcomed them with the love of a longtime family retainer. Feeling a bit more gracious now that he was on his own home soil, Darcy inquired, "Does this acquaintance of yours have a name, dear?"

Georgiana ignored her brother's question and turned towards the housekeeper instead. "Mrs. Reynolds, my brother has given me permission to act as hostess while we are here, and so I would like to meet with you tomorrow regarding the dinner menus and plans, if I may."

Mrs. Reynolds smiled at the young Miss Darcy. "I would be happy to assist you any way you wish. You are growing up so beautifully, my dear."

Georgiana thanked her and then with a quick glance to her brother added, "Mrs. Reynolds, I would like to inform you that we will be having guests arrive next week."

Mrs. Reynolds was pleased hearing her young mistress speak so confidently. "Do you have any particular rooms in mind for your guests?"

Her brother looked at her with such pride; she was secretly entertained to think how his look would change as soon as she revealed her surprise.

Before taking the stairs to her rooms, she mused, "I think the yellow room for my friend, and the double suite with the sage papering for her aunt and uncle will be fine."

"It shall be done, my dear."

Mr. Darcy and Mrs. Reynolds stood watching Georgiana ascend the staircase, both filled with nostalgia, recalling how quickly the years had passed. Georgiana could feel their eyes on her back and waited to turn until she was at the top.

She confirmed that she had their attention before saying, "On second thought, Mrs. Reynolds, place Miss Bennet in the blue room instead." Georgiana smiled as a delighted surprise registered on her brother's face. "It has such a lovely view of the gardens that I think Miss Elizabeth would greatly admire."

At her housekeeper's nod, Georgiana turned and quickly walked to her rooms, satisfied and relieved to have pulled off her scheme. Now it was just a matter of a few machinations once Elizabeth arrived, and she was sure she could get Elizabeth to fall in love with her brother.

Chapter 11

lizabeth is coming to Pemberley! Darcy smiled at the thought. Whereas a week felt like such a short amount of time before he knew the identities of his sister's guests, now it seemed interminable. Their short stay of only four days troubled him though. He doubted he would welcome her departure once he had her in his home. Of course, he would need to speak to his sister about the whole furtive affair. Although quite pleased with the results, he could not condone her secrecy.

He imagined Elizabeth walking around his home, touching the railings, admiring the furnishings. At least, he hoped she would admire them! Suddenly, he worried that she might not approve of the house. *Don't be absurd man! It is a beautiful home. How could she not?* He shook his head to bring order to his jostling emotions and thoughts. One thing was clear: Elizabeth was coming to his home, and he could not be happier.

Contrary to his initial expectation, the first week at Pemberley before their guests were to arrive passed relatively swiftly. Darcy had much to do with his steward, considering the lengthy time he had been away. His discourse with his sister had also been relatively painless, though not entirely without discomfiture on his part and, quite honestly, a little vexing. *When did my sister become so clever?* He wondered how she had outmaneuvered and twisted his words.

She timidly had appeared in his study when he summoned her. He knew that she knew she was caught. "Georgiana, please have a seat. You know why I have asked you to come to me, so I will come right to the point. You should have asked me whether you could invite Miss Bennet to Pemberley."

"But would you have thought to invite her yourself?"

Darcy knew he would have been too craven to suggest such a thing had he known of Elizabeth's northern tour to Derbyshire, but he was not about to concede that to his sister. "I do not think that is pertinent to the topic at hand, Georgiana."

"Do I need to ask you for permission to invite all of my friends? You said in the carriage that you thought I was ready to be a hostess."

"I did and I meant that, dear. But Miss Bennet..."

"...is my friend," she finished for him.

"She is also an attractive, eligible young lady," Darcy countered, satisfied to have made a point she could not refute.

"So I am only allowed to invite unattractive, ineligible old ladies to be guests in my home?"

"Dash it, Georgiana! You know that is not what I meant. Miss Bennet and I are friends, and I should have been consulted first."

"Which is why I did not think you would mind."

Darcy rubbed his temples. When did his sister learn to talk circles around him like this? "I think you understand my meaning."

"Is this all because you are in love with Miss Bennet?"

Darcy's head snapped up to look at his sister who sat innocently in front of him. "Georgiana," he warned, "you forget yourself. That is not an appropriate question to ask me."

"But you do love her, do you not?"

"That is a private matter, Georgie!"

Georgiana was satisfied. "Very well, I will say no more on the matter— except that this pleases me very much."

Darcy groaned and waved his hand to dismiss her from his study. He did not even look up when she added, "Oh, and you should probably play along that the invitation came from you as well, for that is what Elizabeth thinks."

Her parting words had left Darcy confounded, wondering who took whom to task. And now it was the day of Elizabeth's arrival, and Darcy was on tenterhooks as the clock ticked away. The only gratifying element of that exchange a week earlier was the knowledge that Elizabeth had accepted the invitation to his home, believing he had wished it. He hoped that meant something.

He looked out the window towards the road, even though she was not expected until later that day. He allowed himself a brief moment to daydream about bringing Elizabeth to Pemberley, only not as the guest of his sister but as his wife. The master of Pemberley found thinking about Elizabeth there as his wife a worthy way to employ his remaining time before her arrival. And so he did.

ELIZABETH CEASED ENDEAVORING TO HIDE her high spirits and eagerness from her relations after about two miles of Pemberley Woods, admiring every remarkable spot and view. She consciously avoided their amused faces, though.

With cheek, she asked, "Do you think we will make it to Pemberley by dusk?"

Her aunt laughed. "The estate is very expansive. I believe at the top of the hill we shall get our first view of the house."

Elizabeth kept her eyes glued to the window as she scanned the woods for some glimpse of the house. Just as their carriage crested the top of the hill, her eye was instantly caught by Pemberley House, and she audibly gasped. It was elegant with a dignified facade backed by many acres of trees. An exquisite greenway led to a beautifully manicured lake. It could not be equaled in her mind to any of the other estates she had seen thus far—indeed, any estate in existence, she was sure. It was simply stunning—stunning and very large. She had not thought Mr. Darcy so rich.

Her sister's words came to her mind then. *'Perhaps seeing his beautiful home will secure your love.'* Elizabeth laughed to herself as she echoed, *Perhaps, indeed!*

DARCY AND GEORGIANA STOOD ON the steps of the home as the Gardiners' carriage came up the drive and stopped before them. Georgiana rushed to the carriage window to greet her friend even before their door had a chance to open.

Darcy chuckled at his sister's exuberance, wishing he might do the same. Instead, he stepped forward to open the carriage door himself.

Mr. Gardiner stepped out first and turned to hand his wife down. Much to Darcy's chagrin, he also waited and helped his niece out as well, robbing Darcy of the privilege.

"Welcome to Pemberley. I hope you all had a pleasant journey." Darcy allowed his eyes to rest upon Elizabeth. He had, of course watched her descend from the carriage but now took in her full beauty. His eyes had been deprived of her loveliness for far too long.

"Mr. Darcy, sir." Elizabeth's uncle extended his hand. "I thank you. We have had a most pleasurable time; I assure you. Thank you for your kind invitation to Pemberley."

"It is my pleasure, sir. I hope while you are here that you will take advantage of all that the estate has to offer. My stables, hunting, fishing equipment are at your disposal, sir. We are glad you are come." Darcy turned towards the ladies. "And that goes for you ladies as well. If there is anything that we can do to make your stay more agreeable, you need only ask."

Mrs. Gardiner thanked him as she and her niece curtsied.

"Thank you, sir," Elizabeth chimed, her voice ringing as a beautiful song in his ears.

Offering his arm to his sister first, he then extended the other towards Elizabeth. "Miss Bennet, will you permit me?"

Elizabeth slipped her gloved hand around his arm. She was bewitched by his easy manners and wondered whether being at his home was the difference. She remembered that he had seemed more at ease at Darcy House as well. She allowed him to lead the way as they ascended the large staircase towards the immense front doors.

The feel of his arm beneath hers reminded Elizabeth of their time together in his study in London when she had felt his strength through just the thin barrier of his shirt sleeves. By the time they entered the house, Elizabeth found herself quite flushed. When asked whether she would like some refreshment, she conceded that she found the day to be a bit warm and accepted. They were soon introduced to the housekeeper, Mrs. Reynolds, who seemed like an older, more grandmotherly version of his housekeeper in London. She liked her very much at once.

After conversing amiably, the Darcys invited their guests to retire to their rooms to rest and refresh themselves. Darcy saw Elizabeth to the passageway that led to the guest suites before allowing Georgiana to conduct her the rest of the way. Elizabeth in his home promised to be delightful, enchanting even, though perhaps a challenge if he considered the way her blushing cheeks earlier had made him feel. Perhaps he should not have spent the last few hours thinking of Elizabeth as his wife. That kind of mischief could only end with her in his arms, indeed!

ELIZABETH STOOD IN HER DRESSING gown with a cup of tea in her hand, watching the sun rise through her window. *I could get used to this*, she mused. Every morning, Mrs. Reynolds had sent a tray to her room nearly as soon as she woke. It seemed that kind of particular attention was customary at Pemberley because her aunt had commented on the same during a walk around the gardens. To her chagrin, her time at Pemberley was nearing its end. Three of the most charming, blissful days had slipped past, and the next day she would be leaving with her aunt and uncle.

She sat on the window seat and pulled a blanket about her legs as she recollected those last few days at Pemberley. She had joined her aunt in visiting her acquaintances in Lambton while her uncle took advantage of Mr. Darcy's fish. When she was not attending her aunt, she was entertained by Mr. Darcy and his sister. They were engaging, pleasing company and ended spending much of their time wandering the grounds.

Georgiana always seemed to contrive reasons to abandon Elizabeth and Mr. Darcy. These moments seemed to make Mr. Darcy a tad self-conscious. Elizabeth laughed and sipped her tea. Georgiana was nearly as determined as her mother had been in her matchmaking, extolling her brother's fine qualities despite his embarrassment and displeasure at such praise.

During the tour of the house that first day, Georgiana had insisted on showing Elizabeth the manor herself and had brought her around to the principal rooms, highlighting various aspects. Halfway through, she stopped before a door. "This is my brother's studio; he is a fine artist."

Elizabeth was surprised. "I had not heard of this accomplishment."

"Oh yes, he is quite humble about it. He never speaks of it." She turned and knocked on the door, calling for her brother, who she knew was within.

Elizabeth heard some shuffling of papers, and her heart picked up its tempo as the now familiar sound of Mr. Darcy's boots came closer. When he opened the door, he was startled to see Elizabeth with Georgiana and immediately hid his paint-stained hands behind his back and bowed. "Georgiana, Miss Bennet. Is there something I can do for you?" He stepped out into the hallway and attempted to close the door behind him.

Georgiana stepped forward and around him. "I was just showing Elizabeth the house, and I wanted to show her your paintings."

Darcy glanced at Elizabeth to gauge her reaction to his hobby, and finding a curious gleam in her eyes, he stepped aside, allowing her into this sanctuary, albeit with a little hesitancy.

The smell of the oil paints permeated the room, adding to the surprising experience of viewing this side of Darcy for the first time. She glanced around and saw dozens of canvases of all sizes about the room, marveling at his talent. His landscapes were appealing, and although she knew nothing of art, it was his portraits that she found most captivating.

"Mr. Darcy, you hide your light under a bushel. These are truly magnificent!" She handled a painting of Georgiana on a swing in the garden.

She could see her praise both discomfited and pleased him. Looking around then, she noticed that Georgiana had left the room and they were alone. She looked toward him, and he answered her unspoken question. "She remembered she wished to speak to Mrs. Reynolds about . . . something."

Elizabeth nodded and gave a nervous laugh. Despite her efforts to appear indifferent to their plight, she blushed.

Darcy cleared his throat and shifted his feet "She is attempting to manage the job as hostess by herself for the first time, and I admit I am hesitant to suggest she allow Mrs. Reynolds to do more. I do not want her to think she is not managing it well enough." *And I cannot deny the way her 'forgetfulness' has been to my benefit.*

"Of course not; she is doing splendidly." Elizabeth turned and began sifting through a few pencil drawings at a table next to her.

She had only managed to look through a few before Mr. Darcy was by her side and directing her across the room to a painting under a canvas covering. "Miss Bennet, will you permit me to show you one of Georgiana I am working on for her birthday?" He tried to steady his voice despite the close call. Another couple of drawings and she would have been deluged with a dozen or so of her own likeness, as well as another that he was planning to gift her later.

"It would be an honor, sir." Elizabeth's heart was pounding at the gentle pressure of his hands on her arms as he led her across the room and lifted the canvas.

The painting was a good likeness and showed Georgiana's beauty perfectly. They stood talking companionably for a few minutes about the painting. He had just lowered the cover again when Georgiana returned. Elizabeth left with her to continue her tour, and Mr. Darcy retreated back into his studio.

Elizabeth finished her breakfast tea and stood to place the cup back on the tray. She sighed and wished her time at Pemberley were not nearly over. That day they had planned a tour around the lake, and she anticipated it with eagerness. Climbing back into the warm, luxurious comfort of her bed, her mind continued to replay the last couple of days at Pemberley.

When Georgiana had disappeared in the observatory, the music room, the back gardens, and the gallery, Elizabeth and Mr. Darcy had smiled in affectionate amusement at her maiden adventure at hosting. Later, when she had also disappeared from the orangery, the drawing room, the ballroom and the topiary, their smiles indicated more embarrassment than amusement.

However, when Georgiana had deserted them in the library, Elizabeth did not notice for quite some time as the enchantment of the room and the volume of books transfixed her. The lofty room with its upper level contained the most wondrous collection she had ever seen!

Mr. Darcy had quietly followed her through the library and only ventured a comment when she showed marked interest in one book or another. Elizabeth remembered, upon reaching a small alcove in the west end of the room, that he had confessed it was a favorite place to hide as a naughty child. He demonstrated how he would pull the heavy, leather chair in front of the alcove and hide behind it, totally obscured from view.

She smiled now, as she had then, at the thought of Mr. Darcy as an errant boy. She could not picture him engaging in anything more mischievous than possibly stealing a few biscuits from the kitchen before dinner.

Those conversations about their childhoods led Elizabeth to think of Mr. Wickham. She hoped to have a moment to speak to Mr. Darcy about him while at Pemberley; more particularly, she wished to talk to him about the recent rumors regarding Wickham that she heard before leaving Longbourn.

Rolling on her side, she closed her eyes with renewed self-reproach over her complete misjudgment of Mr. Wickham's character. When she had first asked Mr. Darcy about his boyhood friend, he bristled but then related a faithful narrative of every event in which they were concerned together.

"I am embarrassed to admit that I believed Wickham. I, who prided myself on my discernment, was completely fooled by him," she said.

"You could not have known. He can please wherever he wishes." Darcy felt relief discussing this with Elizabeth. He was heartened she was no longer misinformed as to his own character, and he had wondered while at Kent whether she still believed Wickham's lies.

And yet Darcy left out the history pertaining to his sister and Wickham, believing it was Georgiana's choice whether or not to tell Elizabeth since she was her particular friend. Though he had hinted at the events of last summer regarding Georgiana's near ruin when he had accompanied Elizabeth home to Longbourn, he did not indicate the acquaintance had been Wickham.

Later that night, when she retired to bed, Elizabeth mulled over all Darcy's words; her thoughts were so tumultuous that she could get no rest until the early hours of the morning. Alas, she found herself awake at sunrise, as was her habit, despite having slept so ill.

Stretching her limbs, she readied herself for the day regardless of her fatigue. It was her last day at Pemberley, and she did not want to waste a moment. She could fret or reproach herself over Wickham on another day. With a resolved plan to enjoy herself, she pulled the servants' bell to summon the maid to help her dress.

MEANWHILE, IN ANOTHER PART OF the house, Darcy was speaking privately to his sister.

"Georgiana, I know this might sound like an odd request, but later today when we walk the lake path with Elizabeth, I want you to find an excuse to leave us alone."

Georgiana stamped her slippered feet and squeaked, "Are you going to propose, William?"

Darcy threw his head back and rolled his eyes. "Of course not, she is in mourning still, you goose. You know that would be improper, not to mention insensitive. I have made her a small gift that I wish to give her."

Darcy pulled out the miniature he had drawn and handed it to his sister. "Is this her sister?"

Darcy nodded.

"All right, I am sure I can think of something to take me away."

Darcy smiled and kissed her cheek. He tucked the miniature back into his pocket, anticipating giving it to Elizabeth later.

AS HE SET OUT TO walk with Georgiana and Elizabeth, Darcy was nervous. He had wished to give Elizabeth the miniature since the day of her arrival but had not found the right moment. She was to leave the next day with the Gardiners, and he knew his opportunities were dwindling. He had suggested the walk so that he might have an occasion to give it to her beyond the curious eyes of her aunt and uncle.

Disguise of any sort was unnerving for Darcy, and so the knowledge of his subterfuge with his sister only added to his discomfort. He remained silent but attentive enough as the ladies talked animatedly about their surroundings. When they reached the spot in the path where it would lead to the lake, Darcy swallowed the lump in his throat when he heard his sister speak.

"Oh dear, I forgot!"

Elizabeth turned to her with a sly smile. "What is it, Georgiana?"

"I promised Mrs. Reynolds I would meet with her before tea to discuss tonight's menu. It is the last night you are here Elizabeth, and we have planned your favorites."

Elizabeth laughed, and Darcy smiled uneasily at another of his sister's excuses, his better knowledge of her ruse making the excuse sound trifling to his own ears. He was relieved to hear Elizabeth say, "Well, then make haste, my dear. If you wish to feed me all of my favorites, I shall not stand in your way!"

Georgiana giggled and hugged her friend. As she skipped towards the house, she looked over her shoulder to wink at her brother.

"Shall we all go in, or would you like to keep walking, Miss Bennet? I believe you have not had the opportunity to enjoy the path around the lake yet." He thought his voice sounded odd, but thankfully, Elizabeth did not seem to notice.

She smiled sweetly at him. "I think I should like to continue my walk if you will accompany me, Mr. Darcy."

"It would be my pleasure, Miss Bennet."

The two watched Georgiana's retreating figure until she had reached the steps of the great house before turning towards each other. Darcy extended his arm towards the path in an invitation for her to continue. As she smiled up at him, Darcy clasped his hands behind his back simply to prevent them from clasping hers.

As the path meandered through beautiful oaks and Spanish chestnuts, Elizabeth expressed her appreciation for his hospitality towards herself and the Gardiners. Soon the pathway bent around a copse, and they were upon a small, grassy knoll that was covered in wildflowers near the lake.

Elizabeth gasped and brought her hand to her mouth. She had never seen a place for which nature had done more. When she looked up at him with all the admiration in her eyes, his heart nearly leapt from his chest.

Her eyes sparkled pure contentment. "The view is breathtaking, is it not, sir?"

His eyes were intent on her when he murmured, "Yes, it is."

"Bluebells are my favorite of all wildflowers." She bent down to pick a few posies and brought them to her nose. She closed her eyes as she inhaled their fragrant, sweet scent, the picture intoxicating Darcy like never before.

"Then you approve of Pemberley," he said, holding his breath.

Her tinkling laugh delighted him, and he released the air slowly. "I am sure there would be few who would not approve, Mr. Darcy."

He smiled at her words as he reached into his pocket for the miniature. "Miss Elizabeth, I remember your reaction to the last gift I attempted to give you, but I hope that you will make an exception for this one."

He held out the miniature, and her hands came up to receive it instinctively. Elizabeth looked down into the smiling face of Lydia. She shook her head in wonder, her mouth slightly agape as she gazed up at him with wet, questioning eyes.

He hesitated. "Drawing is something of a hobby for me as you have learned. My technique, you will see, is not well developed."

Elizabeth wiped her eyes and hastened to say, "Mr. Darcy, this is such a beautiful likeness. How is it possible that you came to make it?"

"I have an excellent memory, Miss Elizabeth," he said, adding to his embarrassment.

Elizabeth looked at the picture again, marveling at the talent of the artist and its likeness to the subject. A thought came to her mind then of how much pleasure such a picture would give to all her dear family as no one had ever thought to have any of their likenesses taken before. The joy that surged through her at that moment chased away the feelings of sorrow. Her elation expressed itself with such profoundness that she could not have realized the words that she then uttered.

"Mr. Darcy, this is too wonderful. I could kiss you!" She laughed as she ran her finger along the edge of the frame.

Darcy froze and could not help imagining that exact action! His artist's eye was attentive to the sunbeams lighting her soft, chocolate curls. Her dark brown eyes, that had laid the foundation for his love and admiration of her, were sparkling with happiness. He was gratified that she had received his gift with such pleasure but knew better than to imagine her words were in earnest.

But she had said it...so he could not help replying huskily, "I would by no means suspend any pleasure of yours, Miss Bennet."

Elizabeth continued to laugh, still unaware of what affect her previous declaration held on her companion. "I cannot help but wonder why you would trouble yourself with such an undertaking as this, sir"—she held up the miniature—"but I thank you, most sincerely."

Darcy stepped closer to her, his eyes trying to convey all that he felt at the moment. He looked all over her lovely face as he said in a low voice, heavy with significance, "Surely by now you know, Elizabeth. Surely you must know."

Elizabeth looked up at him then and was paralyzed by what she saw. His eyes were focused in the piercing way he often looked at her. At first, she was startled to realize that what she saw there was not displeasure but— Her heart seemed to stop momentarily as the truth settled over her. Looking deeply into Mr. Darcy's eyes, she saw nothing but a passionate expression of raw admiration and desire. His dark eyes swam with intense emotion. *How could I not have seen it before?* Her mind raced through dozens of similar looks she had received from him almost from the beginning of their acquaintance, each of them flashing through her mind with new understanding. That he could have loved her the whole time, she could not fathom.

Her mouth went dry. *Mr. Darcy is in love with me.* The words echoed in her mind, it being unable to contain any other thoughts at the moment. Her new understanding held her under such a power that she had never before experienced. Most surprising to Elizabeth was the fact that his loving her was not an unwelcome discovery. Her heart spoke confidently to her of the truth it had somehow known for some time, a truth that her mind had only just accepted—the truth that she loved him back.

Mr. Darcy saw the change in her expression and became so overwhelmed by the look in her eyes that his body moved on its own accord closer to her. Indeed, he had reached her before he had even realized what he was about.

Elizabeth was spellbound as Mr. Darcy stepped closer to her and brought his hands up to cup her face. She remained still as he leaned his face down towards hers. She closed her eyes just as she heard the sweet timbre of his voice and felt the warmth of his breath on her face.

"Dearest, loveliest Elizabeth," he whispered, and she felt his other hand slip along her cheek and stop at the base of her neck. It was but a moment before she felt his lips meet with hers.

At the exquisite touch of his lips upon hers, triggering a thousand thoughts and emotions, the flowers she had picked slipped through her fingers to the ground. Each of her senses was at once surrounded and embraced by nothing but him. His scent, lemon and sandalwood she remembered, engulfed and delighted her. His caress, so tender, so careful on her neck, her cheek, spoke to her of the gentleness of his spirit. Her closed eyes saw gold from the sun that pierced her lids as her face tilted towards the sky to him. Every sensation she experienced was effected and produced by him. The time felt as if it had stopped, and yet she was aware of her disappointment when the soft, excruciatingly wonderful feel of his lips on hers ended only a moment after it began.

Her eyes remained closed when he pulled away a few inches from her face. His hands were still on her face and neck, and his voice was shaky as he said, "Forgive me, Elizabeth."

She felt an acute sense of loss as he pulled away. She slowly brought her hand up to touch her lips, still tingling from his kiss. She watched him step back again as he drew in a ragged breath and ran his fingers through his hair. She saw his face contort, and she knew he was beginning to rebuke himself.

She stepped towards him then and said, "Mr. Darcy..."

Elizabeth was dismayed to see him step further back and forestall her approach when she had drawn closer to him. She felt the tiniest fraction of relief when he said, "Please, Elizabeth, if you come any nearer, I may not vouchsafe my behavior as a gentleman. Indeed, I have not acted the part just now." Darcy was barely master under his own regulation, and when she stepped towards him, his arms ached to reach out and return to the bliss of that kiss. His heart was still beating rapidly, and his power over his ardor was tenuous. *I should not have kissed her,* he groaned to himself even as the memory of it washed over him again.

She could see his self-censure and said gently, "Mr. Darcy, although I know what just happened should not have happened, especially considering our lack of...of understanding. Even with my own state of mourning, I cannot help but point out to you the fact that I am not complaining, sir."

Darcy stopped his pacing and looked at her for the first time since their kiss. Her eyes were bright and her cheeks pink with the loveliest of blushes—a blush he knew he had given her. One of her impertinent eyebrows was arched charmingly at him. His eyes drifted to her lips, and he unconsciously tasted his own. The taste of her sweet lips was still on his, and he had to look away lest he lose control again. He swallowed several times before he could speak.

"Your forgiveness I know I do not deserve, but I thank you for it, Elizabeth," he finally managed with a half-smile and a sideways glance. He would have proposed marriage right then if he were not so intensely aware of his breech with propriety already. Instead, he turned to her and declared, "I would like to call on you in Hertfordshire when you return."

They both knew that her official mourning would be over by the time she returned to Longbourn. It made his request to call on her all the more significant. Darcy held his breath as he waited for her answer.

Elizabeth could not contain her joy! With her eyes full of delight, she said, "I would like that very much, sir."

Darcy's elation at hearing her words could not be described. He held himself in check as he allowed himself to draw nearer to her. With every nerve in his body on high alert and every muscle commanded to maintain his reserve, he reached for her hand and brought it to his lips for one delicate, lingering kiss.

He allowed her hand to drop only into the crook of his arm as they began walking again. They walked in companionable silence for most of the distance back to the house lost in their own thoughts and sensations of their time amongst the bluebells. Upon reaching the house, it was time for tea. If the Gardiners or Georgiana noticed their heightened color or the tender glances exchanged from time to time, no one said anything.

The rest of Elizabeth's stay at Pemberley was marked by those secret looks and frequent musings of their shared kiss. When she and the Gardiners entered their carriage to take their leave the next day, Darcy was already counting the days until he could leave for his friend's house in Hertfordshire.

Glancing down at his sister standing next to him as they watched the carriage disappear, Darcy said, "Well, Georgie, I think you may have a career as a Bow Street runner with all the sneaky maneuvering you have done on this holiday."

Georgiana smiled at her brother. "I shall consider the option and add that to my list of accomplishments, William."

They both laughed and turned to enter the house, Darcy only pausing once to look over his shoulder at the empty road again.

Chapter 12

Elizabeth bit her lip and fixed her gaze steadily out the carriage window. Her cheeks, she knew, were flushed and warm. It was always the result whenever her thoughts brought her back to Darcy and the kiss, her first kiss, only a few days before. The tingle from it had long since disappeared, but the rapidity of her heart rate often returned with the memory. To have gained such a man's love was beyond Elizabeth's comprehension. She closed her eyes and leaned her head back against the padded seat of the carriage.

Elizabeth had not felt such joy and contentment before in her life, and she laughed to herself at the thought that she was now in love with the last man in the world she thought she could ever be prevailed upon to marry. To think she had held that belief just a short three months ago. She knew that her changed perspective had started with her sister's death; from knowing him better, his disposition was better understood. In this new light, his artless compassion, gentle kindness and understanding nature could be seen, and she could not deny it if she wished.

Her pride still rankled that she had been so deceived by Wickham's character. She believed now, after reflection, that his deception was more her fault than his. Had she not set herself so decidedly against Mr. Darcy because of his slight against her at that first assembly in Meryton last autumn, then she would not have let her wounded dignity be taken in by the charms of Mr. Wickham. Elizabeth struggled with a mixture of wonder and discomfort to think how the tragedy of Lydia's death had shown Mr. Darcy in a new light. She might have gone on forever disliking the man and misjudging his character.

With her new understanding about his feelings for her, she realized that, if Mr. Darcy had allowed his love for her after all these months to compel him to offer her his hand and she had not learned the truth about him, she would have made an even graver mistake in refusing him. For a refusal, she knew she would have given. The very thought of hurting him so, of turning away his love, a love she could not imagine living without now, made her eyes swim beneath their lids.

With overwhelming gratitude, Elizabeth offered up a solemn prayer of thanks for the blessings she'd been given in the face of this adversity. She was certain that he was now the only man she could ever be prevailed upon to marry. Elizabeth smiled as she thought, *It is a good thing then that he plans to call on me soon.*

MADELINE GARDINER HAD NOT SPENT twelve years of blissful matrimony without being able to recognize the look in a man's eyes when he was in love. Neither was she unaware of the look that came into a man's eyes when that love was coupled with desire. Therefore, as much as she had enjoyed her time visiting her friends in Lambton and becoming better acquainted with the Darcys, and as much as she had been gratified exceedingly by the growing attachment between her favorite niece and the master of that beautiful estate, she was glad now to be on their way.

She had seen that look of love in Mr. Darcy's eyes whenever they rested on her niece. She had also seen when it mixed with a bit of the other, especially when they had returned from their walk around the lake. She was happy for Elizabeth. Mr. Darcy would make a fine suitor and husband. She was also glad to see that her niece returned the man's affections. For all Elizabeth's efforts to conceal her feelings, Madeline knew she was in love with Mr. Darcy too. Furthermore, Madeline had not been married these twelve years without knowing the blessed power such a love could have over both one's heart and body—which was all the more reason to separate them until a proper understanding could be had.

She looked at her niece's sleeping form in the carriage. Elizabeth had confessed that Mr. Darcy had asked to call on her upon their return to Hertfordshire. As her aunt, she felt incumbent to discuss with her the significance of such a request. Elizabeth merrily acknowledged the implication and welcomed his return to Hertfordshire. Madeline was gladdened there was at least the hint of an understanding between the two, for surely it would secure the happiness of both. She only wished she were not continuing on to London after returning her niece back home; she would like to have seen for herself how this love affair unfolded. Nevertheless, she would have to content herself in knowing her niece to be a proficient correspondent.

When the carriage rolled to a stop in front of her sister-in-law's house, Madeline gently shook Elizabeth. She opened her eyes immediately, surprised to have reached home.

"You were asleep a long time, dear."

"Oh I was not asleep, Aunt. But I suppose I was too preoccupied to notice the time." Elizabeth was grateful to have shared her love for Mr. Darcy with her dear aunt now that she realized it herself, but she was eager to talk with Jane again and see how her family fared.

Aunt Gardiner smiled knowingly at her niece before turning towards the now open carriage door to be handed down by her own sweetheart.

It seemed her family was doing quite all right, Elizabeth discovered— more than all right. When Elizabeth and the Gardiners entered Longbourn, they were greeted by both her parents and all of her sisters. Everyone was all smiles, and she had to laugh at their warm welcome. After enthusiastic hugs with her sisters, she noticed her parents holding hands. Even as they embraced her, they seemed reluctant to separate.

Elizabeth looked over her mother's shoulder with a raised eyebrow and a look of question to Jane. Smiling, her sister shook her head in return. Elizabeth would have to speak with her sister at the earliest opportunity about their parents' odd behavior.

When Elizabeth and Jane retired for the evening, the former immediately brought up the topic with Jane.

"Papa and Mama, Jane. What has happened?"

Jane laughed and leaned back against the four-poster bed as she pulled her legs up inside her nightgown. She shook her head. "I cannot say for certain, Lizzy. It all started that day when Papa came into the parlor and kissed her in front of everyone. You remember. Since then, they have spent much of each day in conversation together, alone in their chambers. I have even heard Mama laugh."

Elizabeth was all astonishment! "What can you make of it?"

Jane smiled contentedly. "It must be love, Lizzy."

"Love?" Elizabeth was so stunned she could not utter anything else for a few minutes. Surely, her parents did not love each other; their dispositions had grown sufficiently unlike to make it seem impossible. Her sister was leaning her head at an angle against the post with a wistful look.

"And what do you know about love, Jane?" Elizabeth asked with a sly smile. She watched her sister blush and smile back at her.

"Mr. Bingley will speak to Papa tomorrow, Lizzy." She bent her head and picked at her fingernails. "To seek my hand."

Elizabeth leapt across the bed, instantly embracing her sister. "I cannot believe it! Oh, well I can, of course. I knew he loved you, but this is a surprise!"

Jane could have no reserves from Elizabeth where confidence would give pleasure. "Technically, we are out of full mourning, Lizzy, as of two days ago. There is nothing improper about his asking for my hand now." Jane colored and looked away.

Elizabeth laughed heartily. "Yes just two days ago, I suppose I could not have expected Mr. Bingley to wait a moment longer than he had to. I daresay he has been in love with you since he first laid eyes on you last year."

Jane chuckled softly. "You do not disapprove of his haste, do you Lizzy? I could not bear it if you thought he was being insensible to Lydia's death. She will always be in our hearts, but we must try to go on. I think Lydia would wish us happy..." Jane broke off with uncertainty and looked at her sister for assurance.

Elizabeth tilted her head and gently patted her sister's cheek. "Janey, dear, of course, I do not disapprove or think ill of Mr. Bingley. Society cannot condemn his offer." With no little cheek, she added, "Truly, Jane. I think the poor man would have proposed sooner had it been possible. And if he had, I could not have censured him, for he would have secured, perhaps forever, the happiness of a most beloved sister."

Jane smiled in relief and embraced her sister again. "Oh, Lizzy, I cannot tell you how glad I am to hear you say so. I have loved him for so long. How shall I bear so much happiness?" cried Jane. "He has been so much help to me and our whole family during this difficult time. He had a brother once that he lost to an illness when he was just fourteen. His empathy is great."

"Well then, how can I not but approve of such a man for you, Jane. But wait" — Lizzy reached for her sister's hand again — "you have said nothing of his proposal yet. Tell me every detail, Jane; do not leave anything out."

Jane's open and generous heart shared the details of the proposal with her sister, and she flushed when she confessed how Mr. Bingley had then kissed her cheek.

"I know you do not know what that feels like, and I wish I could tell you, but I simply cannot put it into words, Lizzy! It made me quite faint!"

Elizabeth turned her head and smiled as the memory of her own first kiss swept over her. "I do not know what a kiss on the cheek feels like, to be sure..."

Jane leaned forward to see her sister's face better. "No!" Jane cupped her mouth. "No, Lizzy! What are you hiding from me?" When her sister did not respond but did blush a deeper red instead, Jane laughed outright. "Lizzy, you have not said anything of your trip to Derbyshire. Perhaps you have something to tell me?"

Elizabeth bit her bottom lip as she looked towards her sister. She had not even told her aunt about the kiss, but she knew she could not keep it from Jane—not after seeing Jane blush at the memory of her own first kiss.

Elizabeth fell backwards on the bed, dreamily gazing up at the shadows on the ceiling, and sighed. "You may not be able to explain your first kiss, Jane, but that is very well, for I shall never forget the memory of my own."

Jane sat in stunned silence and then burst out, "Why, Elizabeth Rose Bennet! You have been the sly one! To think you have come home engaged to Mr. Darcy and said not a single word!"

Elizabeth laughed. "I am not engaged to Mr. Darcy."

Jane fell to her knees next to her supine sister, her brows lowered in concern. "Not engaged to Mr. Darcy? Then whom have you kissed?"

Jane was confused, for she was convinced that her sister had left Longbourn half in love with Mr. Darcy and only needed to spend time with the man to realize it herself.

"It was Mr. Darcy I kissed—or rather, he kissed me." Elizabeth giggled and covered her warm cheeks again.

"But you said you were not engaged?" Jane sat back on her heels then and rubbed her puckered brow.

Elizabeth raised herself up on her elbow to reach for her sister's hand. She pulled it away from her brow and said softly, a smile pulling at the edges of her lips, "Not yet, anyway. I do believe he would have asked me if I had not been in mourning. He is so proper you know that a few days kept him from asking. But he did say he wished to call on me upon my return to Hertfordshire."

"Yes, Mr. Darcy is very proper."

Both girls were quiet for a minute, looking at each other. Then they erupted into laughter as Jane said, "Well, perhaps not *very* proper, it would seem."

Elizabeth laughed, shaking her head. "Not very, indeed."

Jane clasped her sister's hands. "Well, now you must tell me how it happened."

Elizabeth kissed her sister's hand. "I hardly know where to begin."

"Then you must start with the beginning, when you arrived at Pemberley. Did you like his home?"

Elizabeth nodded her head in exaggeration. "I liked it very much—perhaps, too much."

"And did seeing it render its owner a bit more attractive?"

"Perhaps, a little." Lizzy smiled mischievously. With a sigh she continued, "He was very kind, and every moment I spent with Georgiana and him was most pleasing. Their home is quite grand and handsome, less of splendor but real elegance, and every comfort imaginable was available to me." She recollected their conversations and Georgiana's many attempts to leave them alone. She told her sister about her new knowledge regarding Wickham's character too and her feelings on discovering her own faulty discernment.

"But I cannot believe he could have been so deceitful," Jane said. "There seemed to be truth in all his looks."

Lizzy shook her head sadly. "I know. It seems he is not an honorable man after all. But, Jane, it is in this that I need your advice."

"Of course, Lizzy."

"Do you think we ought to make it known generally what we know of his true character?"

"I cannot think there is a need now—not now that he is gone from the neighborhood."

"I suppose you are right. It can do no good when he is no longer in the area." Elizabeth privately added, *and it would not be good for Mama to blame herself further by finding out she promoted the affections of such a man to Lydia.*

"And perhaps he left to start anew, though it would seem then that the rumors about him have been true after all. They say he left substantial debts and that he dallied with some of the serving girls in Meryton."

Elizabeth sighed heavily. "And as I have learned, Mr. Darcy has all the goodness and Mr. Wickham only the appearance of it." Elizabeth released her sister's hand and slid off the bed. She walked towards her traveling valise and pulled out the miniature of her sister. With her back to Jane, she let her finger trail across Lydia's face as her thoughts trailed across the miles to the artist. He really had all the goodness. With a smile, she turned to her sister and handed her the miniature.

"Mr. Darcy made this for us, and he gave it to me," she said softly, almost reverently.

Jane looked down at the face in the picture. "Oh, our dear Lydia." Tears filled the eyes of both, communicating the moment better than words could have. "It captures her exactly. In fact, I believe that is the very dress that she wore to the Netherfield Ball."

Elizabeth nodded as she had realized that too while traveling. Darcy had said that he had an excellent memory, and he had portrayed Lydia exactly as he remembered her the last time he had been in her company. The portrait depicted Lydia laughing, sitting in a gilded chair. Elizabeth had remembered seeing her sister in that exact pose directly after her dance with Darcy. Their heated argument during their one dance together had ended, and their attention had been momentarily drawn to the loud laughter of Lydia as she sat down, heated after her own dance with an officer. At the time, she knew Mr. Darcy had looked at her sister's behavior with disdain. It had angered her then.

When she had first realized where the scene was from, she had been confused as to why he would choose to draw her like that when at the time he had clearly disapproved of her actions. Upon further retrospection, Elizabeth realized that the setting captured Lydia's zest for life and energy. She was at such a tender age and may never have grown out of her selfish, imprudent ways, but as her sister, Elizabeth could not help loving her for that selfsame exuberant spirit. As soon as she realized it, she knew immediately that, although Darcy had not approved of that behavior, he was wise enough to realize that her family would cherish having her portrayed thus with laughter dancing in her eyes. She could not even argue now with his disapproval of her sister's behavior then; it was not proper behavior for a young lady of gentle birth, to be sure. The truth had caused Elizabeth some mortification until she reminded herself that he had wished to call on her.

Such unguarded absurdities were not enough to frighten him away.

"I wanted to share it with Mama and everyone else. Do you think they would like to see it?"

Jane tenderly touched the pink cheeks of her sister in the portrait. She said softly, "Yes. Mama will love it; I am sure."

Elizabeth sat next to her sister on the bed again, and they both looked at the miniature. After a long while, Elizabeth took the picture and placed it upright on her dressing table. She turned to her sister. "So now we have come to the end, Jane."

Jane raised her eyebrow with incomprehension. "We have? Whatever do you mean, Lizzy?"

Elizabeth's lips twitched in an attempt to smile. "Yes, the end. You said for me to start from the beginning."

Jane's mouth made a perfect 'O' as she remembered that Elizabeth had begun to recount her trip to Derbyshire from the beginning because she had not known how to tell her about Mr. Darcy's kiss. "And so he gave you the picture and you kissed him in return?" she teased her sister.

Lizzy could not hold back her smile then as she laughed. "Not exactly, though it made me so happy, perhaps I could have." She paused as a slip of a memory flitted across her mind, and she recalled Mr. Darcy saying something about not suspending any pleasure of hers. She shook her head, dispelling it as nothing. "No, then I asked him why he drew such a thing for me."

"Mr. Darcy drew it? But of course he did, though I did not know he was so talented."

"Jane, did you know Mr. Darcy was accomplished?"

Jane waved her hand as if it was nothing, "Of course, Lizzy, did you not? Mr. Bingley had said something of it last autumn. He said it was just a hobby of his, but of course, I did not think then that Mr. Darcy was so talented." She nodded towards the miniature.

"Well this is a fine surprise! Why did you not tell me?"

Jane shrugged. "You did not like Mr. Darcy then, Lizzy. I did not think you cared to hear any of his finer accomplishments."

Elizabeth clenched her teeth. Her sister was right. Even if she had been told, she doubted whether she would have cared a jot.

Jane wrapped her arms eagerly about her folded legs. "So you asked him why he drew it..."

Elizabeth sank dreamily down next to her sister. "It was at that moment that I realized he loved me and I loved him." She sighed, remembering the sensation that shot through her when their eyes connected and communicated so profoundly. "I was lost. And before I knew it, he had drawn closer to me and kissed me..." her last words dying out as her eyes glazed over in memory.

Jane brought her hands to her chest over her heart and fell backwards on the mattress in a swoon. "That is so romantic..."

Elizabeth turned to her sister and laughed. Lying beside her, Elizabeth took her hand. "It was and more." She thought of the heat of his kiss and the fire in his eyes—fire that was something altogether unfamiliar to her, though not exactly unpleasant.

Jane stirred from their reverie. "When does Mr. Darcy return to the neighborhood then, Lizzy?"

"I hope soon. I do not know. I suppose we will have to find out from your dear Mr. Bingley."

"He will not stay away long, for I believe Charles plans to ask him to stand up with him at our wedding."

"I would hope he would not stay away *that* long." Elizabeth grimaced at the thought of the common two-month engagement.

"Oh no. Charles and I feel we have waited quite long enough. As soon as we have Papa's consent, we wish to marry as soon as the banns can be read. Three weeks' time is all."

Elizabeth rolled on her side to look at her sister. "That is wonderful! I cannot express how happy I am for you, Jane. You *have* waited long enough."

"And you, Lizzy. You are happy for yourself too, for it will guarantee Mr. Darcy arrives before long. And have you not waited long enough too?"

Lizzy bent and kissed her sister's cheek as she chuckled and lay back again. "There might be a bit of truth in those words, Jane, but I am happy for you."

"And I for you, dear sister."

DARCY GROANED, THREW THE LETTER on his desk and leaned back into his leather chair. He rubbed his eyes and groaned again. Now he could not go to Hertfordshire as soon as he wished. At that very moment, he knew that Elizabeth was home, free of the strictures of society regarding her mourning and, he hoped, waiting for him. He and Georgiana were even prepared to leave for Hertfordshire the next morning. He had hoped to be engaged by the end of the week. Heaven knew he had waited long enough.

Now, he had encountered yet another unexpected delay, separating him from Elizabeth for perhaps another week or two. Blast it all; he wanted to be in Hertfordshire for those few weeks, not in London!

His cousin Colonel Fitzwilliam had written him at Pemberley. Peeved that His Majesty's Post seemed determined to keep him a bachelor, he took up the page and reread the damned letter.

Darcy,

In regards to that matter of business you left me to look into here in London, I have discovered some intelligence about which we must speak at your earliest opportunity. Please send a card around to Matlock House when you arrive in Town.

Regards,
Richard

Chapter 13

Upon reaching his London townhouse after three hard days of travel from Pemberley, Darcy was saved the trouble of writing to his friend Bingley about his wish to visit the following week as the man himself arrived upon his doorstep the next day. Early that morning, as Darcy had reached the bottom of the stairs en route to his study to attend some business before his cousin arrived, Mr. Bingley announced himself.

"Bingley! This is a surprise; I thought you in Hertfordshire." *You are supposed to be in Hertfordshire!* Darcy attempted a smile through his clenched teeth.

His friend beamed from ear to ear as he extended his hand towards Darcy who was a tad slow to accept it. "Darcy, you must congratulate me, for I am to be the happiest of men!"

"Is that so?" Darcy raised his brow and ushered his friend down the hall to the privacy of his study. Closing the door behind them, Darcy continued, "I assume these congratulations concern a certain lady in Hertfordshire then?"

"Indeed, they do! Jane has accepted my suit, and her father has given his consent for our marriage."

If Bingley was now engaged to Miss Bennet, then he was certain to return to the area, hopefully soon. "Then why are you in London if your lovely Miss Bennet is still in Longbourn? She is still at home, I presume."

"Why, to get the license, of course! And I need to pick up my mother's family ring from my townhouse vault."

Darcy relaxed, knowing Bingley's marital felicity was secure. "I wish you joy, my friend! Miss Jane is a jewel, and you will be very happy."

Bingley smiled wistfully. "Yes, she is my angel. I plan to return as soon as possible. How fortunate for me that my butler heard you had arrived just yesterday! That is why I have come—to ask if you wish to travel back with me."

Did he ever! Darcy wished more than anything that he could return so soon. *The devil take you, Wickham!* "I cannot, unfortunately. I had planned to join you in a few days as it turns out, but unexpected business must keep me in town for a little while."

"I hope not too long. I had hoped you would stand up with me. We plan to marry as soon as the banns can be read; the first will be read in Longbourn chapel tomorrow. Will your business be concluded within three weeks?" he asked hopefully.

"Heavens, I hope so! I expect it to be concluded within a week, no more than two." He cursed his old childhood friend under his breath again.

Bingley stood and slapped his friend on the back. "Capital! I shall expect you then in no more than two weeks. My sister will be back from Scarborough by then to come to the wedding and to play hostess." He laughed when he heard his friend groan. "Will you bring Georgiana?"

Darcy walked towards his desk to mark his friend's wedding date in his appointment book. He became momentarily distracted at the thought of seeing Elizabeth again at a wedding, albeit not the one he dreamed of with her eyes lit with happiness and her cheeks pink with pleasure. Her pink cheeks led him naturally to remember the lovely blush on her face after their stolen kiss. He had thought of it often, even sketched her as he remembered she looked after his kiss: her eyes somewhat unfocused, drunk and yet clear and the sunlight that glimmered off her mouth, slightly opened in her dazed state. Heavens, if she knew how she looked then and what a monumental task it had been for him not to take her in his arms again... Darcy swallowed loudly and then choked when his friend's hearty slap on the back pulled him away from his enchanted reminiscence.

"Darcy? Are you all right, man?"

Darcy coughed again and turned to his friend, slightly annoyed. "Of course, I am! What was that for, Bingley?"

"I asked if you were bringing Georgiana to the wedding, and you went blank. Then you turned red; I thought maybe you were in some sort of distress."

Darcy huffed and stood straighter as he smoothed his already impeccable cravat folds. "I am well as you can see. No need to resort to bodily injury."

Bingley chuckled. "My apologies, then, for the misunderstanding. So will you bring Georgiana to the wedding?"

"Yes, I planned to if that is acceptable to you."

"Of course it is; she is like a sister to me" — Bingley laughed and shrugged his shoulders — "maybe more dear to me than my own sweet darlings."

Darcy was clearly amused. "I am happy for you, Charles." Then he conceded, "Again, I am sorry for interfering last autumn. You should have had this moment long before now."

"Fah! Think nothing of it. If you will stand up with me, all is forgiven."

"I would be honored."

Bingley sat down again and observed his friend closely. "While I have a minute, how was your visit to Pemberley?" Jane had hinted to him that Elizabeth was looking forward to it, and Bingley had his own suspicions for quite some time about the object of his friend's interest.

Darcy smiled widely at his friend. If he was soon to fall into a parson's mousetrap himself, he might as well not hide his feelings on it. "It was everything lovely." *She was everything lovely.*

"You mean *she* was everything lovely."

Darcy coughed again when his friend so aptly read his thoughts. "Georgiana and Miss Elizabeth are very dear to each other, you know."

Bingley smiled at his friend's evasiveness. "So, have you no news for me, then, Darcy?"

Darcy's face was unreadable before his twitching lips betrayed him with another smile. "Not yet, my friend, but I hope there will be very soon."

His friend laughed and extended his hand to him. "So it is leg shackles for the two of us then — eh, Darcy?"

"As soon as I can manage it, my friend. As soon as I can manage it."

"Well then, I will leave you to your business so that you may finish it all the sooner. When I return, I will have your rooms prepared for you. Congratulations, my friend. She is almost as lovely as my Jane."

Darcy laughed as he stood to walk his friend to the door. "As fine as your Miss Bennet is, I cannot agree with you there, Bingley. But our argument may be lengthy if we continue to debate that point."

"I could not ask for a better brother, Darcy."

"Although I have reason to feel secure in my suit, I suppose it is still too early to count my good fortune. I envy you that. I can return your sentiment though."

"I will see you soon at Netherfield, Darcy."

"Yes. And give my regards to the Bennet family."

Bingley winked. "I certainly will."

Darcy walked his friend to the door, where his butler was ready with Bingley's hat and gloves. After Bingley left, he returned to the study with a renewed determination to settle things in London so he could secure his own happiness. He penned a quick note to his cousin and rang for Mr. Carroll to have it sent around to Matlock House straight away. Then he poured himself a cup of tea from the sideboard before concentrating on matters at his desk while awaiting the colonel's arrival.

DARCY HANDED HIS COUSIN A glass of port and poured himself one as well. Darcy had been frustrated that his cousin had not come until the dinner hour. He had kept himself occupied for the most part with correspondence and other business while he waited throughout the afternoon; still he had hoped Richard would come sooner than he did.

He waited patiently through dinner, and again after the entertainment on the pianoforte by Georgiana. When his sister finally retired for the evening, the gentlemen could speak freely.

"What has Georgiana in a snit, Darcy?" asked the colonel.

Darcy grumbled and waved his hand at his cousin as he took the seat next to his. He took a sip of his drink before he answered. It was the same reason that had him agitated too. "She is upset that I have delayed our trip to Hertfordshire—business, don't you know." Darcy raised a brow at his cousin to indicate the very business that he came to discuss.

To his surprise, his cousin laughed. "So she is upset with you over that. I warrant this delay is the same reason you are in such high dudgeon as well!"

"I am not in a mood."

"Of course you are not, Darcy. You are always a pleasant bloke to have around." Darcy did not appreciate the sarcasm.

"If it will put an end to your entertainment at my expense, I will admit it. I am not happy to be in London. There is another place with entirely different company that I would much prefer."

Richard clapped his hands. "I take it your visit to Pemberley, or more to the point, Miss Elizabeth Bennet's visit to Pemberley, went well."

Darcy glowered at his cousin. "And how did you know she was at Pemberley?"

"Georgiana told me she would be traveling there before you left town."

"She said nothing to me," Darcy grumbled.

"I do not suppose you minded the surprise though, Cousin."

Darcy eyed his cousin. "The results were to my satisfaction, but I do not like Georgiana keeping secrets. But that is not the topic we need to be discussing now, Richard."

"Hold now, Cousin. Do not be upset with Georgiana. She asked me about whether to tell you, and although I admit it was her idea to surprise you, I encouraged her to stay with her plan. You are sometimes too…bumble-headed to manage your own love life. Somebody has to help."

"I am not bumbleheaded!" Darcy was very much affronted. "And I do not even think that is a word, Richard."

Richard merely laughed, enjoying his cousin's aggravation; Darcy's patience for this conversation was at an end. "You are correct; it is not. I made it up just now. Apt description, though, I dare say. No, of course, Fitzwilliam Darcy is a regular Romeo. What do you call your behavior at Hunsford, then? Is sitting mutely, staring like a buffoon and nearly drooling on your cravat what you call wooing a lady?"

Darcy grimaced. He had been a bumblehead—then. Remembering the many smiles he drew from Elizabeth now, not to mention the kiss they shared, he smiled. He was getting on just fine now. "I will have you know, Richard, that while at Pemberley I managed my own affairs quite well, indeed." Darcy tried to hide his smile behind another drink.

"Oh ho, Darcy! Did you now?"

"Yes, and that is all I will say."

Richard scratched his chin and contemplated his cousin for a moment. He seemed quite content despite his dark mood that evening. "I suppose I am keeping you then from your beautiful maiden."

Darcy turned his head but not before his cousin saw him roll his eyes. "I have already said I wished to be elsewhere. What news have you of Wickham then?"

Colonel Fitzwilliam shrugged his shoulders, consenting to change the topic for the present. He leaned forward, placed his glass on the table with one hand and loosened his neck cloth with the other.

"I think we have discovered a major lead in our search for Wickham."

"Go on," Darcy said, thankful finally to be getting to the point. He wanted to be done with Wickham, and the sooner he knew the dastard was not involved with Lydia's death, the sooner he could put that nasty business behind him—and the sooner he could focus on 'managing his love life' as his cousin had put it.

"We have discovered one of his cronies, a sly and seedy lout who goes by the name of Perkins—sort of a go-between, a lackey for him."

"Of all the double-crossing... If I get my hands on that charlatan..." Darcy was pacing and pulling his hands through his hair with evident anger.

"We have to find the man first. But when we do, Darcy, believe me, I will be your second."

"You do not know where he is?"

"If I knew where he was, I would have told you. Now sit down, Darcy; you are making me dizzy with all that pacing."

"I gave that fabler over one hundred pounds in the course of our despicable acquaintance!" Darcy huffed, angrier with himself for being deceived by his former informant.

"You gave him a whole lot more than that unless you do not count the remuneration for the bequest from your father's will."

Darcy looked at him in confusion. "I am talking about Perkins, not Wickham."

Richard sat up. "You know Perkins?"

Darcy poured himself another glass before answering. He nodded as he held the port to his mouth. "He was my informant—or rather *Mr. Burns's* informant."

Richard scooted to the edge of his seat. "That is fantastic, Darcy! We have him!" He was rubbing his hands together, already planning a strategy when his cousin interrupted him.

"How is this good, Richard? I paid the man to find Wickham for me, and all he did was lead me on a two-week, goose hunt, all the while pocketing my money."

His cousin was already shaking his head. "No, I know his kind, this Perkins. He is motivated by coin. My sources say that Wickham has been on an unusually long winning streak and has become a bit high in the instep with the funds. Furthermore, we know Perkins has only recently become one of Wickham's men. I would wager my quarterly allowance that your Perkins simply jumped ship to what he thought would be more profitable employment."

"More profitable then working for Fitzwilliam Darcy?" he said disbelievingly. They both knew that he was one of the richest men in the realm, a fact that was often discussed in nearly every parlor in London much to Darcy's chagrin. His only satisfaction in being the topic of such boorish discussions was that their rumors of his wealth were only accurate by half.

"Ah, but you are forgetting. The dimwit Perkins only knew you as *Mr. Burns*, not the prominent Mr. Darcy of Pemberley. He saw Burns's pockets then saw Wickham's increasingly deeper pockets and switched sides."

"I can understand now why he may have double-crossed me, inaccurate though his estimations may have been. But that does not explain why you think my prior relationship with Perkins is the key to catching Wickham, especially if, as you say, his allegiances no longer run with Mr. Burns."

"Refill my glass, and I will explain it to you." Richard continued when his glass was returned to him. "A cove like Perkins we know is motivated by money. All we have to do is make him believe you still wish to find Wickham."

"Which we do."

"Right, so we get him to agree to 'continue his search.' And then while he thinks he has landed in the gravy boat, being paid by Mr. Burns and Wickham—"

"Leading me on another goose hunt," Darcy interrupted.

Richard smiled widely. "Yes, and all the while still working for Wickham, we track the fellow and find our real quarry. He will eventually lead us directly to Wickham; I am sure of it."

"If it is that easy, why did you not find Wickham as soon as you learned of Perkins."

Richard shook his head. "Because, Darcy, as I indicated earlier, we do not know where to find Perkins—nor what he looks like for that matter."

Darcy was beginning to feel the weight lift from his shoulders. He could find Wickham, learn the truth about Lydia's death and put it behind him. Part of him wished to end the search before it began; it was that same part of his heart that warned finding Wickham and learning the truth might just cost him more than a few hundred pounds. But his status as a gentleman, his sense of honor—of justice—could not keep him from the truth.

Suddenly he felt very tired.

Darcy rubbed his eyes. "What do you need me to do then?"

Richard smirked, a maniacal grin of triumph. He was forever the soldier and forever would be excited by outsmarting the enemy. "You just need to contact Perkins again—as Burns, of course. Hire him again to try to find Wickham. That is all."

Darcy was quiet. He felt like he was on the edge of a sword. If he found Wickham and the man was guilty, Elizabeth would never want him—not when it meant that her sister's death could have been prevented had he only made Wickham's character known in Hertfordshire. *Blast it! Did I do anything right last autumn?*

When he first set out to find Wickham, employing Perkins, he was driven to find answers. He thought he could help the Bennet family heal—at least Mr. Bennet, to assuage his suspicions. He was now glad he had helped ease the man's concerns because, even if he found out now that Wickham was responsible, he could not tell Mr. Bennet. His purpose in finding out the truth now was mostly for his own conscience since he had not warned the neighborhood in the autumn to stay away from Wickham. Elizabeth was doing so well now; she said her family was coping better, too. Hell and damnation! The eldest Miss Bennets, hopefully both, were getting married soon. At least that was his wish. News of this sort would hurt them. If he was being honest with himself, he had hoped never to find Wickham. After a few weeks on Perkins's goose hunt, he had come to believe he never would. Now they had a real chance at finding him. And finding him might ruin all of Darcy's chances at happiness! With reluctance, Darcy nodded his agreement.

"Fantastic! Now, you do still know how to make contact with Perkins, right?"

"Yes. We had a place we met; I just need to leave a note with the pub owner requesting a meeting. Perkins should show up at the appointed time," Darcy said dispassionately.

"Then write the note. I will have a few of my men at the pub then and begin tracking Perkins."

Darcy nodded.

"I should think you would be more satisfied that we have found a sure way to find Wickham, Darcy. Why are you so downcast?"

Darcy raised his eyes to his cousin and drew in a slow breath before answering. "Have you not considered what finding Wickham might mean? What finding out if he had a hand in Miss Lydia's death might mean for me?"

His cousin remained silent, an altogether rare happenstance.

"She will not have me then," Darcy whispered

"You cannot know that," Richard offered halfheartedly.

Darcy looked up from his glass. "Would you marry someone who could have prevented your sister's death?"

"I am not going to argue your faulty logic. I know how you work, Darcy, and how you take on the responsibility and blame where others would call you blameless. You know, I for one just want to be able to keep better tabs on Wickham. If, once we find him, you do not want to take measures to learn how Wickham fits into this whole dreadful affair, so be it."

"No, I feel honor bound to discover the truth."

"Even if it ruins your chances? No, do not answer that. I do not believe it would anyway."

Colonel Fitzwilliam could see that their business was concluded for the evening. He made to stand and take his leave. "Then you will try to make contact with Perkins tomorrow?"

"I will request a meeting for a few days hence. That will give your men time to become regular visitors to that pillar of high society." Darcy laughed sarcastically, feeling some of his resolve return. The wastrel had cost him too much already. "That way no one can tip Perkins to any new faces."

"Send word when you have secured a meeting."

Darcy nodded, saw his cousin to the study door and shook his hand at his departure. He wished briefly he were not such a gentleman, bound by honor and duty. With a groan, he finished his port and brought one of the candles to his desk to write his note to Perkins.

ELIZABETH WAS IN HER FATHER'S study when she dared to ask him about her mother. "Papa, what have you done with Mama?"

Mr. Bennet looked up from his book, his eyebrows rising above his spectacles in amused surprise. He took off his glasses and smiled at her with affection.

"I am sure she is where I last left her, Lizzy. She was off to speak to Hill about the menu for the wedding breakfast, I believe."

Elizabeth gave her father an arch look, so like his own. "Thank you,

Father, that answers my inquiry perfectly." Bemused, she tried again, her tone lower as she thought about the calm, almost elegant way her mother now comported herself. "I do not recognize her."

"Ah, but I do." There was undisguised tenderness in his voice.

Elizabeth tilted her head to the side as she thought about his words. "She seems happier," Lizzy whispered.

"We both are."

Elizabeth had wished to say more, but at that moment, a knock at the study door produced Mrs. Hill with a letter for her from Georgiana. Smiling, she took the letter and thanked the housekeeper. She looked over to her father with her smile still clearly on her face.

"Who is it from, Lizzy? A secret correspondence with a gentleman?"

Elizabeth laughed at the absurd thought but blushed when she thought about receiving any kind of letter from Mr. Darcy. Unfortunately, her father observed her blush, so she was quick to show him the sender.

"Miss Darcy, I see. You and she have become quite intimate. I can only assume, if you approve of her so much, that she must be of the same good character stock as her brother then."

Lizzy looked up at her father, surprised. "You like Mr. Darcy?"

Mr. Bennet's face slowly drew up into a half smile as he looked into the eager eyes of his daughter. "I do."

"I did not realize you... That is, most people think that he... that Wickham..." Elizabeth twisted her hands in her lap. She was so caught off guard by her father's frankness that she was fumbling to dissemble.

Mr. Bennet chuckled. "I never believed that man, and it seems he was not a good man after all. His debts around town are confirmed, and I, for one, could not be happier he is gone from the neighborhood." Mr. Bennet briefly allowed himself to wonder again whether Lydia's death could have been... No, he would not think of it. He would trust Mr. Darcy.

"I like him, Papa."

"Mr. Wickham? Oh, child, please say that is not so!" Mr. Bennet was already reaching for her hand.

Elizabeth wrinkled her brows and laughed as he took her hand. "No, Papa. I guess I should have been clearer." Sobering, she continued, "I like Mr. Darcy."

"I know, Lizzy."

"You know? But you just thought—"

Mr. Bennet chuckled; he was doing a lot of that lately. "I wanted to hear you say it. But perhaps your feelings run deeper than you have indicated."

Elizabeth puckered her lips, attempting to hide a smile as she blushed and turned her head away. "I think you might be able to say that."

"He is a good man, Lizzy, and will make you happy. Of that, I am sure."

"I believe you are right, Papa," said she, adding to herself, *very happy, indeed.*

"Well you had better see what his sister writes then, Lizzy."

Elizabeth smiled and nodded. She was already breaking the seal and unfolding the paper. Her smile faded as she read through the missive. Her friend was not going to be arriving until the week before the wedding. Her friend stated the reason for their delay being her brother's business in town. Elizabeth was disappointed that she could not see her friend before then. She had looked forward to seeing him so much. *Him?* Of course, she meant *her.*

WILLING HIMSELF NOT TO BREATHE the putrid air too deeply in that part of London, Darcy grabbed his walking stick. It served both as protection and as *Mr. Burns's* prop. Groaning, he stepped out of the hired hackney and walked the block to the pub where he was to meet Perkins. It did not get any easier, knowing what to expect inside.

Thankful for his gloves, he pulled at the door to the drinking establishment and walked in. As he looked around for Perkins, expecting not to see him there yet, he noticed a few of his cousin's hired runners lounging around the tables. They blended in perfectly with the rest of the sordid inhabitants. Darcy looked down at his own black coat and trousers, satisfied to see that they put him above the rest but not so far above as to draw too much speculation. It matched the image Mr. Burns had kept before with Perkins.

Darcy scouted out a table in the back corner of the room. He removed his hat and placed it and his walking stick on the table. When he sat, he drew his hands together in front of him, realizing that his glove had already acquired some kind of sticky substance from the table's surface. *Lovely,* he thought as he scanned the place again for Perkins.

A buxom barmaid sauntered over to take his order and give him an armful of her wares as she bumped into his side. Darcy did his best to hide his disgust, even offering up a small smile as he pushed a coin to her and ordered a strong drink. With a wink and another carefully maneuvered stumble, she left to fill a glass for him, dropping the coin down the front of her dress.

The man at the table in front of Darcy caught his eye. He had his back to him and wore a dank leather hat pulled low on his head. Darcy recognized the slight slant to his shoulders, the unmistakable greasy, dull brown hair visible under the hat and the way the man was even now twirling a coin under the table through his fingers. Perkins had flipped a coin up and around each of his fingers whenever he talked with Mr. Burns before. Darcy smiled, knowing that he had not been fooled this time. He sat back and waited for the man to make his presence known.

Eventually, and to Darcy's growing annoyance, the man turned around about thirty minutes later and took the other seat at Darcy's table.

"Burns."

"Perkins."

"What can I do fur ya gov'ner?"

Darcy leaned forward, controlled and precise. "I have decided to continue searching for the gentleman I hired you to find last time."

Perkins dipped a finger in Darcy's untouched glass of Whiskey and brought his dirty digit to his mouth. Darcy ignored this uncouth scamp's attempt at intimidating him and signaled the barmaid for another drink.

"What's 'e to ya?"

Darcy paused for thought; he must appear calm and collected. "He owes me." That was true. *And I owe him a broken rib or two. Perhaps I could throw in a broken nose for free.* Darcy smiled, somewhat wickedly, causing his companion to swallow and sit back.

"My fees is more now."

Darcy pulled a small purse out of his jacket. He tossed it on the table with a loud jangle of the coins. A few men turned towards the sound, and Perkins frowned as he quickly hid the sack in his jacket. He sat looking at Mr. Burns. He was good for some ready cash, it seemed. He had been making a pretty penny with Wickham while his dibs were in too. His job was to do exactly as he had done before, lead people Wickham owed down false foxholes. He was paid by Wickham and now thought he might gain a bit of the ready from the other half as well. No reason why they cannot pay for him to 'find' Wickham while the man himself pays Perkins to keep him hidden.

Perkins lied. "Might take time, gov'ner. Not on 'is trail, ya see."

Darcy saw the greedy gleam enter his associate's eye and vowed to see him find suitable employment—perhaps on a navy boat bound for the Peninsula—when this was all finished.

"I understand. I will pay you weekly. I expect you to report to me here to receive payment and to fill me in on any developments."

Perkins was obviously pleased with the terms of their agreement and was currently calculating how many weeks he might be able to bleed the man by chasing down fake leads. Darcy collected his personal items from the table, not acknowledging Perkins when the scoundrel tipped his hat to him.

Darcy sighed as he got back into another hired hackney to take him away to a more reputable part of town where he could hire yet another to take him home. His part was done except for meeting weekly with Perkins. Darcy was hopeful, though, that Perkins would lead the runners to Wickham before the week was out.

So it was with great relief that, a few days before he had to venture out to meet again with Perkins, his cousin came striding into his study with news. They had found Wickham.

Chapter 14

Darcy stood looking out his study window to the square below, trying to comprehend his cousin's news. He turned to Colonel Fitzwilliam. "Tell me again why we do not just arrest Wickham?"

"Darcy," Richard said warily, "We cannot arrest a man on speculations."

"Then arrest him for his debts. I will wager they are substantial."

"True, but Wickham has accumulated quite a stash of money with his latest luck at the tables and would probably be able to buy his way out of most of them, leaving the rest holding his vowels and no wish to prosecute. No, the way I see it, all we need is time and we can rid England of him once and for all."

"Time." Something Darcy did not wish to give up. Wickham's location was known, the runners were watching him, and now he was told he must wait—wait for Wickham to make a mistake, which was bound to happen with time. Darcy let out a heavy sigh. "What if there was a way to force his hand. His tongue was always loose when he was in his cups. We could get him drunk and question him."

At the suggestion of drinks, Richard stood and poured himself one. He stood contemplating his cousin's suggestion as he savored his own glass. "It might work, but our involvement must remain a secret. Even foxed, Wickham would never say a thing if he suspected a trap."

"Your runners." Darcy was becoming excited about his plan. "They could ingratiate themselves into some of Wickham's tables. They have to watch him anyway; let him think they are other low-life gamblers."

Richard sat down, shaking his head. "No, Wickham considers himself a gentleman. It would have to be among company he would want to impress, though not so high that Wickham might restrain himself in his speech as not to offend their sensibilities."

Darcy took his seat next to his cousin. They were silent for a while. Suddenly the colonel shot up. "Of course, George and Leigh would be perfect for it." Richard laughed to himself at some memory involving the two. "Major George Whitman and Colonel Leigh Masters, lately of His Majesty's army and friends of mine. They owe me, too, after that little hobble in Bath last year." Richard chuckled again, and Darcy cleared his throat. Richard, now obviously in jovial spirits, refocused. "They could be our men."

"Do you think they can do it then?"

Richard nodded his head confidently. "As long as Wickham is not suspicious, we should be able to find out whether he was involved in Lydia's death."

Darcy nodded. "How soon can we set it up?"

"No more than a few days, I am sure." Richard rubbed his hands together with excitement.

"Well, at least I can drop Perkins. There is a positive side to all this after all."

"No, you have to keep Perkins." Darcy groaned. "Darcy, we have to make sure no one associated with Wickham gets suspicious."

Darcy reached over, took his cousin's glass of port and finished it, stifling the man's protest with a raised brow in his direction.

Wickham leaned his arm against the bar and surveyed the room. Cigar smoke filled the air as thick as wool and heavy enough to block much of the poor light coming from the gas lanterns on the tables. He looked over his shoulder to the barkeep, one of his new friends. He smiled to himself. It was amazing how many friends one could have when flush in the pockets. When his luck was down, the same men would turn, but Wickham never stayed around that long. Wickham raised a finger towards the man who nodded his head, sliding a glass down to him. Picking up the glass of brandy, Wickham turned again to the room.

Men were drinking, cards out, cigars in their mouths. A loud round of laughter drew his attention to a table at his side where a couple of officers and a few regular patrons were playing a game. The men laughed again, the two officers at the table leaning into each other, obviously foxed and losing badly. Neither one seemed to mind; they were drunk as lords and oblivious to the Johnny cardsharps that were bleeding them dry.

Wickham turned back to the bar and set his empty glass down. He motioned to his friend and the man came to him.

"What can you tell me about the two reds over there?"

The barkeep picked up Wickham's discarded glass and began polishing it with his dirty rag. He spit out a bit of tobacco juice to the floor beside him as he put the glass back on the shelf for the next patron. "They come in a few hours ago — swimmin' in lard and lookin' for a good time."

The table erupted with laughter again, drawing Wickham and the barkeep's eyes to it. A barmaid walked by to fill the officers' glasses. One of the men reached for her hand and pulled her close to whisper something in her ear. She tittered, and the man pushed a coin into her grubby palm before allowing her to walk away.

Wickham turned to his friend. "They do not seem to be in luck this evening."

His friend laughed. "I don't suppose their luck'll change neither. Not with Jem and Stoney bleedin' 'em."

"Dipping rather deep, I'd say. How long did you say they have been here?" Wickham was calculating how long they might stay and whether he might cash in on their good times as well.

"Aye, they's regular wells, those uns. Drink like horses. A few hours, I reckon."

Wickham nodded and straightened to his full height. He turned to the barkeep and said he would want a bottle sent to the table.

"What'll ya be drinkin' this time, Wick?"

He tendered a mischievous grin. "The regular for me, and a bit of your blue ruin for the chaps."

Wickham tapped the bar and walked over to the table with the officers just as Jem placed his winning card on the stack. Wickham reached for the man's arm and lifted it up, pulling out the extra cards he knew the man kept hidden in his sleeve.

"I suppose these cards just fell into your coat, eh, Jem?"

Major Whitman, flawlessly acting the soused fuddler, stood up angrily, knocking his chair on the floor. "I say, what gammon is this?"

Swearing a chain of oaths, Colonel Masters stood too, his chair falling behind him. "You both are a bunch of sharps!" He pulled at the other man's collar. Stoney stumbled out of his grasp, losing his stash of secret cards in the process.

Wickham smiled as he knocked the two gamesters into each other. They were his friends, and he would repay them later for their losses. "Get out, the both of you." When they reached for their winnings, Wickham elbowed one of them in the nose, causing him to spill his claret down his shirt. "I believe these two gentlemen deserve their purse after you cheated them." Wickham pushed the pile of coins back in an attempt to placate the drunken officers.

"Right good of you, sir. Major Leigh Masters, and this is my friend"—he hiccupped and swayed on his feet—"Colonel Whitman."

The other officer laughed and grabbed at his friend's arm. "I am the major and you are the colonel." The two men guffawed raucously and thanked Wickham for stepping in and retrieving their swag for them.

Wickham made a magnificent leg and accepted their praise and thanks graciously. Then Masters offered Wickham a chair at their table and invited him to sit for a game. "To thank you properly as a gentleman for your steppin' in, don't you know."

He accepted.

Wickham smiled as he took a seat. He held his arm up and called to the barkeep for a bottle of his favorite and one for his new friends. They raised their glasses to his generosity and shuffled the cards again. The barkeep sent over a bottle for each of them and an empty glass for Wickham.

After pouring his own glass, he surveyed the officers over the rim as he brought it to his lips. They were not nearly so drunk that they could not play cards but too bosky to suspect being fooled again. He was satisfied.

For the next few hours, the three men grew stinking drunk. One got richer, the other two poorer. The bar filled with their loud teasing and ribald comments. The two officers were cautious with their drinks and often managed to empty them onto the floor unnoticed. Wickham, however, seemed to be well on his way to oblivion and a bad headache. With all the finesse of supposed men on the cut, the officers conducted their maneuvers of loosening Wickham's tongue. The conversation grew more bawdy and licentious as the evening progressed.

Near three in the morning, the two officers chortled good-naturedly as they passed the last of their coin to their new friend Wickham. Leigh turned to the other officer. "I suppose it was not our night for Lady Luck, my friend."

They stood and swayed dangerously a few times before they steadied themselves and reached to shake Wickham's hand.

"'Tis a pity to lose, but you're a fine chap to lose to if'n a man has to." Major Whitman covered a gurgle from his throat and placed a hat crookedly on his head.

Wickham was satisfied with his evening of easy pickings from two poor card players. "Any time you gentlemen come back, I would be honored to sit with you." He swayed a bit himself as he stood.

Leigh looked as if he was going to fall asleep on his feet, but he nodded and said, "Maybe next time we meet, it will be your luck that is down, George Wick...umph...Wickham." He pulled a handkerchief from his pocket and dabbed the spittle from his chin.

The two officers attempted a bow but only just managed not to fall to the ground in the process. They turned and sang an old army tune as they stumbled out the door, thanking a patron for holding the door as he exited before them.

Wickham could hear their loud singing for several minutes after they left. He opened up his own purse and swept his winnings into it. Throwing a small pile on the bar for his friend and another bit for Jem and Stoney at the other end, he walked out the back door and up a side alley to a staircase belonging to the boarding house where he kept his rooms.

On the other side of the block, the two officers, as sober as a Sunday, followed the 'patron' from the pub into a waiting hired hackney.

"Well, what do you think?" The patron, Colonel Richard Fitzwilliam, took off a heavy, well-worn coat and hat.

Major Whitman and Colonel Masters shook their heads. The major answered, "The man is the worst kind of sleaze I have ever met! I do not know how he considers himself a gentleman after what we heard in there."

Colonel Fitzwilliam nodded in agreement. "Thank you both for enduring. I suppose it was worse than I thought, so I ought to owe you now."

Masters answered with a laugh. "After meeting Wickham, I would dare say putting him away would be reward enough for me."

Whitman agreed and added, "We will come by your house tomorrow and give you a full report. I am sure you did not catch everything."

Fitzwilliam nodded. "I did not. I could not risk his recognizing me, but I could not stay away; you understand."

The hackney slowed and finally stopped; they exited and walked the distance to their lodgings, leaving Richard to continue on his way back to Mayfair.

"And you are sure?"

Colonel Fitzwilliam walked over to the fireplace and leaned against the mantel before he spoke. "As sure as I can be. I was there, you know. I saw Wickham finish off an entire bottle himself. I saw him ape-drunk."

"What did he say to your friends?"

The colonel waved him off. "Too depraved to repeat. But there was never any hint or suggestion of Wickham laying a hand on Lydia."

Darcy drew in a slow breath and held it. His heart began to beat faster as he was filled with a sense of hope he had not allowed himself to feel since getting his cousin's letter summoning him to London. Could he really be free to go to Elizabeth now? Free in his conscience, too, that Wickham was as despicable, wicked and villainous as ever but not guilty of murder? He released the air he had been holding and looked at his cousin.

"What exactly did they say to him?"

"They bragged about supposed conquests with Haymarket ware…and hinted of convenient, gently bred ladies and"—Richard's face contorted with disgust—"Even spoke of the need to lay a firm hand on ladies sometimes. All the things we previously discussed. All manner of falsehoods that would provoke Wickham to share his own stories."

"And I assume he did."

Richard mumbled a low oath. "Oh yes, he had many stories of his own to share. Of course, his stories are likely true or at least exaggerations."

"And nothing he said was familiar to the story with Lydia?"

"I questioned them thoroughly, Darcy. I assure you, if Wickham had said anything even remotely suspicious, I would have had his hide."

Darcy nodded, satisfied. "Then you do not think he did it."

"I did not say that," Richard mumbled.

"What was that?"

"Oh hell, Darcy! I do not know. Something does not seem to fit. Nothing points to Wickham and yet everything in my gut does. Satisfied?"

No, Darcy was not. It was how he felt, too. He picked up the book on his desk and looked at it. It was the one Elizabeth had been reading the day he found her in his study. He had not returned it to the shelves yet. It was beginning to seem they would never know whether Wickham was guilty or not. That was no reason for Darcy to hold back any longer though. A slow smile grew as he looked down at the plain brown binding.

"So I am free to go to Hertfordshire then."

Richard laughed despite his foul mood. "I suppose you are. Go. Claim your beauty. Who knows, maybe I will get lucky and she will refuse you, professing a fondness for your devilishly handsome cousin the colonel."

Darcy's quiet growl only made his cousin laugh louder. His mind brought him easily back to the feel of Elizabeth in his arms when she was overwrought at Hunsford; Elizabeth smiling at him in his studio at Pemberley, admiring his art; Elizabeth responding to his kiss with sunbeams in her hair. His face spread into a wide grin.

The roguish glint in his eye caught Richard off guard, and his laughter died.

"I do not think that will happen, Richard. I believe I can safely say where the lady's preferences lie, and they are *not* with you."

The colonel grinned before his face turned serious. "You deserve her, William."

Darcy acknowledged the heartfelt sentiment. He knew his cousin only called him 'William' under the most staid of situations. He was always 'Cousin' or 'Darcy'.

Darcy was thrilled to be returning to Hertfordshire—to return to Elizabeth. His heart ached with want to see her lovely face again and to witness the spark in her eyes light up at his entrance.

He stood and walked towards the bellpull to summon his butler. When Mr. Carroll arrived, he asked that the man convey his request for Georgiana's presence in his study.

While he and his cousin waited, he poured them each a glass of wine and toasted his future happiness. He felt freer than he had in weeks and now was eager only to go one place, to be with one person.

Georgiana opened the door and exchanged greetings with her brother and cousin. "You wished to see me, William?"

Darcy smiled at his sister, studying her briefly before answering. She had a powerful combination of innocence and mischief in her eyes. She was no longer a girl but a growing woman. He liked nothing more than to make her happy, and so he said, "Yes, dear. I wanted to inform you to have your maids pack your bags. We leave for Hertfordshire tomorrow."

Georgiana's eyes lit up as she looked from her cousin to her brother. "Then your business is concluded?"

"As much as it can be, Sprite." Richard smiled and kissed her cheek. He made his good-byes and winked at Darcy as he left the room.

Georgiana turned to her brother. "Are we really leaving then?"

Darcy smiled. "Yes, we are really leaving." He walked over to the wall behind his desk and removed a painting from its hanging to reveal a safe in the wall.

His fingers paused momentarily as he retrieved the key from his breast pocket when his sister said, "I am so delighted, William. I cannot wait to see Elizabeth again. I am glad this wretched business of yours is over. What was it anyway?"

Darcy cleared his throat as he turned the key and opened the heavy metal door. "Nothing for you to concern yourself over, dear." He quickly retrieved a small velvet box from the vault and placed it on his desk in front of his sister, effectively deflecting her curiosity from his private matters. "But before we can go, there is something I wanted to show you — to ask your opinion."

Georgiana's eyes filled with tears as she recognized her mother's jewelry case. It had come out of the vault a number of times before. There were a few pieces that her mother had intended for her, and William had given them to her last year. The rest of the pieces, she knew, were left for when he took a wife.

Her small hands came up to her mouth, and she looked at her brother with great tenderness. Darcy's throat was thick too, and his eyes were suspiciously shiny as well. He cleared his throat as he attempted to continue. "As you know these were meant for the woman I shall take as my bride." He paused to regain his composure. She nodded at him to continue; her happiness for him was endearing. "As you may have guessed — indeed, orchestrated in some ways — I hope to ask Miss Elizabeth Bennet to be my wife."

Georgiana squealed as she ran around the side of the desk to embrace her brother. He immediately wrapped his arms around his little sister and held her tightly to him. His voice was full of emotion as he whispered into her hair, "Should you like such a sister, Georgie?"

He felt her head nod up and down as she nearly sobbed, "Oh yes, William!" She pulled back to look up at him. "How soon can we leave? Do you think we can manage to leave tonight?"

Darcy smiled as he pushed a strand of her hair away from her wet cheeks and dabbed at them with his handkerchief. "I wish, Poppet. Tomorrow will come soon enough; you will see."

Georgiana's tender emotions were then transformed into bundled energy as she excitedly thought about having Elizabeth as a sister.

"Oh, it will be so wonderful! We can go shopping and to the park and stay up all night talking—just like real sisters!"

Darcy bit the side of his lip and lowered his brows. "Ha! She may become your sister, Georgie, but you will do well to remember that first she will be my wife." Georgiana waved her hand in dismissal at her brother's words. So he added, "You may go shopping and to the park. But I will not have you keeping my wife up all night." He did not say and would not allow himself to think about keeping her up himself.

"Oh, pssht!" Georgiana laughed. She turned to the velvet box on her brother's desk and remembered. "Oh, can I see it?"

Darcy was confused by her change of topic. "See what?"

Georgiana looked at him as if he had bricks for brains. "Mother's ring of course!"

Darcy, recalling himself to the business before him, laughed. He lifted the lid of the box to reveal a number of exquisite diamond, ruby and sapphire necklaces, bracelets and matching rings. Tucked in the corner was another small velvet box that he reached for.

He opened the box and displayed the ring for his sister. It had been his mother's ring and his grandmother's before that.

Georgiana acted as sensibly as any young lady presented with such a ring was expected to do. She *oohed* and *ahhed* as she tenderly took the box in her hands and turned the ring around to catch the light from the sun streaming through the windows. It sparkled brilliantly, and she confirmed that she was sure Elizabeth would love it.

Darcy was filled with a sense of satisfaction that he had never felt before. He took the ring back from his sister and placed it in his coat pocket. He closed the velvet box and returned it to the safe once more. After it was locked and the picture replaced, he turned to his sister.

"Well?"

Her brows lowered in confusion. "Well, what?"

"Do you not have orders for your maid? Dresses to pick, trunks to pack?"

Georgiana jumped up to kiss her brother's cheek, laughing at the reminder. She bit her lip while she grinned widely.

"How soon will you propose then, William?"

"As soon as I can find a moment alone with her, Georgiana—on that, you may depend."

Chapter 15

Finding a moment alone with Elizabeth was proving to be dashed difficult. Darcy bit back the ungentlemanly oaths that were at the tip of his tongue and politely accepted the cup of tea she was handing him. They were in the drawing room with her family. He looked down at her and allowed a half smile. She was lovely in a sprigged lavender muslin gown with dark purple embroidery. He had forgotten how charming she looked in colors. He had not even considered she would not be in black, or even in half mourning dresses, when he saw her next. That was a few days earlier when he first came into the neighborhood. She stunned him then in all her loveliness in a green-hued summer dress. He had been so discomposed that at first he could do no more than bow politely over her hand as his sister made her delighted greetings.

Elizabeth smiled in return as he took his cup and saucer from her hands. He was as handsome as ever. When he arrived in Hertfordshire and called on her with Georgiana, she had been temporarily overwhelmed with an enchanting memory from a field of bluebells. Her cheeks, she knew, blushed scarlet, and she could not meet his eyes. Now she could, and she looked into his dark brown eyes, thankful to see their usual intensity. If not for his distinctively austere and unwavering stare, she would have wondered whether he had changed his mind. Getting a moment alone with him was proving to be dashed difficult! She swallowed stiffly and sighed.

Remaining at his side, she considered various topics of conversation. Surveying the room, her eyes rested on her mother, demurely sitting with Jane and Mr. Bingley. Her mother was laughing sweetly at something the gentleman said; she was comporting herself in every way the lady. Who would have thought Elizabeth would miss her mother's old scheming ways? She was certain her mother would have artfully contrived a moment alone with Mr. Darcy by now! She would have been locked in the room with him within a few minutes of his arrival a few days before; Elizabeth was sure of it.

Seeing where Elizabeth's gaze was fixed, Darcy was considering the same undeniable change in Mrs. Bennet. The woman had been so ill mannered and uncouth when he was in the neighborhood last autumn; she had been a major reason Darcy had not allowed himself to become totally bewitched by Elizabeth. It would have been unthinkable to attach himself to such a lady and to call Mrs. Bennet his mother, especially when the memory of his own beautiful, charming mother was etched into his mind as the paragon of proper, ladylike comportment. In truth, Elizabeth's mother had been his greatest objection when deciding whether to propose to Elizabeth last April in Kent! Now the lady was preventing his proposing to her now—albeit, Darcy admitted, not intentionally! He had been counting on her matchmaking agenda to help him find a moment to speak with Elizabeth privately.

He could not complain about her changed behavior, really—only observe it with astonishment. He had been in company with the Bennet family several times since arriving in Hertfordshire, and she had yet to revert to her nervous and invariably silly ways. To add to his amazement, she was not the only Bennet whose transformation nearly made his jaw drop in disbelief. On more than one occasion since his arrival, Elizabeth's father had entered the room, greeting his wife tenderly with a kiss to her fingers before seating himself beside her! This was the same man who before, as far as Darcy had ever witnessed, kept more than a room's distance from his wife whenever possible. It was foul timing in Darcy's mind that the two of them should decide to become proper just when he could have capitalized on either *his* negligence or *her* matchmaking with respect to their second daughter.

Thinking of this, Darcy looked at her next to him. He ached to take her arm and thread it through his own in a proprietary fashion—much the way Miss Bingley often did—almost claiming him. The thought of Elizabeth placing claim on him brought a smile to his face. Her silken curls were arranged with a few purple flowers woven in a beautiful twist on the top of her head. From his height, he could not see her face below the curls. He had to see her bright eyes, so he cleared his throat to garner her attention.

Elizabeth looked up at Mr. Darcy and smiled. She had been enjoying reacquainting herself with his manly scent. "They are much changed, are they not?"

Darcy's face registered no understanding for a moment before he saw her indicate with her small chin towards where her father and mother were now sitting conversing with each other across the room.

"I could not say," Darcy said politely.

Elizabeth laughed. "Oh, come now, Mr. Darcy. There is no need to preserve propriety and not speak of the obvious with me."

Darcy could not help but smile a little wider and bow his head to acknowledge her statement. He was not in the habit of commenting on another's behavior, but he ventured, "Your parents do seem to be..." He thought about it and could find no other word than "Happy."

Elizabeth sighed and returned her gaze to them. "Yes, I believe they are."

Darcy could not then resent their change in behavior or their failure to aid his suit, not with Elizabeth looking so content, her eyes dancing with happiness as she observed her parents. Of course, he knew he should have requested a private audience with Elizabeth as soon as he arrived or any time in between, but he had never been an open man. He had never been one for display or sharing his personal matters. If he could not find a private moment with her on his own before the wedding, he vowed he would swallow his pride and request one.

"You know, my father says that they married for love."

Darcy did not know what to say, so he only nodded and studied the couple.

Elizabeth sighed. "Of all the changes that have come to our home since Lydia's death, this was not one we could have foreseen."

"I would suppose not." Darcy returned the small smile she offered him. Then a thought struck him. She had once requested a private meeting with him; why could he not ask her? "Miss Elizabeth," he began with his voice lowered, "I believe there is a set of benches behind the hedge in —"

"Mr. Darcy!" Miss Bingley's shrill voice could not have reached his ears at a more inopportune time. Elizabeth watched his eyes cloud and his jaw tense before he turned towards Miss Bingley just as the lady slid her gloved hand through his arm. "There you are, sir. Forgive me for neglecting you; I was detained by that insufferable Sir William —"

Darcy cleared his throat to stop her, stepping backwards to allow her to notice Elizabeth for the first time at his other side. Miss Bingley barely colored at her barb before she addressed Darcy's other companion. "Why, Miss Eliza! I did not see you there. Your dress makes you blend so splendidly into the room." She waved a delicate hand around to point out the purpled hues of the wallpaper.

Darcy frowned slightly; he thought Elizabeth stood out like a midnight star, a lighthouse to a lost ship, a glass of water to a dying man, and the very breath of life at his lips. Her breath at his lips… He cleared his throat again, this time to dispel his thoughts so he could address Miss Bingley. He spoke rather coldly. "Miss Bingley, I do not recall hearing you extend your congratulations to Miss Elizabeth on the happy upcoming marriage of her sister to your brother."

Elizabeth bit the inside of her lip, first to stifle her own cutting retort for Miss Bingley and then to keep from laughing aloud at the way Darcy forced her to display a pretense of civility.

Glancing at Darcy, Miss Bingley presented an insincere smile to Elizabeth. "My congratulations, Miss Eliza."

With a dangerously sweet smile, Elizabeth parried, "Thank you, Miss Bingley. And of course, my continued congratulations to you on your brother's happiness." When Miss Bingley nodded stiffly, Elizabeth could no longer help her riposte. "It seems we are to be sisters."

Darcy felt Miss Bingley's hand tighten at his arm, but he carefully kept his face from betraying his amusement.

"Indeed," was all Miss Bingley could manage.

At the best of times, Miss Bingley was merely tolerable if only for her brother's sake. Throughout the week, she had intruded upon his conversations with Elizabeth, and now she interfered as he was about to request the privilege of speaking to Elizabeth alone! His patience with the woman was hanging by a thread. If his friend were not getting married in just two days, he would have given over to his frustration days ago! He did not want to create an unpleasant atmosphere at the time of his friend's triumph and felicity, and for that reason, he bit his tongue.

Since traveling impetuously to Hertfordshire earlier in the week, he had called at Longbourn two times, each surprisingly accompanied by an insistent Caroline Bingley wishing to see her 'dear Jane.' Each time, she had spent more of her energy trying to engage him in conversation than talking with 'dear Jane.'

He had suggested a walk on a bright day, knowing that Miss Bingley did not walk, especially when there was a chance the sun might penetrate her enormous bonnets and freckle her porcelain skin. He had thought then that he might be successful in speaking with Elizabeth, especially when he knew his clever sister would come along but might lag behind — overcome by a timely bout of fatigue, of course. As luck would have it, Miss Catherine offered to join their walk. Darcy thought nothing of it until it became apparent that Kitty was determined not to stray far behind, pulling Georgiana along with her.

Foiled yet again, Darcy never anticipated Kitty would prove to be such a tenacious chaperone. It had made him wonder whether she felt any responsibility towards her sister's fall, having not been close enough to see around the bend in the path when Lydia fell. He quickly pushed the thought from his mind, not wishing to acknowledge any uncertainties he had there. They had found Wickham and decided the proof was simply not there to cry foul play. *Besides*, he told himself, *what motive could Wickham have had to hurt Lydia?*

Across the room, Georgiana excused herself from speaking with the Gardiners, newly arrived from London for the wedding, and made her way towards where her brother, Miss Bingley and Elizabeth were talking. She had been watching her brother converse with Elizabeth. Both had smiled brightly, had looked wistfully into each other's eyes and seemed pleasantly engaged with each other. Then she saw Miss Bingley spoil the moment. What did a frustrated matchmaker like Georgiana have to do? How could she get her brother and Miss Elizabeth pleasantly engaged in a more *official* capacity when people like Bingley's and Elizabeth's sisters stepped on all of her efforts?

She shook her head as she cursed under her breath — of course, not real curses; she was a gently bred lady. When she reached the threesome, two sets of eyes registered relief; the other feigned welcome. So Miss Bingley did not appreciate her several attempts to separate her from William since they arrived. *No matter*, Georgiana thought. *If she would just give up, we would not have to play this tiresome game.*

"Miss Bingley," Georgiana began, noticing the slight hitch in the lady's insincerity. "Would you do me the honor of playing this evening? I believe they are about to open the instrument. For myself, I am not yet comfortable exhibiting before such an audience, but I so enjoy seeing you display your talents. What say you? Will you give me another opportunity to observe your confident bearing, so that I might learn by your example?"

Miss Bingley swallowed her irritation at the interfering miss and sagely agreed as she patted the girl's hand. "Why, Miss Darcy, of course I will. I am sure by the time you make your curtsey, you will be one of the most accomplished young ladies of my acquaintance." She released Mr. Darcy's hand with a meaningful smile, making sure he noted her attentions to his sister. While she walked away with Miss Darcy she thought, *And after I am married to your brother, I shall see that you are married off to the first nabob I can find. And good riddance!*

After watching his sister leave with Miss Bingley, Darcy looked down at Elizabeth, his lips pulling up into a smile as he watched her press her own lips together to keep from laughing.

"And what do you find so amusing this evening, Miss Elizabeth?"

Elizabeth kept her eyes firmly in front of her and did not dare look up at him. She knew she would lose her composure. "I am sure the same thing that you find amusing this evening, sir," she managed, covering her mouth with a gloved hand.

To hell with propriety, Darcy thought, as he boldly reached for that gloved hand and placed it on his arm. To the room, it looked as if he were simply escorting her to the refreshment table to deposit her glass there. He ignored her impertinent look when she lifted her chin in reaction to his behavior. When they reached the table, she released his arm to place her cup on the table and then turned to take his from him. When he retrieved her arm and placed it again on his to escort her back to their corner of the room, he raised his eyebrow at her in challenge when she tilted her head again to him.

If it could be said that their conversation thereafter was natural and unaffected, the same could not be said about the feelings coursing through them by their slight touch; those were completely affected.

Unfortunately for both of them, before Darcy could solicit a private audience, their exchange was again interrupted from another quarter. When Darcy saw the man approach, he felt every bit the errant schoolboy as he attempted then to discretely remove Elizabeth's arm from his. She was having none of it and tightened her grasp on his sleeve. He stood straighter, trying to convince himself that he had no reason to feel uneasy; the man was just . . .

"Mr. Bennet, sir." Darcy bowed stiffly. *Elizabeth's father.* And judging from his face, Darcy could see the man was not best pleased. Where Elizabeth's arm was before a pleasant patch of warmth, now it felt like fire, one that was currently drawing her father's eyes. Darcy swallowed and again attempted to slip his arm away. It was not as if he did not wish Mr. Bennet to know his intentions towards his daughter; he had just not informed him yet. Moreover, Darcy felt as if the man could read his very thoughts, some of which he would rather not have Elizabeth's father know.

Elizabeth tightened her hold. "Papa, how are you this evening?" His face was worried, though she could tell by the way Darcy was fidgeting beside her that he was misinterpreting her father's look as disapproval or possibly anger. It was a common enough misunderstanding.

Mr. Bennet looked up from Elizabeth's hand at Darcy's sleeve to her face. She was contented, happy, and he did not wish to cause her any grief. Even though he knew that, of all his daughters, her sensibilities would survive the topic he wished to speak with Darcy about, he still did not wish to burden her. No, he could not have her present when he spoke to Darcy. Besides, why upset her unnecessarily if it turned out to be nothing after all?

"I am well, my dear, though I am feeling a bit parched. Tea is perfectly fine for you young people, but an old man like me needs something a bit more lasting. Lizzy, would you be so kind as to go to my book room and smuggle a glass of my brandy back to me?"

Elizabeth smiled and slid her arm out of Mr. Darcy's, a touch peevish that he seemed relieved. "Of course, Papa."

Mr. Bennet bent and placed a tender kiss on his daughter's cheek as he said, "I will keep your place here, so no other ladies steal your beau." His teasing caused her cheeks to flash bright red. A quick glance at Mr. Darcy confirmed that he was similarly affected. She nodded quickly and curtsied before she departed swiftly out the parlor door.

Mr. Darcy watched her retreat, lifting his chin and trying to affect his familiar ascetic façade to hide his own embarrassment at her father's jest.

"Mr. Darcy," Mr. Bennet began in hushed tones without preamble. "We cannot speak privately without causing some talk, and I would rather not have them speculate. I am sure you understand."

Darcy did understand. He understood, with growing alarm, that perhaps his suit would not be sanctioned by Elizabeth's father! It was a possibility he had never considered, its being so absurd to him. His mind was too much in turmoil to respond.

"So I must speak to you in company, though I know you will understand my wishes not to draw any attention."

Darcy nodded his head numbly.

Mr. Bennet breathed a sigh of relief that only made Darcy feel more despondent. In a more conversational tone, surprising Darcy, Mr. Bennet said, "Mr. Darcy, when we last spoke—" He paused and looked the younger man in the eye, willing him to remember their last conversation. Darcy expelled the breath he had been holding. *Of course! He wants to talk about Wickham.* When Mr. Bennet was sure that Darcy understood his reference, he continued, "When we last spoke, you said you had some business that you were going to look into. Might I ask how your business investigations panned out?"

His expression grave, he replied, "That business was concluded just last week, sir—I believe satisfactorily to all those concerned."

Suddenly Darcy felt endeared to the older man when he saw that he was struggling with his emotions. It was some time before he responded. "I am glad to hear it." Mr. Bennet swallowed thickly and said, "So you did not find any reason to worry—that is, about the business, of course."

Darcy understood the man's need to know—his need to dispel any questions about his daughter's death. Compelled to reassure the older man, he smiled and nodded. "Nothing at all, sir. I believe all those affected by the nature of my business can rest easy now that it has been concluded with positive results."

Mr. Bennet could only nod. He was overwhelmed for a moment with acute relief, his happiness complete. When he was mere days away from giving the hand of his oldest daughter away to a man who loved her—and when he had only just found the love of his life again—Mr. Darcy's words of reassurance that Lydia's death was an accident could not have been sweeter.

When he gathered enough of his composure to turn to the younger gentleman, he extended his hand and said, forgetting to code his words for others, "Thank you, Mr. Darcy. You have given this old father—" He coughed, struggling again. "If there is anything I can give you in return, you have only to ask." They both knew he was referring to Elizabeth's hand.

Mr. Darcy glanced away from Mr. Bennet only to smile at Elizabeth as she entered the parlor again. "I do have something in mind, sir."

Mr. Bennet could laugh now, feeling light as a feather. "Then I will look forward to seeing you soon in my library, perhaps for a game of chess?"

Mr. Darcy tore his eyes from Elizabeth to address her father again. "I hope not before too long, sir."

Elizabeth had reached the men then and was relieved to see them smiling. She handed her father his drink, and he excused himself to return to the couch beside her mother. Mr. Bennet's last words gave Mr. Darcy such joy that he felt he must bring her hand to his lips! But before he could resign himself to take her arm in his instead, she made the movement herself, claiming him as he had wished earlier. He looked at her and smiled so brightly that his dimpled cheeks forced her to catch her breath.

THE SKY WAS SUNNY AND clear on the day that Miss Jane Bennet resigned the name of her childhood and took the name of Bingley. It was a lovely assemblage of friends and family who gathered to witness them bind their love and make their vows before man and God. Elizabeth had been so delighted with her sister's happiness that she did not know the effect her bright, sparkling eyes had on the best man standing beside Mr. Bingley. Every time she looked at him, he trembled, praying for the day when she would stand with him as his bride.

He still had not had the time to speak to her privately, but he was not as concerned. He was still eager, to be sure, but he did not seek some rushed affair, hurried because they had stolen a few moments of private conversation. No, when he told Miss Elizabeth Bennet that he loved her for the first time and how bewitched he was by her, he wanted all her attention. So he tarried, his family ring always in his pocket, waiting for the perfect time.

Fortunately for both of them, their duties as wedding attendants to the bride and groom allowed them to spend much of the day's festivities in each other's presence. The day seemed as magical to them as it did to the new Mr. and Mrs. Bingley. It was during their dance that evening at the wedding ball that Mr. Darcy made the first steps to secure her life to his.

"Miss Bennet, I feel it imperative to inform you that tomorrow I am going to call at your house with Georgiana."

Elizabeth laughed at his formal recital of his plans for the next day. "I thank you for informing me, sir. I will try to remain at home for your visit then."

Darcy looked her in the eye in that intense way that she had come to love so much. "And then I am going to leave my sister with your sisters to request permission from your father for a private audience with you."

Elizabeth faltered, almost missing the ladies' next turn in the dance. With all the love in her heart, she looked towards him then and replied, "I will look forward to it, sir." She raised a brow in that saucy way he had loved since he first met her. "Though what you can have to speak privately to me about, I cannot guess..."

"Minx!" He laughed loudly, shaking his head and causing others to look towards them.

Elizabeth laughed too, though butterflies had begun to swirl around her insides. How she could be so nervous suddenly when she had expected and known for weeks that this day would come, she did not know. Part of her still wondered how she could have garnered the affections of such a man.

Mr. Darcy parted ways with Elizabeth that evening with an equal measure of anticipation, anxiety and impatience. He had only one night to sleep before he could lay claim to her heart forevermore. If it also meant reclaiming her lips... well, who was he to complain?

Chapter 16

Elizabeth could not sleep. Who could be expected to sleep when filled with such anticipation and excitement? No, she could not find any way to relax. Though she lay in her bed all night, she was not tired. Her mind kept sleep at bay while evoking every one of her favorite moments with Mr. Darcy. In the quiet peace of the morning, first light was already chasing the night's shadows away. Elizabeth decided she needed to calm her excited nerves with a walk about the countryside.

She quietly rose and went to her dressing table. She could not hide the smile that pulled at her cheeks. Elizabeth was anxious to share with Jane the blissful tumult in her mind. But Jane, of course, was gone away with Bingley. Without Jane's steady nature, Elizabeth was restless with nervous excitement. A walk was indeed needed.

After pinning up her hair, Elizabeth walked towards her dressing room, opening the door quietly so as to not wake the rest of the house with its creaky hinge. She had the door opened only an inch when she heard whispered voices on the other side. Two of the maids were putting away the starched and folded laundry in her dressing room. Not wishing to disturb their work, she quietly leaned against the wall and smiled dazedly. Waiting for them to finish, she could not help but overhear part of their conversation that wafted through the cracked door.

"I 'ear 'e left 'er in London, ruined, 'e did."

"But ya say she's a come 'ome now?"

"Aye, and lucky she is; 'er uncle owns the inn, or she'd 'ave no place."

"No man'll 'av 'er now."

Elizabeth turned her ear towards the door then, curious as she realized they were talking about the missing girl from the Meryton Inn.

"I 'ear she's a breedin' too, poor mop."

"An' there's more, Bess." The maid lowered her voice even further, causing Elizabeth to steal closer to the door to catch what was said. "She 'as said the bastard b'longs to that gent who 'ad been always callin' on Miss Lydia, bless 'er soul." The maid shook her head again.

"The off'cer?"

"Aye, Wick somethin' er other. Told 'er they'd get hitched, 'e did."

"Not Miss Lydia?" she gasped.

"No, ya ninny! The mop at the inn."

Elizabeth was glad she was leaning against the wall then because she had very little strength in her legs anymore. Her knees had gone weak, and her head was still spinning when the voices of the maids faded away down the servants' staircase. *Mr. Wickham was the man who took the girl from the inn?* She could not fathom it, even knowing all she did about his character. Still, all she knew for certain was that he was a liar, a cheat and a gambler. *But a libertine?* Darcy had not said anything about that.

Elizabeth shook her head, more than a little shaken. She regained her strength and walked into the dressing room to ready herself for the day. She was eager to see Mr. Darcy and relate to him what she had just learned of Mr. Wickham. It was simply too astonishing not to tell him! When she remembered his intentions for that morning, all her earlier excitement returned and she hurried to dress for her walk.

When she exited her bedchamber, a thought stopped her in her tracks. Never had she once thought that Mr. Wickham could have been dishonorable with Lydia, but now she wondered. If she had not heard about Wickham's behavior with the maid at the inn, she would have disregarded the errant thought as ridiculous. But something nagged at her mind, and she began to panic. He had spent so much time with Lydia. If he was of such loose morals, could he not have been capable of coercing her sister to commit some breach of propriety or even something more sinister? Instead of turning towards the stairs to go down for her walk, Elizabeth turned the other way and nearly ran up the back stairs to the attic. She quickly found the trunk that held all of Lydia's belongings.

With no small amount of determination, Elizabeth managed to move the heavy trunk away from the wall so as to open the lid. Her sister's belongings before her eyes caused them to tear. She rifled through the trunk until she found what she was looking for. Pulling out the worn leather diary, Elizabeth sat back against her heels. She held it, experiencing a moment of indecision about whether she ought to read her sister's private thoughts.

Covered with dust and cobwebs, Elizabeth decided she had to know. After closing the trunk, she secreted the small book into the pocket of her dress and then rushed down the stairs and out the door. A sinking feeling in her heart drove her forward, as far away from the house as she could possibly go on foot. She would not attempt to read any of it until she had reached the secluded peace of Oakham Mount.

DARCY HAD HARDLY SLEPT A wink. He was rehearsing all he wished to say to Elizabeth that morning. After so many months—so much heartache, personal assessment, and humility—Darcy was ready to place his heart before Elizabeth and hope she would receive it. What had she not done for him? During the course of the months after her sister's death, Elizabeth had taught him more about himself through her judgments of him than he had ever known before—hard lessons at first, but necessary to learn what it took to please a woman worthy of being pleased.

He did not want to consider what a disaster it would have been to propose to her in Kent. He was positive now that she would have refused him. The relief that filled his breast was immeasurable. Darcy swept away the troubling thought. It was irrelevant now.

Unable to stay indoors any longer, he decided to ride that morning to relieve some of his nervous energy. When he slipped out to the stables, narrowly missing Miss Bingley on his way, he asked the groom for directions to Oakham Mount. He had never visited it when he was in town last autumn, though it was always acclaimed as possessing an excellent view.

After receiving directions, Darcy mounted his horse and kicked him into a steady gallop. The breeze was in his face, and he felt the sting of the cool morning air in his lungs. When he was near the summit, he stopped his horse and dismounted. The sun was just beginning to crest the horizon. He tied his horse loosely to a nearby tree, so it could graze as he began his final ascent up the hill.

Upon reaching the top, his breath was taken away by the picturesque view—not the surrounding vista of hills and lush green farmland and not the rainbow of colors painted across the sky as the sun rose higher but that of his sweet Elizabeth. She was sitting on a small boulder, her back to him, reading. He marveled at how delicate and feminine she looked, her back arched in a curve over the book.

Recovering from his surprise and with a smile on his face, Darcy quietly approached her. When he was but a few feet away, he called her name softly, not wishing to startle her. When she did not respond, he stepped closer. His smile broadened at her distracted state. "Elizabeth . . . "

His brows knit together when she did not react again to his call. *Must be a very good book.* He quickly crossed the last of the distance between where she sat and where he stood, kneeling in front of her to finally catch her attention.

What he saw on her face caused him to fall back on his heels. Her eyes were red and her face covered in tears. Her face was painted in an anguish he had only seen once before: when he had discovered Georgiana with Wickham before the intended elopement. He recovered himself then and instinctively reached for her shoulders to bring her to his embrace.

"Elizabeth! What is the matter, my dear? Please, what is wrong?" He felt a rush of panic when she resisted his embrace and pushed against his chest for him to release her. He immediately complied.

Elizabeth could not speak; she could hardly think. He was pleading with her; she could hear his voice, but she could not communicate what she felt. It was as if she were drowning. She silently handed him the book, covering her face with her hands to weep.

Mr. Darcy took the book from her with questioning eyes. He reached into his coat and pulled out his handkerchief for her. Carefully, he pulled at one of her hands, to uncover her face again. "Elizabeth," was all he could manage. Her sorrow affected him too powerfully for him to voice anything more. His throat closed, and he patted her cheek tenderly with the soft linen. She took it from him to wipe her face as she indicated again towards the book.

"It is Lydia's," she finally replied in a throaty whisper.

Darcy sighed; he understood then. He was saddened that her tender heart was still so grieved by her sister's death, but it was something he loved about her: her full, compassionate heart. He patted her back and took the seat next to her. "I know it is difficult, Elizabeth. You need never hide your feelings from me."

Elizabeth shook her head; she needed him to understand. What she knew now was not just in the past between two individuals. It affected her life too. It affected Darcy's, and he deserved to know. Her heart was breaking, anticipating the moment when he would learn of her shame and no longer want her.

With a voice barely above a whisper, she pushed the book back to him again and said, "Read it."

Darcy frowned. He looked down at the worn binding and opened the book to the first page. It was filled with an embellished, feminine handwriting he did not recognize. The first words, "Dear Diary," stopped his examination and he closed the book again.

"Elizabeth, I cannot. These are your sister's private thoughts. It is perfectly acceptable that you read them, but it would not be appropriate for me."

Elizabeth took the book from him and opened to the last entry. She looked up at him with such painful eyes that his heart turned to ice at the sight. She mouthed, "Read it."

He would rather not but for those eyes. They pleaded with him. He would do anything to make her happy again, and if Elizabeth wished that he read her sister's diary, it was an easy request to fulfill.

Nodding, Darcy looked down and began reading.

Dear Diary,

La! What a perfect day for a walk. I shall laugh when I see the faces of my family when I return with Mr. Wickham and announce our engagement.

Engagement? Darcy's heart sank to his feet, but he read on.

To think we have been secretly engaged for two months and not a soul knows about it. Not even Kitty! My dear George said we must keep it a secret until his sister marries and he inherits the money he was to have been given from the settlements or some such detail. La! We shall be rich as lords—for I just heard from Mrs. Forster that Wickham has requested leave for his sister's wedding. So it is done! I shall insist we announce today when he comes to call on me. He would want to tell his family at the wedding about his own intended, I am sure. Besides, I cannot wait much longer. My dresses are already getting tighter. Oh, how happy George shall be to know that he will be a father before long! Oh, but he is here; I can hear him being announced below. When next I write, I shall sign 'Mrs. Wickham.' Oh, how droll that sounds! For now, the future Mrs. George Wickham!

He was frozen; he could not move, react or think. *No, no, no!* Elizabeth was looking at him with a steady, piercing gaze. *How could she not blame me?* He thought. It was his fault for not revealing Mr. Wickham's true character to the good people of Meryton last autumn. He, who could have prevented Elizabeth's family from the licentious designs of such a man. He knew Wickham would never have married the girl! Now he was beginning to accept that Wickham was likely guilty when it came to Lydia's accident—an accident that was looking to be nothing of the sort.

What words could he say to atone for such devilry? Her own sister ruined, and at the hands of a man from whom Darcy should have protected society. *If only I had been more open with my neighbors.* He felt as if his own future were crumbling around him.

What words could she say to atone for such devilry? Her own sister ruined, and at the hands of his enemy. *Who could possibly wish to connect themselves with the family of a fallen woman?* Even with Lydia's death and the secret of the loss of her maidenhood—a secret Elizabeth would never allow anyone to know—she knew Darcy could not wish to have such connections. And to think there was a baby. The loss she felt for her sister and her foolishness was only compounded by the defeat Elizabeth was now feeling for herself. She felt as if her own future was crumbling around her.

Darcy found his voice. "I cannot say...cannot find words to express how sorry I am."

Elizabeth's eyes dried, and she lifted her chin. She could not show him the affect his words were causing her. Of course he was sorry—sorry he could no longer honor his intentions towards her. "I am sorry too, though I understand your feelings."

She did? He could not think so; it was his fault after all. Of course, she was sorry about what this meant for their own future. It was too painful to think about.

She wished she had not felt honor-bound to show him the diary. But she would die if the shame became generally known. Her parents! *Lord, they would be brokenhearted.* No, she had to have his word. Elizabeth could not meet his eyes when she asked, "You will not tell, will you?"

"Of course not, Elizabeth."

Darcy was already transferring the searing pain in his heart into justified anger toward the man who caused all the torture in Elizabeth's eyes—anger toward the man who once again intruded on his life, this time dashing Darcy's chances for happiness. He had to go to London at once to speak with Wickham. He had to rid himself of the man for good. It would not change the situation with Elizabeth, but at least he could bring Lydia some justice, even if no one knew it but himself.

"I can see you have long desired my absence, nor have I anything to plead in excuse of my stay but real, though unavailing, concern. Would that I could do something…" *Something to make you love me still.*

Elizabeth nodded. Her heart was numb, and the hole in her chest was expanding. "This I fear will prevent you and your sister from visiting Longbourn this afternoon."

He made no response. Mr. Darcy seemed scarcely to hear her. He was now pacing in front of her in earnest meditation, his brow contracted and his air gloomy. He seemed to come to himself after several long minutes and was distracted as he said, "Ah, yes. Please make my excuses. I must be off to London as soon as I can."

"Of course."

Elizabeth's dejected voice brought Darcy's mind back from where it was in London, already planning what he would do to Wickham. He was grateful that his cousin was still watching the villain. He kneeled in front of Elizabeth then and took up her hands in his. They were so slight, so fragile. He turned them over in his hands. He thought about confessing his love to her right then. Surely, she must know even though he had not said the words.

He almost did, but he could not put her through the agony of hearing it when she could not possibly want him now. Instead, he carefully took off her gloves and turned her palms up. Holding her hands in his, he allowed his face to fall into her hands. Elizabeth's eyes filled with tears again as she looked down at her lap, at Darcy's dark curls, his face hidden in her hands. She could feel his breath on her fingers. A tear escaped the confines of her eyes, rolled down her cheek and fell into his hair. She watched it glisten in the morning sun. For a brief moment, Elizabeth allowed herself to lean down and rest her cheek against the feathery curls. If that moment were all she could have from him, she would take it.

A moment later, she felt him kiss each of her palms tenderly, whisper a good-bye and stand to leave. He could not meet her eyes, and she watched him walk away, every step taking him farther from her and breaking her heart into more pieces. She looked down at her hands when she could no longer see his form. They were wet with his tears.

Chapter 17

With every pound against the saddle and every hoofbeat on the hard road, Darcy closed his heart further. He could not think about his own pain; he had a nightmarish task ahead of him. It would be the last gift he could ever give Elizabeth — the gift of justice for her sister. The fact that Elizabeth would never know was no consequence. The least he could do was secure that Wickham never caused pain elsewhere, for him or anyone else. He had to do this for himself and for Elizabeth. Darcy kicked his stallion's flank and rode harder.

He had left a note with his sister, informing her of his departure and instructing her to have her trunks packed and to return to London in the coach. His valet was instructed to accompany her and her maid. He could not wait until their trunks were packed; he had to be on the road, his need for a distraction from his pain driving him forward. Harder, he pressed his horse. The sooner he could reach London, the sooner he could find his cousin and close the books on George Wickham.

He was tired, physically and mentally spent from the ride by the time he reached Grosvenor Square and the mews behind his London home. The horse was panting, lathered from its exertion. He threw the reins to the waiting groom and took the stairs into Darcy House two at a time.

Bellowing for Mr. Carroll, Darcy headed to his bedchamber at the same pace, pulling at his road dust-covered clothing. He was already half dressed in the dull black clothes he used to meet Perkins when his butler arrived at the door.

"Send a footman to Matlock House for Colonel Fitzwilliam immediately.

Send one to his clubs, too, in case he is not at home."

"Yes, sir. At once!" Mr. Carroll bowed and made a hasty exit. To see his master home so early and with such blue devils was more than a surprise for the loyal retainer. His was the best of masters, and Mr. Carroll knew that some dire circumstance had occurred to pull Mr. Darcy away from Hertfordshire and a certain lady there. He hurriedly issued the orders to the footmen and sent them on their way. Within thirty minutes, he was escorting an equally concerned and surprised Colonel Fitzwilliam into his master's study.

"What in the world has you back so soon, Darcy?"

Darcy spun around to face his cousin. The color drained from his cousin's face when he saw him. Turning away, he caught a glance in the mirror. He barely recognized himself as the drowning man he saw in his reflection.

"Do you still know where Wickham is, Richard?"

"Of course, I have my men near him at all times. Why?"

"We have to find him. He did it. Blast that man! He did it!"

The colonel's jaw firmed, and he spit into the empty fireplace. "Tell me everything."

Darcy sank into one of the armchairs, momentarily defeated. "He ruined her..."

"What! That bastard! But how could it be? We have been watching him here. I swear he could not have gone to Hertfordshire."

Darcy glared at his cousin. "I did not mean Elizabeth. God help me, not her. Thank goodness. He ruined her sister, got her breeding, telling her that they would marry. On the day she fell, she had written in her diary that she was going to insist he announce the engagement because her, ah, condition was beginning to show." His look told his cousin that he could guess what happened next.

Richard ran both his hands through his hair, growling, "Then we have to get him for sure this time." They were silent — Richard contemplating plans, Darcy trying to breathe.

Richard looked at his cousin, dressed to meet with Perkins. "What is your plan then?"

"Other than to get my hands on Wickham's neck and send him to hell?" Anger was good. It kept him from feeling the other painful emotions that threatened to overcome him.

"Yes, besides that."

"I was going to meet with Perkins; I care nothing for that man either. I was going to reveal that I know his game and insist he take me to Wickham."

"But we already know where Wickham is."

"I want him to confess, Richard. I have to hear him say it. I do not know why, but I feel as if having Perkins there will help. The man knows too much, has been watching Wickham for too long not to. And if he is useless, well, I will just arrange for him to travel to the colonies or some such."

"It is a good plan. What do you want me to do?"

"I need your friends to help me to convince Perkins. We get him to take us immediately to Wickham and then we need to see that we have a place to *talk* with him."

Richard nodded, standing. "Then we are off?"

"I have already sent a note to the pub owner requesting Perkins's appearance as soon as possible."

"Well, let's get to it!" Richard laughed with malice. Within a few minutes, they quitted the house.

Georgiana was worried — really quite worried. She had received her brother's note and had done as he instructed, but she had insisted on paying a farewell call to Elizabeth before leaving the area. She had to know what was going on. Something had obviously upset her brother. She knew he had gone riding that morning, and she knew he never would miss their planned call on Elizabeth later that day. He had told her that he planned to propose to Elizabeth that morning during their visit.

What had her more worried was the fact that, when she called on Longbourn to pay her respects, Georgiana was told that Miss Elizabeth was indisposed. She had come home feeling ill from her walk and was not taking visitors. Georgiana had been hurt at first until the thought hit her that perhaps her brother had encountered Elizabeth on his ride. *He must have proposed and been refused!* But it did not make sense; she knew Elizabeth loved her brother. She was sure of it. *Didn't she?* Georgiana's concern then turned to her brother. To have been refused when he was so sure, so happy and so in love — it was unfathomable. She instructed her coachmen to make all due haste to London. Her brother needed her, and she would be there for him. If only she knew what was wrong.

A DETERMINED DARCY, HIS EAGER cousin and a visibly shaken Perkins were currently encased in a small hackney on their way to a set of boarding rooms where Perkins claimed Wickham was presently lodging. Darcy looked at his cousin when Perkins gave the driver the direction. His cousin's nod was almost imperceptible. Perkins at least was telling the truth that time. Darcy had clearly shown the man he was not best pleased to have been misled by him. Perkins was not fool enough to try to deny it, especially when three burly men stood up from their tables throughout the pub and surrounded him. He recognized the men as some of those who had been often at the other places Wickham frequented.

Their conveyance stopped in front of the building. Perkins gulped; he was not yet sure whether Wickham's men might be worse to face or not. Either way, his employment was surely at an end. Everyone exited the carriage, another one behind them emptying of the men from the pub. The man Perkins knew as 'Burns' left him in the custody of his burly associates from the pub as he and the officer went up the steps of the building.

"Keep him down here until we call for him," Colonel Fitzwilliam instructed the bruisers.

At the top of the stairs in front of the door Perkins had indicated, Richard turned to his cousin. "Darcy, let me go in first. I do not know whether he is armed."

Darcy protested but finally agreed. He stepped aside, out of view of the door. Richard kicked the door in and called for Wickham. A moment later, Wickham sauntered out of a back room, followed quickly by a servant girl who was readjusting her dress as she slipped out.

"Richard, how pleasant of you to visit!" Wickham pretended not to be concerned at the sudden appearance of Colonel Fitzwilliam at his door, or what was left of it, surreptitiously surveying his options for escape. The window to his right was too high off the ground. *Damn!* He usually preferred ground floor apartments for times likes this.

"Put off, George. I did not come for a social call."

Darcy could not wait another minute. He charged into the room and planted Wickham a facer that sent him sprawling to the floor, down for the count.

"Well, great, Darcy. Now, how are we going to question him?"

Darcy was rubbing his cut knuckles. "He will come to eventually. Blast, if I have not wanted to do that for so long!"

Richard slowly started to laugh. After a few moments, Darcy did too. Richard shook his head and went to call the others up to the room. When the rest of his men and Perkins entered the room, Darcy noticed how Perkins's eyes went wide at the sight of an unconscious Wickham on the dirty floor, his nose bleeding. The men sat Perkins down in the corner and ordered him to stay there.

After a few more minutes, Darcy went to the wash jug at the side of the room and poured its contents on Wickham. He sputtered and started to come around, cursing as he reached for his broken nose.

"What the bloody hell?" His voice died in his throat when he saw the fury on the face of Darcy. If he was concerned before at Richard's appearance, now he was truly alarmed at the rage in Darcy's eyes.

"Tell me now, Wickham; did you do it?"

"He is talking about Lydia," Richard clarified as Wickham was yet oblivious.

Wickham looked between the two men and considered his options again. "I do not know what you are talking about. Lydia Bennet? The girl from Hertfordshire?" he said, feigning indifference upon hearing her name.

"Cut line, Wickham." Darcy roared, "I know you ruined the girl. Furthermore, I know you left her with child, too."

Wickham gulped and looked again between the men. He sputtered, "What does it matter now? I heard the girl died! It's not like her father can make me do the pretty to a dead girl. Did she say something before?" He was beginning to panic.

Darcy nearly punched him again for his careless disregard for Lydia's death, an event that had affected his beloved Elizabeth profoundly. *No, not mine anymore.* His vehemence grew, and he stepped towards Wickham again, his fists clenched.

Richard stepped in his way. "No, Darcy."

Darcy's irritated eyes set upon his cousin. "And why not?"

Richard motioned to two of his men to get Wickham into a chair and off the floor. Then he instructed them to guard both Perkins and Wickham while he stepped outside with his cousin.

Darcy was reluctant to go, of course. How many years had he waited to finally deal with Wickham? How many times had he been hurt, cheated and deceived by him?

As soon as they reached the hallway and out of earshot of the room, Richard spoke through clenched teeth. "Get a hold of yourself, Darcy!"

"I am surprised to hear this from you, Richard. You know what that blackguard has done to me."

"Yes and here's the rub. Firstly, Wickham cannot talk when he is unconscious on the floor. Second, if you kill the man, you will be hanged." When Darcy huffed, Richard asked, "What about Elizabeth and Georgiana?"

"There is no Elizabeth!" Darcy spoke so coldly that Richard had to step back.

"What?"

"She would not have me after that man"—Darcy pointed down the hall towards the door—"ruined and killed her sister."

Richard cursed and ran his hands through his hair. He mumbled to himself, "I cannot believe she holds you accountable."

"Why would she not when I could have prevented it?"

Richard was still confused; the letter he received from Georgiana while they were in Hertfordshire had related how well they got on. He looked at Darcy then and caught a glimpse of the drowning man again. There was nothing to be done about her today; they had to deal with Wickham first.

"Put that aside now, Darcy. You have to think of Georgiana at least. So you cannot kill Wickham even if you should like to."

Darcy closed his eyes and groaned.

"Thirdly..."

Darcy opened his eyes and gave a look of exasperation at his cousin. "Thirdly? There is more?"

Richard nodded. "Yes, thirdly, you have to get hold of yourself because this is not you, Darcy. You are not this man: violent, a quick switch. I will allow you that first punch; heaven knows, I'd have liked to spill his claret myself. But you are a gentleman, and you are not this man."

Darcy quietly looked at his cousin for a minute. He knew he was right. As much as he had enjoyed dimming Wickham's lights, he was raised to be a better man than that. *She* would have expected better from him too. He was here for her after all; it was the only honorable thing he could do to atone for what was lost. He nodded to his cousin.

"Besides, I have a plan." The colonel smiled wickedly at his cousin. Wickham had asked what Lydia had said. Allowing him to think she had said something of import before she died might not be such a bad idea.

Darcy followed him back into the room.

If possible, Wickham thought the new controlled, reserved Darcy who entered the room was even more threatening than the anger-filled lion that left. He swallowed and tried to ignore the man's steady gaze.

Richard leaned casually against a bare wall. "I think you know what Miss Lydia would have said before she died, Wickham."

Wickham's eyes went wide for a minute, but he kept silent at first. "I do not have the pleasure of understanding you, Richard," he finally said, although his voice faltered, stripped of all its bravado.

"I suppose I ought to just hand you over to the magistrate to fit your hemp neckcloth. But I had thought you would want to plead your case—you know, explain yourself. Lord knows the evidence is stacked against you." They had no real evidence, but Wickham need not know that. "You know, long-time standing with the family and all that."

Wickham considered his options again. "I do not suppose you would believe then that it was an accident?"

Darcy's fists clenched again, but he now understood his cousin's plan and added, "Not when the girl herself had named you." She had called out his name before she was given the draught.

Wickham cursed aloud.

Perkins spoke up. "I knowd he'd done it, gov'ner."

All eyes went to the man. He gulped and went on to say how he had been following Wickham since he came to London, first hired by another gentleman for the debts owed to him. He had often been in the presence of Wickham when he had been in his cups and bragging to his friends about a girl named Lydia, and about how he had escaped the parson's mousetrap by her "conveniently timed demise."

Wickham cursed again. Darcy and Richard looked at each other. They had gotten him drunk and had not gotten anything out of him. Perkins could be trying to save his own skin now. Wickham saw the suspicion in their eyes.

"The man is lying. Why, anyone can see he is trying to save himself!"

"No, gov'ner. I swear!" Perkins spilled. He told Richard and Darcy all about Wickham's gambling operation: how the barkeep was in his pay; how he got unsuspecting gentleman drunk while he stripped the table, his own drink being nothing but coffee-darkened water.

Richard looked towards his cousin, and Darcy gave him a wide grin. Wickham cursed again.

"Well, Wickham," Richard began, "we gave you the chance to tell your side, and you lied to us. I suppose there is nothing left for us but to call the magistrate." And he meant it.

"I swear, I did not mean to kill the girl." Now Wickham was scared. "I only wanted to, you know, get rid of the babe."

The men were even more revolted by him. Darcy could see that his cousin really was going to call the magistrate next. He could see Wickham was sweating bullets, too. As much as it went against every fiber of his being, he needed to stop it. He called his cousin to follow him out the door again.

"What is it Darcy?"

"You cannot call the magistrate, Richard," Darcy said softly.

"What? I know that I said you had to get hold of yourself, Cousin, but you cannot be thinking of letting him get away again."

"No, he cannot get away. But I cannot have you call the magistrate either."

Richard leaned against the wall and began to run his hands through his hair then, realizing the grime they had accumulated in the dirty boarding house, thought better of it.

"Then what do you propose we do with the devil?"

"Ship him to Australia." He raised his hand to stop his cousin's near outburst by adding, "Richard, I cannot let Elizabeth's family go through the humiliation of a trial. I cannot let Lydia's previously untainted reputation be challenged. I cannot do that to them. It would break them. It would break her." He was not just thinking of Elizabeth then but of the relief he saw in Mr. Bennet's eyes when he had assured him there was nothing to worry about.

Richard sighed heavily. "I suppose there is no chance of keeping it quiet with a trial."

"No, there is not. And besides, I gave my word to Elizabeth not to allow Lydia's ruination to become known."

"Then she does not even know that Wickham killed —"

Darcy shook his head. Richard nodded in understanding.

"We have a problem then, Darcy. As a colonel in the army, I am duty bound to bring about a trial in one form or another—either a civilian trial for murder or his court-martial for desertion from the militia."

"Then court-martial him. These things can be quiet affairs. Certainly you can see to that."

Richard paced as he considered his options, looking grave but satisfied when he finally realized a solution. "A field general court-martial—it requires less than a general court-martial. It can be done quietly. Transportation is usually the sentence, though it is an automatic death penalty if he returns to England. All right, Australia it is. I do not like it; indeed, it is far better than he deserves."

It tasted bitter to Darcy too, and he said as much. "Perhaps we will get lucky, and Wickham will not survive the passage."

The two men reentered the room, and Darcy addressed Wickham. "You have two options, Wickham: the noose or Australia." The tone of his voice suggested that the noose would be fitted personally—and that evening—if he did not choose Australia. Besides, Wickham was too smart not to see this for what it was: another slip of the coin and a chance to get away, even if he had to go to God-forsaken Australia.

"Australia," he grumbled.

"Good choice." Darcy turned to his cousin. "What do you want to do with that one?" He pointed towards Perkins.

Richard smiled at his cousin and winked. "I have been considering that one for a little while. He is a downy cove even if he is slick as a stick. I think the army could use the likes of him. I have a buddy bound for the continent next week who could take on a new plebe and teach him some discipline."

Perkins gulped but nodded his head vigorously, recognizing his own option at avoiding a more serious punishment. "King 'n' count'ry, gov," he said as he tipped his hat.

Richard acknowledged his compliance and ordered two of the men to take him to the recruiting office and to ask for Colonel Masters. His lip twitched in amusement when he saw Wickham swallow at the mention of the man's name.

When the two men left, dragging Perkins along, Darcy turned towards his cousin again. He looked at him only briefly before stepping forward and dimming Wickham's lights again with another swing of his fist. He shrugged at his cousin's raised eyebrow. "One for the road, you know."

Richard laughed and patted his cousin's back. "Of course." He was still laughing when he instructed the last of his men to send another message in a different direction.

Wickham was still out when the man returned with Major George Whitman. The army officer took one look around the dirty room, noting the bleeding knuckles of his friend's cousin and the slumped body of Wickham, and cursed. "I do not suppose you could have waited for me before having all the fun?"

After he had spent the evening with Wickham in that vile pub, pretending to get drunk and hearing all of his sordid tales, Major Whitman had asked that Richard allow him to partake in bringing him down. Now he was informed that he was to watch over Wickham, personally escort him to the major general's office for his court-martial, and then escort him to a ship was bound for Australia as soon as may be.

Richard smiled. "You have my permission to have all the fun you want after we leave," he said to his now-smirking friend. "If he is a little worse for wear for the journey, so be it."

Darcy stood to leave, feeling all the weight of the day come upon him in full force. Now that he had defeated Wickham, he was left with only the threads of his broken heart. He did not even have enough energy to hold onto his anger anymore. The embers had burned out, leaving ashes inside.

He motioned to his cousin that he wished to leave. Richard said he would meet him at the waiting carriage. Darcy slowly walked down the stairs of the boarding house. He hailed the coach and climbed in. Now that he had washed his hands of Wickham, he was left to think about the events of the day. Had he really seen Elizabeth only that morning? Seen her lovely face darkened by pain and scandal? The day seemed one long nightmare.

Richard climbed into the coach and looked at his cousin with a satisfied grin on his face. "It feels good to be rid of the man, does it not?"

Darcy nodded and turned his head to look out the window.

"SOMEBODY HAD BETTER TELL ME what the blazes is going on!" Georgiana shouted to her cousin.

"Georgiana! A lady does not speak in that manner."

"A lady! You have the nerve to tell me how to comport myself as a lady when my brother has not been seen for three days?"

"What are you talking about, Georgie? I brought him here myself a few days ago." Richard was becoming concerned, though he would not show Georgiana as much. He had worried about his cousin when he dropped him off after returning from Wickham's. Darcy had said nothing the entire ride home, and Richard had not had a word from him since then. He was actually at Darcy House to inquire about his cousin when Georgiana had accosted him in the entryway and nearly dragged him through the closed parlor doors.

"He refuses to see anyone. He has not left his rooms since he came home that evening he was with you, and all of his food trays come back barely touched. Three days, Richard!"

"I will go see him." Richard sighed as he walked toward the door.

"No you will not, Richard. You are not going anywhere until you tell me what is going on. My brother can wait, but I cannot."

Her voice faltered, and her lip quivered, causing her cousin to stop in his tracks. He turned to her then and opened his arms. Georgiana walked into his embrace and began to cry.

"Shh, sprite, all will be well. I will see to it; I promise you."

Georgiana pushed away. "I am not a child, you clutch. Tell me now."

Richard sighed. He did not think she needed to know about Wickham, but he could explain something of Elizabeth. Nevertheless, he was sure that was the real reason for Darcy's current behavior.

"He is a man disappointed, my dear."

"Then she refused him after all," Georgiana mumbled as she sank slowly into a nearby chair.

"No. At least, I do not think he even got that far."

Georgiana looked up, encouraged by his words. If he had not proposed and been refused, then things could be fixed; she was sure of it. They loved each other; what could come between that?

Richard sat next to her and took her hand, deciding an explanation about Wickham was unavoidable after all. "What I am going to tell you may make you upset, my dear. Do you still wish to hear it?"

The look she gave him indicated she did.

"Your brother found out that Wickham compromised Elizabeth's sister before she died. Wickham told her he was going to marry her, but of course, you know he had no such intentions."

"Oh." Georgiana's eyes watered again as she thought of the pain Elizabeth must have felt on finding out such news. "But what has that to do with William?"

"She blames him for it—believes he should have exposed Wickham for who he was in Hertfordshire last autumn."

"Elizabeth could not think that! I know her. She loves him."

Richard merely shrugged his shoulders. "That is what your brother believes."

Georgiana looked at her cousin. He was not telling all; she could tell by the way he was eager to get away. She narrowed her eyes. "Richard Fitzwilliam, you may be my guardian and a good deal my senior"—she did not laugh when he protested her reference to his age—"but do not think for a moment that I will tolerate your being anything less than honest with me. I know Elizabeth, and this simply does not make sense to me. Why did my brother leave in such haste for London? Where were you both until late that evening, and what are you not telling me?"

She crossed her arms across her chest, and for a moment, Richard thought she looked a lot like her brother, only more like an adorable, angry kitten. But he could not deny that she had grown up, and considering the state of her brother upstairs, perhaps she needed to know the whole sorry tale after all.

He sighed and acknowledged there was more to the story. He related how Darcy had learned of Wickham's deeds with Lydia, encountering Elizabeth on the walk as Georgiana had suspected. He told his young cousin about how Wickham's behavior after Lydia's fall had been suspicious and how they had tracked him down and found him in London—nor did not spare her from Wickham's confession about how Lydia really died. He ended with Wickham's court-martial and exile to Australia and Darcy's hand in it.

"He did not want to put Elizabeth or her family through the pain of a trial, so we arranged to have him deported. I am glad to say, I personally saw him leave on a ship yesterday."

Georgiana was saddened by the news, especially when she considered her own past with Wickham. She knew her brother had not exposed Wickham to save her the possible humiliation of having her name bandied about. She considered her cousin's account of Lydia's death. She knew that would be the most difficult part for Elizabeth. Georgiana ached to comfort her friend.

The only way she could think to do so would be painful. She thanked her cousin and dismissed him to deal with her brother. After another few minutes gathering her thoughts, she stood up and went to her room where she spent the rest of the evening penning probably the most important letter she would ever write. She hoped it would make a difference to the two people she loved most in this world.

Chapter 18

Her fingers paused, the shears ready to clip another bloom for her basket. As had often occurred since returning home from her encounter with Mr. Darcy and the discovery of Lydia's secret, Elizabeth's mind seized, and she was left reviewing their meeting.

Long after the sound of his horse's hoofbeats no longer reached her ears, Elizabeth had remained sitting on the rock where Mr. Darcy had left her. Numbly she sat there absorbing what had occurred. Her heart could not connect with any emotion for some time, protecting itself from further sorrow. Absentmindedly, she retrieved Lydia's diary from the seat beside her, resting her hand in the place it had laid, where moments before Mr. Darcy had sat. The cool, hard rock seemed apt to describe her new understanding.

Standing slowly, she had unconsciously smoothed the wrinkles from her dress. A flash of white caught the corner of her eye. She looked down to see the handkerchief Mr. Darcy had given her earlier. She looked at it almost incredulously. Then a small gust of wind picked it up, and it tossed, danced and rolled across the ground to tangle itself on a low fern. It seemed to mock her — a symbol of her fleeting hold on the man, only to have him pulled from her grasp and tossed away from her. Elizabeth rushed to seize the linen, feeling a sudden wish to hold on to the only thing she could possess that once was his. She knew he would not be coming back for it. She had to claim it as her own.

Pulling the soft fabric to her face, she had dried her cheeks, only to have them wet again when his scent from the fabric reached her senses. She lowered her hands and looked at the freshly laundered linen. It was damp from her tears. She rotated it to study the embroidered initials on the corner: '*FD*'. Sighing, she ran her finger delicately across the script—his initials, simply stitched, with no other adornment. It suited him, she thought. His classical, distinguished, unaffected demeanor matched the fine texture and simplicity of the expert stitching.

Elizabeth had laughed at herself without humor for spending so much time contemplating the handkerchief and comparing it to its owner. It was not as if any of that mattered any longer. She had returned all of his others. This one she could not part with. Reverently, she had folded the square, placed it in her pocket and begun her slow, solemn walk back home.

A rustling in the bushes near her feet roused Elizabeth back to her task at hand. She saw a rabbit dart across the garden to another bush, and she cut another flower.

After allowing herself to grieve Mr. Darcy's departure that morning three days ago, taking her future with him, Elizabeth stirred herself to calm her disturbed, unequal spirits. After all, she knew that living in a village like Meryton, gossip would run wild if she showed her loss. She could not bear to expose him to the censure of the world for caprice and instability, or herself to its derision for disappointed hopes. The world could not know their reasons, and she would not give it a source to involve either of them in further misery of the acutest kind. Her resolve allowed her to walk and talk amongst her family with all the blithe ambivalence she did not feel.

At night when she was alone, she would take out her handkerchief—his handkerchief—and sob without restraint. The torment of the last few days had wearied her spirits.

Elizabeth sighed as she placed the last bloom in her basket. She made her way slowly back to the house. When she reached the side door, she was met by her mother. Mrs. Bennet had watched her daughter in the garden. Her noticeable lapses in concentration those last few days had concerned her parents. Although appearing to walk through her day with composure, her manner did not have the same vivacity. Furthermore, Mrs. Bennet had observed her daughter withdraw into herself when she thought no one was looking, her eyes revealing a sorrow that pricked their hearts.

Mrs. Bennet had never been a keen observer, and although she was delighted with the attentions Mr. Darcy had given her daughter during the wedding week, she had not suspected a serious attachment between them until he had left. His departure from the area must be the source of her daughter's unhappiness.

"Thank you, my dear," she said as she took the basket of flowers from Elizabeth.

Elizabeth managed a half smile for her mother before she turned to walk past her. Mrs. Bennet looked down at the basket in her hands, noticing that all the blooms selected were half wilted and certainly not the best of those available. She frowned, considering again her daughter's situation.

"Have you written back to Miss Darcy yet, Lizzy?"

Elizabeth stopped and turned slowly to her mother with a quizzical brow. Then she remembered that Miss Darcy had left her a note when she did not come down to see her before she took her leave. It had been too much to face Darcy's sister, the girl she had grown to love as her own.

"Not yet, Mama," Elizabeth whispered.

"I suppose you are waiting until she is settled again in London. It has been a few days now, though," her mother suggested kindly.

Elizabeth nodded and walked towards the stairs to her room. She had not written Georgiana because she did not think he would wish for the reminder. As much as it pained her to disappoint her friend, she did not think that either should further the acquaintance. His best friend was already married to her sister. They would often be thrown into each other's presence, and eventually he would marry. She quickened her steps until she reached her door.

Stepping across the threshold, she turned and closed the door behind her, sinking against the wood. The very thought of his marrying anyone turned her stomach and caused her heart to beat painfully. He had a legacy to continue—an heir to secure for Pemberley. It was reasonable to assume that he would eventually overcome his affections and resolve himself to find another. She vowed she could not. She had no legacy, not without Mr. Darcy.

Walking towards her bed, Elizabeth sank heavily onto it. It had only been three days, and she was tortured with the thought of his moving on. She knew he loved her, knew he must be suffering with her now, but somehow she could not believe her hold on him could last forever. As for herself, she was his and would be until her last.

WHEN COLONEL FITZWILLIAM KNOCKED ON his cousin's bedchamber door, he received no answer. He suspected such would be the case, and so he raised his voice to be heard through the wood paneling.

"Darcy! It's Richard! You have about three minutes to ready yourself before I open this door!"

A movement down the hall made Richard look in that direction. A chambermaid who had heard his declaration looked scandalized as she hurriedly entered another room. Richard smiled, amused. He took out his pocket watch and looked at the time. There were no sounds from within, and though the exacted time had not passed, Richard retrieved the key he had charmed off of Mrs. Carroll earlier and put it into the locked door.

Turning the key and entering the room, his senses were assaulted by a surfeit of unpleasantness. The room was stiflingly warm with a roaring fire in the hearth in the middle of August. The heavy drapes were pulled closed, trapping the heat inside and the light out. His eyes adjusted to the dimness and found his cousin.

Darcy was sprawled in front of the fire with his legs stretched before him, still in the same coat and waistcoat in which Richard last saw him days ago. His neckcloth was discarded, a crumpled heap on the floor. A three-day beard darkened the already dismal look on his cousin's face. Walking further into the room, Richard was assaulted by the stench of an unwashed body and strong spirits. Disgusted, he did not attempt to lower his voice as he allowed a few choice expletives to escape.

Immediately, he tore open the drapes and unlatched the window to allow in a fresh, cool breeze. Turning towards his cousin, the colonel said, "I have seen barracks of footwablers in better shape then you and this room, Cousin." He shook his head, taking in a deep breath of air by the open window.

Darcy took no notice of his cousin's words and remained still, staring into the fire.

"Ignoring me, I see," Richard droned — still no response from his cousin.

"Very well, it suits my purpose better this way. I will not have to endure your insipid arguments, and you have a lot to hear from me."

Richard waited to see whether his hard words had any effect. They did not. Although he had genuine concern for his cousin, he grew livid thinking of the worry that Georgiana had suffered while his cousin nursed his sorrows with brandy.

"You, sir, are a coward." Richard was satisfied to see his cousin wince. "You claim to be in love with the girl, and yet you will not fight for her. So she tells you she will not have you because of your negligence with Wickham? Give over! Convince the chit you deserve her anyway!"

Nearly startling his cousin, Darcy's voice was low and incensed. "Do not refer to that lady so disrespectfully, Richard."

Richard smiled. At least he got a response. "And why should I not? If Miss Bennet has no more sense than to see the man you are through what has happened, then she does not deserve my respect."

Darcy clenched his teeth and brought the glass to his mouth for a practiced swig. He had already engaged in more of this conversation than he had wanted to.

"Deuces, man! Perhaps it is she who does not deserve you." Darcy growled, yet his cousin went on. "She laid blame on you for the whole of it, did she? I have to say I am disappointed. I had not thought Miss Bennet so unfeeling. What were her exact words?"

Though preferring his own silence, Darcy could not let his cousin disparage her. "She had no words; I saw the condemnation in her eyes."

Richard groaned into his hands and tried to control his sudden aggravation. "Are you telling me that, after encountering Miss Bennet and learning of Wickham's deception with her sister, you *saw* her assign the blame to you in her *eyes?*"

Darcy did not deem his cousin's sarcasm worthy of a reply.

"If you will not answer, I will assume it was so. Well then, I take back everything I have said. I am only sorry for what my own feelings have been." He stood up to leave.

Darcy said nothing, still irritated at the interruption and frustrated by his cousin's mockery.

Richard turned one last time to his cousin. "I came here out of concern for you, and I saw the anxiety that your wallowing has caused Georgiana. I see now that I have no reason to feel pity for you—not when I see that you are determined to be the blasted, honorable idiot that you think you are. I did not think Miss Bennet could have spoken such words. It did not seem in her nature be so unreasonable. Her eyes—humph!" Richard laughed mockingly.

Darcy shook his head; his cousin did not understand, and he could not expect him to.

190

"What seems more likely is that the lady would be concerned that *you* would not have *her*—certainly, not after having knowledge of her fallen sister."

Darcy's head snapped up. "Don't be ridiculous! I could not love her less were *all* her sisters ruined."

"But does she know that?"

Darcy returned to his drink; his only response was the rapid blinking of his eyes as he considered his cousin's words.

Richard was getting tired of his cousin's sour mood, the putrid room and its stifling heat. His tone was clipped and irritated. "So your plan to win her favor is to languish in this room brooding? Growing more dissolute by the hour, is it? A fine plan, Darcy."

Richard walked towards the door and turned only when he had opened it. "And take a bath, Cousin; you stink."

Darcy flinched at the loud sound of his chamber door slamming shut. If there had been any possibility Elizabeth did not hold him culpable, he would jump at it and prove to her his worthiness, but he had not the slightest hope. However, his cousin was right about one thing. He could not shut himself in his chambers forever, especially not when he considered Georgiana. Richard's reminder of his duty to his sister pierced him. For the first time in days, he felt the stifling heat of the fire he had requested to be lit in an attempt to stave off the chill in his heart. He rang for his valet. The man was much relieved to receive his master's request for a bath and a shave. Darcy was humbled. His staff and Georgiana had been worried about him. Although he knew he could never forget Elizabeth, he could no longer disregard his responsibilities.

After a bath and a shave, Darcy fell into his bed exhausted. He had not slept for most of the last few days and now that he had resolved to attempt normalcy again, his body succumbed. He noted the cleanliness of his room, obviously done while he bathed. The thought of his housekeeper's efficiency being his last, Darcy drifted into numbing sleep.

As GEORGIANA EXPELLED A DEEP breath, her shoulders sagged. She reached for her sealing wax and held it above the candle over her letter. Watching the deep purple of the wax drip onto the crisp paper, she said a small prayer that her efforts would help. Georgiana then pressed her Darcy seal into the hot wax. Her writing table was covered with the edges of her pen as she had mended it throughout the course of writing her letter to Elizabeth. Bits of the quill were scattered everywhere and blotted sheets of previous drafts were crumbled and discarded to the side.

Although it was difficult to relive the events of her past, it was liberating at the same time. For the first time, she felt that she had moved beyond the horrible events of last summer in Ramsgate. She loved Elizabeth, and she loved her brother. Furthermore, she knew they loved each other and deserved happiness ever after.

Her motives were not totally altruistic. Elizabeth had become quite dear to Georgiana. She had been guided by Elizabeth's bright, lively personality, strengthening her own confidence to step beyond her timid tendencies. Their shared friendship was more important to her than any other friendship she had known. She was apprehensive that the contents she had shared in her letter would change Elizabeth's opinion of her, but it was a risk she must take.

Standing, Georgiana pulled the cord, summoning a servant to collect the letter. She instructed it to be posted by way of express. Then she said another little prayer.

Mr. Bennet thanked Mr. Hill when he brought the post into his study. While he flipped through the letters of correspondence and business, he looked over to his favorite daughter, reading a book in her chair by the hearth. Mr. Bennet frowned; he did not like to see her so lost. Even now as she was looking down at her book, he could see that her eyes were not focused on the words on the page but somewhere beyond his study.

Mr. Bennet pursed his lips and looked down again at the letters in his hand. He placed them on the stack of other matters of business to which he had yet to attend and thought about what he ought to say to his daughter. Just as he was about to address her, there was a knock on the door and Mr. Hill entered with another letter. This one was marked express, and it was addressed to Elizabeth from Miss Darcy. Mr. Bennet thanked Mr. Hill and placed the letter in his pocket when he saw that his daughter had not even noticed the interruption.

He walked over to the chair next to her and reached for her hand. Elizabeth started in surprise but gave him a small smile.

"Are you enjoying that book, Lizzy? You seem quite engrossed in it."

Elizabeth cleared her throat and attempted to put a bit of levity into her voice. "Yes, Papa. It is very diverting."

Mr. Bennet smiled sadly at his daughter and then reached for the book and placed it back in her hands with the text facing the right way up. "I suppose it would be quite diverting to read upside down and backwards," he teased.

Elizabeth colored in embarrassment for having been caught thus. Shame-facedly, she looked at her father, only to see his sympathetic eyes looking back. Elizabeth could not repress a small chuckle for her mistake and his teasing words. "I suppose I was a bit distracted."

"You have been a bit distracted, my dear. I would say for about four days now."

Elizabeth blushed again and closed the book in her hands, keeping her eyes trained strictly on its binding. "I miss Jane, I guess."

"You must think your old Papa is 'attics-to-let' if you think I believe such nonsense."

Elizabeth blinked and then laughed at her father. "You know it is not always a good thing to have one's parent know you so well."

Mr. Bennet was pleased to see her smile and laugh, though it did not quite reach her eyes. "I know you miss Jane, but that is not what has you so forlorn."

"I am not forlorn."

"Attics-to-let."

Elizabeth lowered her eyes again to the book and smiled as she shook her head.

"Perhaps a certain gentleman has something to do with your distraction." Mr. Bennet frowned as he saw his daughter's eyes cloud over at his reference to Mr. Darcy. "It seemed to me that your 'arts and allurements' were very close to working their magic on the gentleman."

Hot tears stung at Elizabeth's eyes, but she held her breath and attempted to push them back. "I do not wish to speak of this, Papa."

She could not explain to her parents what had caused Mr. Darcy to leave so suddenly because doing so would require her to reveal Lydia's indiscretions. That she could not do, not when they seemed so happy; they were finally finding peace with her sister's death.

Mr. Bennet could see that the topic distressed his daughter exceedingly. With a gentler tone and with much tenderness, he said, "Very well, child. I will not press you if that is your wish." He reached into his pocket and retrieved the letter from Miss Darcy.

Reaching over, he gently slipped the letter under his daughter's hands that were gracefully folded on her closed book. He watched Elizabeth note the direction on the envelope and then saw her hopeless eyes water again. Something had happened, some kind of misunderstanding between the two of them. Mr. Bennet cleared his throat and went to kneel beside his daughter.

Taking her hand in his, he forced her to look at him. "Lizzy, dear, I know that you have always had your own mind and rarely yield to persuasion... But please listen to your old, attics-to-let father."

At that Elizabeth giggled and smiled at her father with affection as she placed a hand on his cheek.

Mr. Bennet tipped his head into her hand to return the sentiment as he continued. "I know from experience the sorrow of losing years of happiness to a misunderstanding. Please do not make my mistake." He indicated the letter in her lap. "Nothing can be lost that love cannot find if you will but allow it."

Elizabeth closed her eyes, releasing the tears down the sides of her face. When she opened her eyes to her father, she could not miss all the love, earnest concern and affection that he had for her. Even though she did not feel she had reason to hope, she nodded to him to relieve him of his worry. She closed her eyes again when he placed a gentle kiss on her cheek and stood.

Looking down at the letter in her hand, she thought about the other note from Miss Darcy. She had not yet even responded to that one. She felt wretched that Georgiana had written again. Surely, by now her brother would have informed her that their acquaintance was at an end. She examined the envelope and noticed the markings on it that indicated it had indeed come by express. She could not help then wondering at the reason for such haste in writing to her. Thoughts of Mr. Darcy's welfare flashed in her mind, and she panicked at the thought that some accident may have befallen him. Excusing herself from her father's study, Elizabeth took the letter and raced to the privacy of her room.

WHEN ELIZABETH REACHED HER BEDROOM, she was most anxious to read the letter. By the time she had closed the door and locked it, she was filled with quite another feeling. Setting the unopened letter on her bed, she walked to her window. Georgiana was her link to Mr. Darcy, and the pain she had felt at his departure was still a fresh binding around her heart. No matter what the letter contained, she knew it would pain her. Elizabeth looked at the letter. She needed to know he was well. She needed to brace herself for the onslaught of emotions that she was sure would come. Drawing in a fortifying breath, Elizabeth took up the letter again and held it in her hands.

Sitting on the bed, she pulled her legs up underneath her and pulled the counterpane over them before she turned the letter over to reveal the seal. Swallowing, she pushed her finger through, breaking the wax.

Another deep breath and she unfolded the letter, pressing it flat against her legs, before beginning to read.

Dearest Elizabeth,

Be not alarmed, dear friend, upon receiving this letter, by the apprehension of its containing a reminder of those events or those discoveries about your sister's past that were so distressing to you a few days ago. I write without intention of paining you or anyone else by dwelling on history that, for the happiness of so many, cannot be too soon forgotten.

Elizabeth closed her eyes and suppressed the urge to cry again. She could not blame Mr. Darcy for sharing what they both knew of Lydia's past with Georgiana. It was probably a necessary part of his explanation as to why she must end her acquaintance with Elizabeth. Oddly, she felt comforted by her friend's words. Opening her eyes, she returned them to the pages in her hands.

It has come to my knowledge that an offense has been laid at the door of my brother by you, one that I feel it is incumbent on me to defend. However significant in its severity it may seem to you, I hope that after the recital of all that I have to relate, you will acquit my brother of wrongdoing. If, in the explanation of which I feel is due to him, I am under the necessity of stirring feelings that may be distressful to you, I can only say—I am sorry.

Elizabeth's brows furrowed, and she became worried. *What offense have I laid at Mr. Darcy's door?* She did not understand at all. It was her sister whose loss of virtue prevented him from connecting himself with her! But

Mr. Darcy was not to blame. She read on.

My only hope at regaining your esteem for my brother is to lay before you the whole of Wickham's connection to my family. I am unaware of what part of this you may already know, of what my brother may have related, so forgive me if I recount parts with which you are already acquainted.

Elizabeth shook her head, confused further. "Regain my esteem? It cannot be that Mr. Darcy should doubt my affections for him. And what had Wickham to do with it?" Elizabeth whispered aloud before returning to the letter, hoping to find clarity for her confusion.

Elizabeth then read a repeat of everything Darcy had related to her in his library at Pemberley regarding Wickham's history with their family. Then to Elizabeth's astonishment and horror, Georgiana began to relate an entirely new part of that history—a part that left Elizabeth in tears, this time with compassion for her young friend.

Last summer, he once again most painfully intruded upon our family's notice. I must now mention a circumstance about which I would wish to forget myself and which no obligation less than the present should induce me to unfold to any human being. Having said this much, I know I can be assured of your secrecy. I have been left under the guardianship of both my brother and my cousin Colonel Fitzwilliam. About a year ago, I was taken from school in London and, with my companion at the time, a Mrs. Younge, left for the seaside resort of Ramsgate. Hitherto also went Mr. Wickham, I know now by design. He and Mrs. Younge, in whose character we were most unhappily deceived, seemed to hold a prior acquaintance—a fact that, as you must realize, my brother and cousin knew nothing. Mr. Wickham began calling on me with the permission of my companion, and through the memories of his kindness to me as a child and with my natural diffidence, I was persuaded to believe that I was in love with him. It was his design that it be so. It was through this belief that I consented to an elopement with him.

My brother, who happened to surprise me at Ramsgate a day or so before the intended elopement, knew nothing of our plans. I could not bear the thought of paining a most beloved brother, and so I divulged to him all our plans for the elopement. You may imagine how he felt and how he acted. Mr.

Wickham's design, it seemed, hinged on obtaining my fortune, being thirty thousand pounds.

And now I come to the reason for telling you all of this. William's regard for my credit and consideration for my feelings prevented him from any public exposure of Mr. Wickham in Hertfordshire last autumn.

Elizabeth was stunned beyond belief and had to reread the account twice before she felt she comprehended it all. All proper feeling went out to Georgiana in her distress and for the mortifications she had to endure to share such a personal narrative with her. Suddenly, she remembered a moment with Mr. Darcy on their ride back to Longbourn directly after Lydia's death. He had told her then he approved of their correspondence because of his belief that Elizabeth would be helpful to Georgiana. He had hinted only at a painful experience the girl had recently endured. Elizabeth covered her mouth with her hand, realizing that he was then referring to Ramsgate. The old acquaintance he mentioned would then have been Mr. Wickham. Still, she could not understand what Georgiana's history had to do with her own situation with Mr. Darcy and had yet to determine with what offense she felt Elizabeth had charged him.

You see, dearest Elizabeth, that it was with the hope of protecting another's secret that he did not expose Mr. Wickham to your society. Please consider my words and do not persist in holding my brother accountable for the tragedy your sister has encountered at Mr. Wickham's hands. I know that he carries all the guilt on his shoulders, and I realize that, if he had exposed the man, Wickham could not have imposed on your family, especially your sister, in such a way. If anyone is to blame, it is I, whose history with him prevented others from knowing his true character. Please forgive my brother, Elizabeth.

Georgiana's plea was so sincere and heartfelt that Elizabeth nearly wept again. She retrieved Mr. Darcy's handkerchief from her pocket and dried her eyes. *So this is what he thinks?* A small hope began to spring within her chest. She had never considered blaming Mr. Darcy for anything regarding her sister and Mr. Wickham! But there was more, and she returned her eyes to the last page.

Forgive me if I offend you by being too forward, but I know that my brother loves you. Concern that he has lost you has driven him to depths I have never seen him suffer before. Immediately upon reaching London, my brother sought out the whereabouts of Mr. Wickham and, together with my cousin, was able to get him to confess his violence against your sister. My brother's love for you and his consideration for your feelings as well as the wellbeing of your family alone prevented him from turning Wickham over to the magistrate immediately. Instead, they hastened a court-martial for Mr. Wickham's desertion from the militia and brought about his passage to Australia, thus ensuring that he would never again be able to cause your family or mine pain again. If this does not prove his unaltered affection for you, I do not know what may be said that will. With an urgency that I know you will understand, I shall endeavor to put this letter into your hands as soon as may be by sending it express. I will only add,

God Bless You,
Georgiana Darcy

Elizabeth's fingers went numb as she sat shocked, grieved at Georgiana's final revelation. Words from it kept crashing through her mind unaccountably. *'Violence against your sister.' 'The magistrate.'* Elizabeth could feel her head ache as the realization began to dawn on her. Suspicion was not in her nature, and detection could not have been in her power. That her sister's death was not an accident had never occurred to her and inflicted upon her a new wave of grief. Unable to contemplate anything more, Elizabeth sank under her blankets and tried to summon sleep to relieve her mind.

Some hours later, she awoke clutching Darcy's handkerchief in her hand. Sleep had aided in healing her heart and mind. Somehow, the nature of Lydia's death did not pain her further, for it did not change that she was gone. Her thoughts about the man whose hands were responsible only caused her to think of the great kindness Mr. Darcy had done in saving her family the humiliation of a trial. She was relieved that Wickham was gone and felt satisfaction in knowing justice had served Lydia. There were many who could have prevented Lydia's death beyond Mr. Darcy and his reticence about Wickham; she decided harboring guilt would not change history, and it resolved nothing. She concluded Mr. Darcy should not hold onto his guilt if she did not.

Elizabeth turned and reached for the well-loved leather book resting on the side table near her bed. It was her mourning book from Mr. Darcy. As she held it in her hands, the pages opened naturally to where she had placed a few flowers for pressing. They were bluebells from her trip to Pemberley. Gently tracing her fingers across the tissue-soft petals, she was transported back to that field. A feeling of warmth surrounded her as she recalled the tenderness she felt from Mr. Darcy and the recognition of his love that she discovered standing amongst the bluebells. It was a bright spot, an ethereal moment of beauty in the dark months of mourning for Lydia. *Think only of the past as its remembrances give you pleasure.* Elizabeth realized then that, although Lydia's death was a terrible tragedy, a preventable one perhaps, it had been the catalyst for "bluebell moments" in the lives of many in her family. Jane and her Mr. Bingley were reunited where there had been no hope. Her parents' affection for each other had been reborn through their sorrow as well. All that was left now was for Elizabeth to find a way to reconcile with Mr. Darcy.

Although Elizabeth was worried about his reaction, her mind began to formulate how she might signal to Mr. Darcy her true feelings while allowing him to decide whether he still wanted her and her connections. Leaving her bed, Elizabeth went in search of the first thing she would need to accomplish her task — a needle.

Chapter 19

Darcy was at his desk, attempting to keep his attention on the business before him. He would not allow himself to think of Elizabeth, though it took great effort. When Richard had burst into his bedchamber a few days prior and berated Darcy for what his cousin believed were misinterpretations regarding Elizabeth's feelings, he had at least succeeded in getting Darcy to leave his room. His heart still ached, but to everyone else he was a master under good regulation. If he dedicated more time than was usual to estate business usually left to his stewards, then so be it. Most of the time, these distractions succeeded in keeping him from losing himself in regret.

Darcy rubbed his eyes and shook his head to return his thoughts to the paper before him. When he heard a knock at the door, he was grateful for the interruption. "Enter."

Georgiana walked in with a skip to her step. His eyes narrowed a little to see her looking so mischievously playful. In the past couple of days since he left his chambers, his sister had taken to avoiding him and his mercurial moods. He worried as she seemed to be on edge herself. Darcy noted she had not received any letters from Elizabeth and knew he was responsible. Suddenly he was sorry for his sister. Placing his pen in its stand, Darcy attempted to return his sister's smile. She held something behind her back and he was then curious as to her reason for visiting his study.

"Is there some way I can oblige you, Georgiana?"

Unbeknownst to Darcy, she had asked Mr. Carroll to see that all her letters came directly to her rather than the silver salver in the hall with the rest of the correspondence. Georgiana smiled, thinking of the letter she had just received.

"I hope I am not disturbing you," she said with winsome appeal.

Darcy's smile returned, this time more genuinely. He loved his sister, and before him stood his only family. He sat back and laced his hands behind his head. "Of course not, my dear. Would you like me to accompany you on a walk in the park? Or is there something else?"

She smiled and shook her head. Georgiana seemed to vibrate with excitement. "No, thank you. I came here to give you this." She pulled a small tissue wrapped parcel from behind her back and placed it before him on his desk. He looked at her intently before reaching for the package.

"Georgiana, this is very good of you. What is the occasion that warrants giving me a gift?" he asked as his hands closed around the small package.

"Oh it is not from me, William."

Darcy looked up at her. "Oh?"

"It is from Elizabeth."

Darcy fumbled upon hearing her name, and the package slipped through his fingers to his desk. His heart began to beat violently as he considered what Elizabeth could have sent him and, more importantly, why. His mind was flying. He could think of no circumstance for Elizabeth to send him anything. He realized he had not said a word when his sister spoke.

"Well? Are you not going to open it?" Her eagerness was transparent.

Darcy lifted his eyes from the package to her ardent face. He swallowed and looked down at the package again.

"Eliz...Miss Bennet sent this to you, you say?"

Georgiana almost whimpered with impatience. "Yes...well, no." Giggling then, she continued, "I mean she sent it to me, but I do not know what it is, for her letter said it was for you."

"I see." Only he did not at all. He dared not hope that Elizabeth had forgiven him.

"William! Open it! I cannot wait a moment longer!" Georgiana was mad with curiosity. Elizabeth's letter had indicated that she did not hold her brother accountable at all and never had. *That is good news, is it not?* She thought so at the time she read it. Furthermore, her letter had been full of all the right sentiments of understanding and compassion, and Georgiana no longer worried that her friend may think poorly of her for being deceived by Wickham.

Darcy laughed at his sister's impatience. Her levity and the budding hope springing in his chest lifted his own spirits in a way he had thought never to experience again. "Very well then, I will."

His fingers trembled only slightly as he reached again for the package. He carefully pulled at the cords binding the tissue together. His heart beat loudly in his ears. Hesitating only a moment, he pulled back the tissue paper and immediately recognized his own handkerchief. He did not even need to turn it over to see his initials. He was sure it was the one he gave Elizabeth at Oakham Mount when he saw her last. With that realization, his heart sank.

"Leave me, Georgiana," he said more gruffly than he had intended. Nevertheless, the pain of having his hopes dashed in such a way made it nearly impossible for him to control the emotion in his voice.

"But what is it?" Georgiana started, concerned as a sudden dark shadow crossed her brother's countenance.

"It is nothing but my handkerchief being returned. Now leave me, Georgiana." His voice was low but obviously pained.

Georgiana stood there a moment, confused. Elizabeth's letter was so positive and full of allusion as to her own dreams and wishes. She had said she was not angry with her brother and had indicated that she held him in the highest esteem. *There has to be more to it than just returning his handkerchief!* Elizabeth could not have been so cruel as to say such things to her in the letter, giving such hope, and then coldly return the handkerchief. Thinking there must be a note or something else hidden in the package, Georgiana reached for it.

"That cannot be all there is!" she said with heightened emotion. "There must be something else in there!"

Darcy slammed his hand on top of the opened package atop the desk, preventing her from taking it. "I said leave me, Georgiana!" His anguished voice bellowed through his study, startling her, her hand frozen in place, extended towards the package.

She blinked, having never been chastised in such a manner by her brother—by anyone, for that matter. Slowly she backed away, her arm still numbly extended in front of her.

"Please." His voice was softer then but full of pain. Georgiana lifted her hand to her mouth to stifle a cry and quickly ran out of the room. Darcy watched her leave and then lowered his head to the desk, defeated.

He had not meant to speak in such a way to his sister, but he could not bear to hold back his feelings a moment longer. The infinitesimal bit of hope that he had allowed to creep into his heart because of his sister's excitement had left him falling farther and harder when he saw his returned handkerchief. *Why could she not have simply kept it?* If she did not wish to have anything as a reminder of him, then could she not have considered his feelings and burned the cloth? But to return it felt like a slap in the face. It was cruel, and he was mortified to have been so exposed in front of his sister.

Sighing, he rolled his head to the side, unwittingly onto the handkerchief. He heard a crunching sound. Unnerved, his head shot up, and he immediately pulled the cloth away to reveal a small note hidden underneath the linen. Darcy swallowed as he looked at the note, his name written in her beautiful script. He did not know how long he stared at the note, his handkerchief in his hand. He conceded he was ill prepared to read whatever she might wish to convey. He had not the least bit of hope the letter contained anything more than a carefully worded thank you for the loan of the handkerchief, and he was not interested in her empty sentiments just then.

Placing the folded square back on top of her missive where he could not see it anymore, Darcy then slid the package to the corner of his desk and pulled the letter from his solicitor back into place in front of him.

He read the first lines of the correspondence three times, each time struggling to comprehend even a word. His thoughts and eventually his traitorous eyes harassed him to read her note. Bringing his hand to his face in a fist, Darcy drew in a ragged breath. He closed his eyes and counted to five before trying again to concentrate on his business.

Inevitably, his gaze returned to the opened package, and his eyes bored through that cloth to where he knew his name had been written — written in her beautiful script by her beautiful, slender fingers. Shaking off those treacherous thoughts, Darcy stood and walked towards the window; if he were to continue down that mental path, he was certain it would lead him to visions of her beautiful arms, neck, face, lips… It was too much for any man to bear.

Placing his hands on either side of the window, he looked out onto the square. It was a scene he had often looked upon without really seeing it. As was his habit, he often stood there when he was too full of thoughts. He bit his top lip and looked over his shoulder again, contemplating the package.

Cursing, he crossed to the decanter on the sideboard to pour himself a bit of liquid courage. He knew he would get no work done until he could put it all behind him once and for all.

Resuming his seat, Darcy nursed his drink, all the while eyeing the package. In his distraction, he spilled a splash of brandy onto his waistcoat.

"Blast!" He instinctively reached for the handkerchief to daub at his coat, stopping himself only when it was inches from his chest. He returned the linen and grabbed the one from his pocket instead. He felt the sentimental fool. Although he accepted he must give up Elizabeth, he was not about to stain the one item he knew was last in her possession.

Rigorously dabbing at the brandy until it had long been soaked up, Darcy laughed at himself for being such a coward. *Quit stalling man.* He drew in a breath; with one hand, he picked up the handkerchief and, with the other, the note. Unfolding it slowly, he looked down and began to read her words.

Dear sir,

I hope this gives you as much comfort as it has given me, and I hope that you do not mind the alterations I have made.

As ever,
Elizabeth

Darcy chewed over her words, undecided whether he should be further distressed by the 'sir' or encouraged by the 'As ever, Elizabeth'. Reading it quickly, he was intrigued by her hopes it would bring him comfort. However, he could not understand how that could be as it brought him no comfort that she had not wished to keep it. The reference to the alterations confused him further. Putting the note down, Darcy opened the folded square for the first time, turning it over in his hand.

A slow smile began to grow at the edges of his mouth and his heart came alive in his chest as he saw the 'alterations' she had made. His initials, before so elegantly alone, were now surrounded by dozens of tiny whimsical bluebells. Bluebells were her favorite wildflower, he remembered, and more significantly, they were the flowers that surrounded them at Pemberley when they shared their first kiss — their only kiss.

Darcy all but wept with relief, and his hand began to shake with the feelings that were coursing through him. He looked at his other handkerchief, the one soiled with brandy stains, and compared his decorous initials with the one he held in his hand. He rather preferred this decidedly feminine alteration.

He was astounded by what he thought she was intimating by embroidering the bluebells. *Could she really still love me? Could she really have forgiven me?* The thought was so delicious to Darcy that he laughed out loud and cried out a prayer of thanks.

He seized the short note and read it again, smiling so widely that his face began to hurt. She wished to give him comfort. It was more than he deserved, but he was not fool enough to let such an opportunity pass him by if indeed she was offering him another chance. Springing up from his desk, he placed the now cherished note into his pocket, and while still holding the returned linen, Darcy hastened out the door to find his sister.

He found her sitting in the music room at her piano. Her hands were at her face, and he could hear her quietly weeping. Immediately, he felt terrible remorse for the way he had spoken to her, forcing her to flee the room. Joining her directly at the instrument, Darcy lifted her chin with his finger until she looked at him.

"I am so sorry, Georgiana. Please say you will forgive me for my abominable behavior just now. I should not have spoken to you as I did."

Georgiana sniffled. "It is all right, William. I am more disappointed in Elizabeth's package than I am upset with you. Her response to my letter made me think that she wished for... for something else," Georgiana stammered, realizing she did not wish to upset her brother further by expressing what she had hoped.

"You wrote Eliz... Elizabeth a letter?" She had been Elizabeth to him for so long, and now with his renewed hope, he cared not what it suggested to his sister.

Georgiana's eyes twitched when he used Elizabeth's Christian name, unsure whether she should proceed. "I wrote to her when Richard told me why you had been so distressed. I told her all about my past with Wickham, hoping she would not blame you."

Darcy reached for his sister's hand and squeezed it. "I am sure you found her to be a sympathetic and understanding friend." His heart soared again, thinking of how lovely and good Elizabeth was and that there was still a chance he might convince her to be his.

"Yes, she was very gracious, but I had thought—"

Darcy interrupted her. "Darling, you were correct in your assumptions, at least I think you were. I hope we both are." He handed her the cloth, and she looked at it without comprehension.

"It is my handkerchief, only she added bluebells," he said triumphantly.

"It looks beautiful, but I do not understand. How are the bluebells significant?" She looked up at him with clear, innocent eyes.

Darcy swallowed, realizing, of course, that she would not know about their first kiss. Naturally, he had said nothing to her about it, and certainly, he did not wish to discuss it with her now. He laughed as he mused that an event so significant to his life and one of the happiest moments, thus far, was obviously not significant to anyone else. *Had not the world stopped spinning at that moment?* He was sure that it had. How was he to explain why Elizabeth's needlework was so monumental?

"When we were at Pemberley, Elizabeth seemed to enjoy the field of bluebells near the lake very much, my dear." *I know I did.*

Georgiana's face lit up. "Then she is saying she loves you! Why else would she hint at her happy time at Pemberley with us? Oh, that is so romantic, William!"

Darcy smiled back at his sister. "I do not know whether she is quite professing her love, but I am determined to find out."

"Will you go to her then?" Georgiana clutched at her brother's sleeve with excitement.

Darcy was suddenly overcome with emotion: the happiness he was experiencing, coupled with his sister's, and the thought of seeing Elizabeth again. He could only manage a nod. She threw her hands around his neck for a quick hug and then pushed him quite forcefully off of the piano bench, nearly causing him to fall onto the floor.

"Georgiana!"

"Oh!" She covered her mouth with her hand. "I am sorry, William, but you really must go to her this instant. Hurry! You have not a moment to lose!"

Darcy laughed and agreed with her. With purpose, he quickly strode out the music room door. He issued the requisite orders to have his trunks packed and then called for a carriage. He had two stops to make in Town before he could be on his way. He was not taking chances this time that anything would delay his marriage to Elizabeth if he were fortunate enough to gain her hand. A stop at his solicitor's office for the copies of the settlements that he had drawn up before going to Bingley's wedding and then another to the Archbishop for a special license were in order.

ALTHOUGH ELIZABETH'S MOOD HAD LIFTED significantly since receiving Georgiana's letter, she was still anxious about how her own response might be received. She surmised at least by now that he would have received her package and seen its contents. Her heartbeat quickened every time she thought of it. She bit her lip and looked back down at the sampler she was attempting; the occupation of her needlework was not helping her to think of something else. Every attempt to concentrate failed her. She even found herself embroidering bluebells, regardless of whether they were the intended flower. She would then have to un-stitch the flowers and begin anew.

She looked at the rest of her family assembled about her. Her father, with a book, had chosen to sit with the family that evening after dinner instead of retreating into his book room as he had for nearly twenty years. His arm was draped casually across the back of the settee behind her mother who was helping Kitty trim an old bonnet. Mary, of course, was reading too. She liked having her father spend the evenings with them. There was something comforting to Elizabeth about having her family spend time together, and she was pleased to see that his attention to her mother was so happily received.

Everyone looked up, then, when they heard the hoofbeats of an approaching rider. Glancing at her father, Elizabeth raised her brows in question. He shrugged his shoulders, but put his book down and waited with everyone else for Mr. Hill to announce their guest.

To everyone's surprise, Mr. Darcy was led into the parlor. Elizabeth hardly knew where to look. She could not believe that he would have come so soon! For a minute, no one said anything, and the silence in the air was deafening but for Elizabeth's heart that was pounding so powerfully she was certain everyone could hear it.

Darcy was struck motionless from nearly the moment his eyes found Elizabeth. She was everything lovely, especially the way she blushed and nervously fingered her dress where her hands were hanging by her side. Suddenly, he remembered himself and bowed to the rest of the family.

"Mr. Darcy, you are welcome to Longbourn," Mr. Bennet said with a twinkle in his eye and a quick glance at his second daughter.

Darcy mumbled a quick thank you and then was silent again. He looked at everyone in the room and then rested his eyes once again on Elizabeth. He knew his appearance at that hour was untoward. He had only arrived from London, and instead of going to Netherfield—where he hoped to convince the housekeeper to let him stay even though the Bingleys were not expected home from their wedding trip for a few days—he had ridden directly to Longbourn.

His reason for coming strengthened his resolve, and without further delay, his words spilled out. "Mr. Bennet, I request a private audience with Miss Bennet."

The room was thick with silence. Elizabeth blinked several times, trying to convince herself she had heard him correctly. The heaviness that had settled over her heart lifted, and her mouth turned up into a small smile. Before her father could respond to Mr. Darcy's request, they heard her mother blurt, "Good Lord! It is about time!"

Elizabeth gasped at her mother's outburst, so much like her old behavior, and she blushed profusely. Risking a quick glance at Mr. Darcy, she noticed he was blushing too and looking at his boots. Then her father began to laugh, followed by her sisters. Next, Elizabeth heard Mr. Darcy's soft baritone join in, relieving her of her embarrassment. She could not help herself then and began to giggle, too.

Between chuckles and affectionate looks at his wife, Mr. Bennet said, "You have my permission, Mr. Darcy."

"Thank you, Mr. Bennet." He bowed to the rest of the room and waited for Elizabeth to join him.

Elizabeth moved by instinct, still dizzy from the whole remarkable scene. She kept her head down as she led Mr. Darcy out through the parlor doors and into the garden where they might find some privacy. She was not surprised when he took her hand, placing it on his arm. They went to the set of benches behind the hedge, out of sight of the four expectant faces pressed to the window in the parlor.

Chapter 20

There was a cool breeze, though the weather was still warm for early September. Elizabeth looked everywhere but at Mr. Darcy, who was intently looking at her as they walked further into the garden. Her heart was now feeling fairly light compared to only moments before. The sun had not quite set, but the blue hour approached, casting the garden in shadow. Absently, Elizabeth reached for a sprig of lavender as they walked past. Breaking it off with her hand, she twisted it nervously in front of her, releasing the sharp, fresh fragrance.

She was thankful for their privacy now as she felt the heat on her cheeks when she looked back at her home, only to see the eager faces of her family. When they reached the benches, Elizabeth began to draw her hand from Mr. Darcy's sleeve. She looked up at him when he took her small hand in his and brought it slowly, mesmerizingly so, up to his face to place a feather light kiss on the back of her ungloved fingers.

Darcy looked into her eyes and was lost in their depths. They had so much to express, but for now, he could not speak a word. For what seemed like minutes, they simply stood in each other's presence, feeling relief and disbelief at their being together and looking on each other once again.

Remembering their last conversation in that location, Elizabeth smiled and sat down on the bench. Darcy smiled too and quietly took up the seat next to her.

Believing that he ought to be the one to begin, he said, "My sister's letter..."

Keeping her eyes on her lap, she whispered, "Yes, I received it."

Darcy tentatively reached across the short space and took her hand in his, hoping she would allow him that liberty. In the deep and saturating blues of twilight, he could barely make out her slight blush, but her acceptance of his holding her hand satisfied him, and the press of her fingers comforted him.

Finding her voice, Elizabeth straightened her shoulders and lifted her eyes to him. "It taught me to hope as I had scarcely allowed myself to hope before."

"Yes!" Darcy said with relieved understanding.

"I knew enough of your disposition to be certain that, had you been absolutely, irrevocably decided against me, you would not have thought yourself the wounded party."

"Never, my dear!" He positioned himself closer to her. "I could more easily convince the swallow in the sky to cease its flight forever than I could forsake you, dearest Elizabeth."

Elizabeth saw his earnest look. "It was too much to hope, after Lydia's disgrace, that you would come again. I had hoped that my handkerchief..." Laughing softly, she corrected herself. "...*your* handkerchief would prompt you to reconsider."

Darcy shook his head slowly in disbelief but said nothing at first. With a twitch to his lips, he said, "I liked your rather singular 'alterations' to my handkerchief."

Elizabeth looked up at him. "Is it not the accustomed fashion among London gentlemen then, sir?"

His lips twitched again as he tried to keep from laughing at her tease. "Not that I am aware of, madam."

"I can unstitch it for you. I would not wish for you to become the laughingstock at your clubs, Mr. Darcy."

"No!" He spoke quickly and then gently added, "I would not have you remove the first thing to give me hope in the past few days. Let the other men laugh. I will smile." He said the last with an endearing sideways glance at her. He was still unsure of her feelings after all that they had endured over the past few days.

Elizabeth held his hand tightly in her own. "Are you sure of your path, sir? Could you connect yourself with such a family having fallen into disgrace?"

"Elizabeth, did you really think that I left you because I could not forgive Lydia's imprudence?" He tempered his voice. "No, I can see from your face that you did. Oh, my dear, how I have made you suffer!"

Her heart reacted wildly when he spoke such endearments. It seemed more than she deserved and all still a dream. She looked at him with questioning eyes. "Then why *did* you leave me, Mr. Darcy?"

Darcy gently smoothed away a strand of her hair that had escaped her pins near her temple, sending a shiver down her spine. He could not meet her eyes, however, when he said, "Because I knew that you would see, and rightly so, that I could have prevented everything."

"And how could you have prevented anything, Mr. Darcy? Was it your responsibility to chaperone my sister and Mr. Wickham?"

"No." He shook his head. If she had not thought him responsible before, revealing his reasons for guilt now surely would open her eyes to it. Reluctantly he continued. "If I had exposed Wickham long ago, he could not have intruded upon your family, and your sister would have been safe from him—thus, you see, protecting her reputation, preventing her accident and, of course, her death." He risked looking into her eyes then.

"I know it was not an accident, Mr. Darcy," she whispered, saddened only by the guilt she saw in his eyes. "I also know the great lengths, the many mortifications you had to endure to discover Mr. Wickham. I cannot thank you enough, for I also know that you ensured he could not harm us further by exposing my family to a public trial. If my family knew, I would have more than my own gratitude to express."

He was not surprised that she knew of his dealings with Wickham or his part in shipping him off to Australia. Darcy lowered his eyes and removed his hand from hers. Standing, he stepped away from her a few paces. "If you will thank me, thank me only for yourself. I believe I thought only of you." Pausing just a moment, he continued, "I am so sorry, El... Miss Bennet. Truly, I am. Would that I could have done something before to prevent it!"

Elizabeth was bewildered by his removal and the distant sound in his voice. What hurt more was his reverting back to his formal address of her. In the short time they had been in the garden, she had grown pleased with his endearments and use of her Christian name. It was a soothing caress to hear her name on his lips. Now to lapse back to 'Miss Bennet' cut her to the core. Swallowing the melancholy welling up in her throat, she determined that no more misunderstandings would come between them. Her father had wasted most of his life's happiness because of one, and she had promised him not to make that same mistake.

"Fitzwilliam," Elizabeth began, embarrassed, having never addressed him so informally before. Such familiarity made her blush, but she had purposely used it to gain his attention and to make a point. She was satisfied when he turned abruptly to her, his face registering a powerful range of emotions. "Please do not pain me by assuming responsibility for actions with which you are so wholly unconnected. Mr. Wickham was a cad — a despicable spendthrift, a gambler. My sister was imprudent, spoiled and reckless. Although I never would have wished this, their choices *together* led to that end. You, sir, are not responsible."

Darcy struggled to remain firmly where he stood. The determination in her eyes demanded he ought to allow her to finish her speech, but after hearing her sweet lips speak his name, he wished only to take her in his arms and kiss them. Never had he expected to have such an overwhelming feeling of love, admiration and desire by hearing her say his given name. Considering her words, he responded, "But, if I had exposed —"

"If you had exposed him, my dear, he would have gone on to hurt someone else in another shire that did not know him or his reputation. You could not follow him to every village in England."

Mr. Darcy shook his head and drew in a steadying breath. *She called me 'my dear'!* "Elizabeth, you must return to calling me 'Mr. Darcy' or 'sir' — at least until we finish this discussion. I am finding your familiarity uncommonly distracting."

"I see." Elizabeth colored with shame. "Forgive me, Mr. Darcy."

Seeing she misinterpreted his meaning, Mr. Darcy came to her side immediately. He took up her hand in his and pressed it to his lips. "You misunderstand, Elizabeth. Please believe me when I say that I am affected in a *positive* way. I like it. I like it very much — more than I should."

When she looked up innocently but with obvious uncertainty as to his meaning, he smiled roguishly at her. "Forgive me. I feel I must speak plainly now, Elizabeth. I believe we must make certain the topic at hand is properly addressed. But when you refer to me so charmingly, I can only think of taking you in my arms and kissing you."

"Oh!" Elizabeth blushed and bit her lip as she lowered her head. Her heart beat wildly, her momentary shame turning into relief and more at his words.

He lowered his voice to a husky timbre. "And perhaps, you might further ease my suffering and not bite your lip in that bewitching manner."

Elizabeth peeked up at him through her lashes. "I understand your meaning now, sir. But you have been calling me 'Elizabeth' for quite some time."

Darcy lifted his eyes to the now dark sky and sighed. *Oh, how I love you, Elizabeth.* How he was to return to the serious subject of her sister and Wickham, he knew not. "You are correct, of course. I will endeavor to be mindful of that now."

"I do not mind, sir," she said quietly.

Smilingly tenderly, he took up her hand. "Let us return to our previous topic, as distasteful as it is. For the sooner we resolve it, the sooner we can speak of more pleasant things," he said significantly.

"I believe we had finished our discussion, sir. You were just about to agree with me that there was no reason for you to feel guilty over Wickham's actions."

Darcy lifted an eyebrow in amusement. "Was I?"

"Yes, sir. I have always found you to be a wise man, and as such, you were about to agree with me. Doing so is undoubtedly the wisest course of action for you." Elizabeth challenged him with the fine arch of her impertinent brow.

Darcy admired her comely face, lit by the moon above. "Of course, you are right, madam."

"So you agree that you are not to blame for Wickham or Lydia's actions?"

Darcy's jaw clenched; he was amused by Elizabeth's teasing words but could not help still blaming himself. He saw tenderness in her eyes and sighed. If she did not blame him, then he could not blame himself. Besides, she believed him to be a wise man, and a wise man always knows when to yield. "Yes, my love."

Darcy moved closer to her and placed his other hand on her cheek. He felt her cheek's heat under his touch. Unable to resist her any further, he leaned his head closer to hers, resting his forehead against hers. "Elizabeth, will you forgive me for being so stupid and leaving you to wonder at my affections?"

Suddenly, Elizabeth seized his hands in hers, bringing them to her lips. She shook her head in wonderment. "Forgive me, Mr. Darcy. But I had to prove to myself that you — and indeed, your words — were not part of the sweetest dream I have ever had!"

His heart swelled as Darcy captured Elizabeth in his embrace. Correcting her, he whispered, "Fitzwilliam."

Elizabeth pushed futilely at his chest, teasing. "But you said I should not refer to you so familiarly, *Mr. Darcy*." She laughed delightedly at his mock frown.

"Fitzwilliam," he repeated again, leaning closer.

Elizabeth reached her hand up to cup his cheek, marveling at the feel of his rough skin. She had never touched his face before—had only dreamed of it. The shadow of a beard made his face look roguish and masculine, and she tenderly ran her fingers along his jaw as she savored the feel of his face under her fingertips. Reaching further, she caught an errant curl that always fell across his forehead. Twisting it between the tips of her fingers, she sighed.

Surrendering, she said almost reverently, "Fitzwilliam."

Darcy smiled and closed his eyes to capture her lips with his for a sweet, second kiss. He did not allow himself any more than a chaste moment of bliss before he forced himself to pull away from her. He looked down at her enchanting face, her eyes still closed after his kiss. Slowly, she opened her eyes and looked into his.

"Elizabeth, please tell me we can wed by the end of the week."

Elizabeth's breath hitched in her throat. Of course, she expected after his requesting a private audience and after all their confessions and declarations that he would propose. But still, somehow the words caught her by surprise. She teased him. "I do not see how that can be possible, my dear."

Darcy's smile widened. "Too far away, love? I agree; let us marry tomorrow."

"Tomorrow?!" Elizabeth laughed happily. "No, my dear, what I meant is, that you are too hasty. You forget I cannot give you an answer, for in truth you have not asked me to marry you."

Darcy threw his head back and laughed, shaking his head. He withdrew his arms from about her and spoke to himself. "After waiting nearly four months to propose, you would think I would remember the essential part of actually doing so."

Elizabeth laughed, too, reaching for his hand with a tender smile. Then her brows furrowed. "Four months?"

Darcy tipped his head towards her. "Indeed, I came to the parsonage that night to propose to you, Elizabeth."

"No!" she gasped, amazed. "So then—all this time?"

Darcy nodded and smiled at her. "All this time."

"I had no idea," she said quietly. "I admit I had some indication of your feelings when we were at Pemberley." She was thinking of her discovery of what his dark stares actually meant and how she had realized she loved him too. At the time, she had been surprised to see his feelings for her but had not thought that they had been so longstanding or of such a magnitude as to persuade him to propose to her.

Darcy, on the other hand, was thinking of their first kiss. "I would certainly hope you had some indication of my feelings, my dear, for I can assure you, I do not kiss ladies every day. Indeed, I would not have kissed you had I not wished to make you my wife."

The tenderness in his voice caused Elizabeth to look at him. "I am glad to hear *that*, sir."

"Sir?"

Elizabeth smiled cheekily at him, "I believe you are getting distracted from the topic at hand, and so it must again be 'sir.'"

Darcy laughed. "Indeed."

He then stood before her, preparing himself to ask her properly the question he had wished to ask for so long. They both knew this moment was but a formality. On the ride from London, he had tried to formulate his thoughts, rehearse what he would say, and how he would finally propose. Remembering the speech he had prepared, he looked at her, ready to begin. Realizing he had been pacing, he smiled in apology first.

"Miss Bennet"—he winked—"you must allow me to tell you how ardently I admire and love you." He saw her smile and color, and thus encouraged, continued, "Almost from the beginning of my acquaintance with you, I have come to feel an affection and admiration that has led me to believe that we would suit amicably together. I am in possession of a sizable estate as you well know, and I am capable of supporting you—"

He stopped, seeing that she was chuckling quietly to herself. Frowning, he walked towards her but said good-humoredly, "And what, pray tell, my dear, do you find so humorous in my declaration?"

Elizabeth shook her head, waving her hand, but could not keep herself from laughing more audibly then. "Forgive me; please, go on, sir," she said, carelessly laughing.

If she had not been so beautiful when she laughed, her eyes sparkling with mirth, Darcy easily could have found himself affronted that she found his prepared words so humorous. He began again when she looked as if she had herself more under control.

"I can provide for you the necessities—" Her burst of laughter interrupted him again, and this time he laughed too. "Miss Bennet, I must ask you to refrain from laughing at me while I propose!"

This only made her laugh harder. With tears welling in her eyes, she said, "I must ask that you forgive me again, sir. It is only that, after all the wonderful things you have ever said to me before, I find your rote method of proposal diverting."

Darcy shook his head at her, ever amazed at her lively impudence. He came and sat next to her again, not at all discouraged by her words. "Well since you are so adept as to the manner in which a proposal ought to be accomplished, and I have never given one, perhaps you might school me in what I should say."

Elizabeth looked at him to see whether she had indeed offended him with her nonsense, but seeing the love and tenderness in his eyes, she said playfully, "Very well, sir. First, you must not pace in front of the lady."

Darcy slid to one knee in front of her and tenderly brought both her hands to rest on top of one of his, stroking them gently with his other hand. "Better, my dear?"

Elizabeth's heart filled with love at the look he gave her then. Sobered by his romantic gesture, she nodded and went on. "And you must not recite all of your qualifications as a spouse. You are not a stallion at auction, sir."

Darcy's eyes narrowed at her words. He, indeed, had wished to expound upon his merits. "And how else am I to convince you of my ability and wish to care for you, my love?"

Elizabeth stroked her hand down the length of his face from his temple to his jaw. "I need not your money or your grand estate, Fitzwilliam. I need only assurance of your love and care."

His heart skipped a beat upon hearing her sweet words. They were a balm to his previously broken heart, sealing the pieces together once again. "Duly noted, my dear. Anything else?"

Elizabeth smiled. "You must remember to say you love me."

"A thousand times, yes. I do."

With unshed tears, she looked at him still kneeling in front of her.

Darcy swallowed, suddenly overcome with emotion. A small smile pricked at the edges of his lips. "Very well, Elizabeth. Shall I begin again?"

Elizabeth nodded.

Darcy paused, considering her artless beauty. When the words came, they were undoubtedly unrehearsed. "Elizabeth, sweetest, dearest, Elizabeth. You are in possession of my heart and have been since almost the first I laid eyes on you. I find that I can no more live without a heart than I could live without you. Come home to me, my dear. Make your home be my love, and I will endeavor always to keep you safe and warm. Will you honor me by consenting to be my wife?"

Elizabeth's eyes, already filled with tears, spilled over. She could not immediately manage her voice but finally whispered a small "yes" while she nodded happily at him.

Darcy pulled her to him at once and held her close. Never in his life had he been so content—or elated. In all of his twenty-eight years, he had never felt such love and fulfillment as he did at that moment. Finally, she was his, and it felt so right. She rested her head beneath his chin, and he kissed her velvet curls.

"Better, my love?" he asked sweetly.

He could feel her shoulders shake with gentle laughter before she lifted her face up to his. "Much."

Darcy beamed. His eyes moved slowly down to her lips. His smile softened, as his eyes grew darker. Swallowing, Darcy said, "Elizabeth, may I kiss you?"

Wrapping her arms around his neck, she teased, "I do not believe you have ever asked permission before, my dear."

Darcy laughed. "My gracious! How I do love you, Elizabeth!"

"And I love you, too," she replied bashfully.

Darcy, at hearing her first words of love spoken, expressed himself on the occasion as sensibly and as warmly as a man violently in love can be expected to do as he immediately took her face in his hands to kiss her quite soundly.

THUS HAPPILY OCCUPIED, THE COUPLE did not hear Elizabeth's father approach. Upon encountering this romantic scene, he cleared his throat. When the couple did not take notice of him, Mr. Bennet did not hesitate to act as sensibly and as warmly as a father—finding his daughter held passionately by a gentleman—could be expected to do. He immediately poked the guilty gentleman with his walking stick!

"What was that?" Mr. Darcy said, as he pulled away from his betrothed. They both looked up when Elizabeth's father cleared his throat again.

"Kindly unhand my daughter, sir," Mr. Bennet said sternly.

Although embarrassed, Elizabeth could see the gleam in her father's eye, indicating he was not really as upset as he appeared. Nevertheless, Mr. Darcy quickly stepped back from her, looking sheepishly at her father.

"I assume, sir, that you have some business you would like to discuss with me in my study?" Mr. Bennet asked in a firm voice.

Mr. Darcy, decidedly alarmed and already chastising himself for placing Elizabeth in such an indelicate situation, nodded his head. "Yes, sir, I do."

"Very good, sir. I will see you in my study shortly. You may go and wait for me there."

Darcy nodded, and as he bent to kiss Elizabeth's hand properly, he was waylaid when Mr. Bennet cleared his throat again. The master of Pemberley winced and looked at his intended with embarrassment as he was forced simply to bow over her hand. Elizabeth could not help winking and encouraging him with her smiles when their eyes met. Darcy then straightened to his full height and left the garden, walking directly to the house.

When Darcy was sufficiently out of hearing, Mr. Bennet said to his daughter, "I assume then that you have managed to work through your misunderstanding with the gentleman, Lizzy."

Elizabeth laughed. "Yes, Papa, I believe we have."

"I would hope so after what I have witnessed!"

Elizabeth had the good sense to blush. "Do not be too hard on him, Papa. I know you are not as angry as you wish for him to think."

Mr. Bennet laughed as he took the seat next to his daughter and rested a hand on her knee. "Yes, but a father's job is to intimidate into better behavior the gentlemen who wish to court his daughters."

"He does not wish only to court me, Papa. He asked me to marry him."

"I am glad to hear it, my dear, after that kiss, but you are wrong about one thing."

"What is that?" Elizabeth asked, her eyes twinkling and her face smiling at her father.

"When I am through speaking to him, Lizzy, he will understand it is his responsibility to court you for the rest of his life, even after the ceremony." Mr. Bennet thought about his own marriage and wished, for a moment, that he had made the effort to always court his dear wife. Brushing aside his regret, he patted his daughter's leg. "I suppose I ought to go see the

218

gentleman. Do you think I have left him long enough?"

Elizabeth laughed and pushed her father's shoulder. "Go, Papa, and be kind to him. I love him so. And it would be to your advantage to be on his good side."

Mr. Bennet raised his eyebrows. "Oh, and why is that?"

"Because I have seen both his libraries in London and at Pemberley, Papa."

Interested and amused, Mr. Bennet said, "Ahh, and are they very grand, Lizzy?"

"A more exquisite sight you will not see," she assured him.

Mr. Bennet looked at his daughter, seeing the light in her eyes, the love and happiness glowing from her. After all the sorrows of losing Lydia and then to see how downtrodden Elizabeth had been the past few days when Mr. Darcy left, he was now pleased to see her happiness was complete. She looked radiant, and fatherly pride welled up inside his chest. He did not think all the libraries in England could rival the beauty he saw displayed on her face.

"Well then, let me not delay further!" he teased as he stood up. Mr. Bennet turned and offered his hand to his daughter and assisted her to stand. "Perhaps you ought to fix your hair, dear, before coming back into the house. We would not wish to give your mother a fit of nerves."

Elizabeth reached up to feel that a few of her pins had come undone. She blushed deep red then and heard him chuckle at his little joke. "Do not tarry too long. I suspect your Mr. Darcy will wish to bid you good-bye after our interview."

"Yes, Papa."

Chapter 21

By the time Elizabeth finally made her way back into the house, her siblings and mother were in near hysterics. Their excitement was uncontained, and Elizabeth could no longer feign her own composure. She shared the happy news, confident in her father's blessing. Wishing to see Mr. Darcy again, she excused herself from her family to wait for him outside her father's study.

As the time passed though, she found the waiting worrisome. Certainly, her father would grant his blessing. Even so, she did not anticipate the process taking so long, and she became uneasy. When her father opened the door, she immediately rushed past him to her intended—her impatience giving her father much amusement.

"Come, Lizzy, I left him in once piece—no need to fret. Shall we go and tell your mother the happy news?"

"I already have, Papa," Elizabeth said to her father, keeping her eyes fixed on Darcy.

Darcy was feeling a mix of relief and joy, perhaps the former still taking precedence after his interview with Elizabeth's father. Mr. Bennet had not been hard on him, but Darcy had no practice in asking a father for his daughter's hand. He found himself the object of her father's mirth when, in his nervousness, he nearly repeated his practiced proposal to him! The only difference being that Mr. Bennet was not his charming daughter, and therefore, Darcy could not maintain his good humor on being laughed at a second time in one evening.

Eventually, however, the older man granted him his blessing only after ensuring a promise from Darcy that he would always endeavor to please Elizabeth as much as he aimed to now. That was an easy promise for Darcy to make as he had intended to spend the rest of his life making sure his wife was happy.

"I should like to greet my new sisters and mother, Elizabeth," he said with a slight smile.

Elizabeth raised her brows in surprise but nodded and boldly took his hand in hers to lead him back to the parlor. Darcy colored when he looked to see that, indeed, Mr. Bennet had seen her actions. Their visit in the parlor consisted of many well wishes and congratulations. Darcy bore the attention well with the help of the comforting grasp of Elizabeth's hand. When the matter of a wedding date arose and Mrs. Bennet began speaking of dates several months into the future, Darcy had to intervene.

Darcy insisted on no more than two weeks, ignoring the raised brows of his intended's father. Elizabeth smiled at her betrothed and seconded his wish for a short engagement. Mrs. Bennet at first wanted more time than she could get, of course, but at length was reduced to be reasonable. The date was set for two weeks hence.

When it came time for Darcy to take his leave, Elizabeth walked him out. "Fitzwilliam, what about your Aunt Catherine? I cannot imagine she will be happy to hear of our engagement."

Darcy placed a finger under her chin and raised her face to look at him. "Do not worry, my dear. She is no obstacle to us. I already have a plan."

WHEN JANE AND BINGLEY RETURNED from their wedding trip, they were surprised to see Mr. Darcy at Netherfield. As Bingley's particular friend, he was always welcome, of course. They were not home long before they became aware of his reason for being in the neighborhood.

Jane was in raptures for her sister and not at all surprised by the turn of events. She had been away since her wedding and was not even aware of her sister's distress afterwards. Elizabeth and Darcy did not speak of it and allowed them to believe everything went as smoothly after their wedding as the groom and bride had assumed it would.

Jane happily accompanied Elizabeth on all her shopping and, to the relief of the engaged couple, often invited Elizabeth to take tea at Netherfield.

Anne sat in the large parlor with her mother when the post came and the footman handed her a letter from her cousin.

"Who is that from, Anne? I must know who sent you a letter," her mother demanded.

Anne looked at the name on the letter and replied that it was from her cousin Fitzwilliam.

Lady Catherine beamed, highly gratified to see her nephew finally making steps towards his courtship with her daughter. "Well, what does he say, child? Open it, or better yet, give it to me, and I will read it. Your eyes are much too weak in this poor light."

Anne pulled the letter to herself and surprised her mother when she refused to hand over the paper. Lady Catherine did not protest, happy to gloat over the fact that her nephew had written.

Anne puzzled over the letter as she opened it. Darcy was an inconstant writer with her; Georgiana was a more reliable correspondent. As she read through the missive, she began to smile. He was engaged to the amusing Miss Elizabeth Bennet, who had visited them at Easter. Anne and Darcy had long ago decided that they would not suit and would never marry. Only her mother wished for their union. Anne was happy for her cousin and determined to facilitate his request for help.

"Well, what does he write?" her mother demanded again.

Anne folded the missive and placed it in her pocket. "It is just a review of his life since he left in April, Mother."

"That was kind of him. I told you, his attachment to Rosings increases."

Anne excused herself from her mother to carry out her cousin's tasks. She first spoke to the butler and requested that the London newspapers come to her first. The servants, who were endeared more to Miss de Bourgh than to their demanding mistress, complied readily. Next, Anne ordered her phaeton and ponies readied so she might go for a drive.

When she pulled up in front of the parsonage, Mr. Collins, pulling his wife along behind him, immediately exited his house and rushed to pay his respects to her. She expected this and thus began, "Mr. Collins, you ought not to keep your wife out in all this wind. Go now and retrieve her wrap."

The unctuous parson bowed and apologized profusely, more to Anne than to his wife, and left the two ladies as he scurried back into the parsonage.

"Mrs. Collins, I wished to speak to you in private about a matter of some consequence."

"Of course, Miss de Bourgh; speak freely."

"I need your help, Mrs. Collins. If you have not heard already, you will soon that my cousin has recently become engaged to be married to your friend Miss Bennet."

"Mr. Darcy!" Mrs. Collins beamed.

Anne smiled, sharing her neighbor's excitement. "Yes. My cousin requested that we keep the news of his wedding a secret from my mother as he fears she may try to stop the wedding or insult Miss Bennet in some way."

Charlotte nodded and, as she could hear her husband returning behind her, said quickly, "I will make sure to intercept any letters from home and the newspapers as well, so that my husband does not hear of the happy news either."

"That is precisely what I would wish for," Anne said with a grin.

Mr. Collins arrived then and hastily gave his wife the wrap before turning his attentions again to Miss de Bourgh. Before he could extol his usual reverence, she forestalled him by speaking.

"Mr. Collins, you have a lovely wife, and I have enjoyed visiting with her, but I must be on my way now. Thank you and good-bye." Anne hastily left the man to shout out his praise to her back as she pulled forward in the phaeton and began her return to Rosings Park.

"My dear Charlotte, she pays you a great honor to stop in such a manner."

"Yes, Mr. Collins. Shall we return to the house?" Charlotte was already walking towards her home, leaving Mr. Collins behind to watch until Miss de Bourgh was out of sight. She was happy for her friend and eager to watch for any letters from her.

WHEN THE DAY OF THE wedding arrived, it seemed that everyone except the bride and groom was nervous. They had endured enough strain in the times before their engagement, leaving them entirely content on the day of the wedding.

Elizabeth laughed at each of her sisters as they fretted over her dress, kissed her mother on the cheek when she fussed over her hair, and smiled at her father when he paced in the church's vestibule before the service.

As the church bell rang, signaling the hour was at hand, Mr. Bennet took his daughter's arm. "Well, Lizzy, it looks as if it is time. Do not worry, my dear; all will be well."

Elizabeth breathed deeply, feeling that sentiment ring true throughout her body. She thanked her father and ushered him to the church doors. With a gentle press at his arm, she looked forward as the doors opened into the sanctuary.

As her eyes traveled down the aisle to her beloved Fitzwilliam, her lips drew up into a delighted smile. She saw herself run to him, wrap her arms around him and laugh as he kissed her eyelids while he swung her around. As she reached the front of the church, still on the arm of her father, she smiled at her daydream. Nevertheless, she was there, now standing happily beside her love.

Her eyes misted as she looked up into his and took his arm. He felt an overwhelming satisfaction realizing that forevermore her place would be at his side.

Luckily for both the bride and groom, the words the vicar had them repeat kept them present for enough of the ceremony to know their parts and not to drift into their own happy world, oblivious to the rest of the witnesses. The moment they were introduced to the assembled guests as Mr. and Mrs. Fitzwilliam Darcy was perhaps the happiest either had experienced.

Mr. Darcy turned to his new wife as they walked down the aisle. With pride coloring his voice, he said, "Have I told you how fine you look today, Mrs. Darcy?"

Elizabeth smiled brightly at her husband. "You have not, Mr. Darcy."

Darcy laughed gently as he placed his other hand to cover hers. "Then allow me to do so immediately. You, Elizabeth, are more beautiful to me today then you have ever been before."

"Thank you, Mr. Darcy. I am glad to hear it."

LATER, AT THE WEDDING BREAKFAST, Mr. Bennet was proudly looking around at his friends and family as they conversed with each other. The bride looked luminous on her husband's arm as they spoke with the Gardiners. His neighbors were each engaged with other members of his family. Mr. Bennet became overwhelmed as he considered how blessed he was. Looking about for his greatest blessing, he frowned when he could not find his wife.

Just as he was about to stand and look for her, Mrs. Hill approached him and handed him a note. Thanking the housekeeper, Mr. Bennet slipped out of the breakfast room, where the guests were assembled, and went to his study to read the note.

A few minutes later, a dazed Mr. Bennet made his way up the stairs slowly. His mind was reeling at the news he just read in the note. He was trying desperately to make sense of it and to control both the fear and happiness that were warring in his breast as a result.

Coming to his wife's bedchamber door, he knocked and waited for her summons. As soon as he entered, closing the door firmly behind him, he asked, "Is it true?"

Fanny Bennet sat nervously at her dressing table, ringing her hands in her lap. She turned around to face him and replied with a feeble, "Yes."

"How can it be? I mean, it is at the same time wonderful as it is..." Mr. Bennet shook his head. "How can it be?" he repeated.

His wife blushed. "I believe you know how it could be, sir. The process has not changed since the last time."

Mr. Bennet stood there for just a moment absorbing it all. Slowly his face broke into a wide smile as he went to his wife and took her into his arms. "Congratulations, my dear!"

Nervously, his wife looked up into his face. "Then you are not unhappy to hear it?"

"Unhappy? Of course not. Concerned for your health — terrified really — but unhappy? Not at all."

Mrs. Bennet laughed uneasily. "It was quite a surprise for me; I assure you."

Mr. Bennet nodded. "I did not realize there was still a chance..."

"I am not that old, sir!" she stated with offense.

Mr. Bennet smiled wider at his wife. "No you are not that old, Fan. You are more handsome today than the day of our own wedding, my dear."

He laughed as his wife blushed. Still a little bewildered at the news, he whispered disbelievingly, "A baby."

Her own eyes clouded over with disbelief. "A baby."

ELIZABETH LOOKED ANXIOUSLY FOR HER parents. The newlyweds had taken their leave of the rest of the family after the wedding breakfast, and they were even then at the carriage ready to leave on their wedding trip. But she did not see her mother or father anywhere. Unhappily, she turned towards the carriage, preparing to enter it with resignation and disappointment at not being able to say goodbye.

As Darcy was handing her into the carriage, her father called out to her from the door of the house.

"Just a moment, my dear!"

He rushed to her, with her mother's hand in his, coming along behind him.

Elizabeth stepped down and turned quickly to give her father a warm embrace.

"Where were you both?" she asked. "I was worried I would have to leave without saying goodbye."

Mrs. Bennet answered, "That was my fault, my dear. I had a matter of importance to speak to your father about. Come here, child, and give your mother a hug."

Elizabeth happily complied and held her mother tightly, filled with tenderness for the woman. "I will miss you, Mama."

"Shh, Lizzy, you have a husband now. Think no more of us, but do come and visit often."

"I will."

She released her mother as her father shook her husband's hand. Mr. Darcy gave her a smile as he extended his hand again to assist her into the carriage. This time she was ready. When they were both comfortably settled, she looked out the window and waved goodbye to her friends and family as the carriage began to roll away.

Turning in her seat, Elizabeth looked across to her husband. "Did you ever think that, when you brought me back from Rosings in this very carriage, you would take me away from here one day as your wife?"

"I had certainly hoped such would be the case."

Elizabeth switched sides and pulled her husband's arm around her as she snuggled into his side. Sighing, she said, "I admit, I had never considered the possibility at the time."

"Well I, for one, am glad that you have come around to my way of thinking, Elizabeth."

They laughed together for a moment until Darcy asked, "When did you first fall in love with me, Elizabeth? I can imagine you going on charmingly once you started, but—" Darcy laughed as he squirmed away from her jab in his side.

226

"I suppose I could say something highly romantic like, 'I was in the middle before I knew I had begun.' But I shall not deceive you. I believe I first knew I loved you after seeing the beautiful grounds of Pemberley," she teased.

Darcy laughed and pulled her closer to him. "Then it *was* my fortune and home that you were after."

Elizabeth reached up and placed a hand on his cheek. She smiled when he turned his face and kissed her palm. "It was in the field of bluebells, Fitzwilliam. That is where I first realized you loved me and that I loved you."

"Then it was not my home after all," he said with a smile.

"No, but you did promise me when you proposed that I could make my home your love."

Darcy kissed each of her cheeks before placing a gentle kiss on her lips. "Indeed, I did, my love. Welcome home."

The End

Epilogue

Within seven months of their second daughter's wedding, each month more stressful and agonizing than the next for both Mr. and Mrs. Bennet, the birth date for their surprise baby came. While Mr. Bennet paced his study, running his hands through his hair and praying for his wife, his two sons-in-law looked on helplessly. Neither had ever experienced having his wife in labor and certainly had never expected to be present when the situation visited their mother-in-law. Darcy offered his father-in-law a drink to help calm his nerves.

Mr. Bennet took it in his hands gratefully but, in his distraction, never drank it. Darcy looked towards Bingley who simply shrugged his shoulders.

Upstairs in her bedchamber, Fanny Bennet was surrounded by the midwife and all of her daughters as was their wont. Fanny had not been easy in her confinement. She had never imagined being with child again at two and forty years when her other children were grown — not to mention her fears of a repetition of Sammy's birth. But here she was, supported by her daughters, crying the tears of a mother about to be renewed again.

Elizabeth had insisted on being there as soon as she received word from her parents that they were expecting a new sibling. She marveled at the thought, stunned beyond words at first when she learned of it. After a few minutes, she began to cry happy tears as she realized that this child was the blessed result of her parents' reconciliation.

"It is time, ma'am," the midwife said.

Elizabeth took one of her mother's hands and Jane took the other. She smiled as she looked across her mother to her older sister, the first signs of life just beginning to swell in her belly. Jane noticed Elizabeth's smile and smiled knowingly in return. Elizabeth was excited for her sister and Mr. Bingley. They would be excellent parents. Elizabeth placed her hand on her own flat belly in satisfaction.

Her mother's moans brought Elizabeth back from her thoughts, and she turned to give her mother words of encouragement. Emotions were high, and the excitement of the moment filled everyone. After several more arduous minutes, Mrs. Bennet cried out loudly through her last push before delivering her seventh child.

The gentlemen all locked eyes with each other when they heard Mrs. Bennet's voice cry out. Her husband grew white and sat himself slowly into a chair, terrified. Mr. Bingley and Mr. Darcy stood quickly and went towards the door, determined to do something, though neither knew what. Opening the door, they both tried to exit together, their broad shoulders thwarting their departure.

Elizabeth ran down the stairs at that moment and came rushing towards the room, calling for her father. Running to her father's side, she knelt beside him. "Papa! It is finished, and Mama and the babe are both healthy and fine."

Mr. Bennet's unfocused eyes rested upon his daughter as he processed her words. As color returned to his cheeks, he stood and walked to where he had placed his drink and swallowed it down.

He turned to the stunned faces of his sons-in-law and smiled triumphantly. "Well, boys, did you hear that? I am a father again!" He laughed and kissed his daughter on the cheek as he quickly exited the room and bounded up the stairs as if he were twenty years younger. Mr. Bingley followed, eager to see his wife, having been a little shaken by the experience he knew was to be his in a few short months. Mr. Darcy remained with Elizabeth and pulled her into his embrace.

"I cannot say I enjoyed that experience, my dear. I have never seen your father so shaken."

Elizabeth snuggled into her husband's chest, wrapping her arms around his back. "I shall remember not to tell you when my time comes then, so you may remain unaffected."

Darcy tightened his arms and rested his chin on her head. "No, you must tell me. I shall just have to prepare myself."

Elizabeth smiled against his chest, feeling so much love for him in that moment. "And how much time do you think you will need to prepare, my dear husband?" she asked as she looked up at him.

Darcy puffed out his cheeks and shook his head, "A very long time, I think."

"Well, then, you may wish to begin preparing now, Fitzwilliam."

Darcy's brows lowered as he looked down at his wife, trying to discern whether he heard her correctly. Upon seeing her smiling eyes, his own began to crinkle at the corners as his mouth drew up into a wide smile. "Really?" he asked incredulously.

Elizabeth nodded and then was crushed instantly against his chest as he lifted her up off the floor and swung her around in his excitement. Realizing her new condition warranted extra care, he immediately put her down and worriedly looked towards her abdomen. "Oh, I am sorry, Elizabeth. Did I... Are you all right?"

Elizabeth laughed and reached up to place a quick kiss on the concerned lips of her husband. "I am well, my dear."

Meanwhile, upstairs Mr. Bennet hesitated only a moment before knocking on the bedroom door. When Kitty opened the door widely for him, all he could see was his lovely wife on the bed, flanked by Jane and Mary, and holding a tiny bundle in her arms. Slowly, he entered the room.

As he approached the bed, he roamed his eyes all over his wife, assuring his mind that, indeed, she was well. When his eyes met hers, she said, "Come here, my dear, and meet your new son."

Mr. Bennet's eyes welled with water as he looked down at the tiny body in her arms. The thought crossed his mind that he had forgotten how small they started out as he slowly reached for the little hand. His voice broke as he said, "My son."

Edward Samuel Bennet grew up in the warmth of his parents' love, and he was doted on by every one of his older sisters, their husbands and his nieces and nephews — many of whom were very close to his age. The entail to the estate was broken, of course, with his birth. He was especially close to his older sister, Mary, who never married but instead went on to write several popular romantic novels. She lived with him and his eventual family the rest of her life.

Kitty Bennet often visited her eldest sisters at their homes. She became especially close to Georgiana, and together they were introduced to society.

One year, shortly after her twenty-first birthday, she was introduced to the handsome Major George Whitman, a friend of Colonel Fitzwilliam. The two of them fell quite in love at first sight, and they were married not long after.

Georgiana lived happily for several years with her brother and new sister until her heart was swept away by a young gentleman by the name of Mr. Cummings. He was a second son who inherited a pretty property that was located in a neighboring county to Derbyshire after his older brother died in a carriage accident.

Their courtship was long and as filled with misunderstandings as was her brother's with Elizabeth until one day she found herself locked in the library with him at Pemberley. Neither her brother nor Elizabeth would admit to having locked them in, though both had a very innocent look about them when questioned later. The result of their incarceration was fortuitous though, as it forced the two to clarify their misunderstandings. Miraculously, the missing key to the library was found not long after the happy couple came to an understanding. Upon telling her brother the happy news, Georgiana could have sworn she heard him call her a 'bumblehead' under his breath.

When Darcy received the news a few months after his wedding that Wickham did not survive his voyage to Australia, he did not seem much affected. After hearing of the condition in which Wickham boarded the ship, he was not altogether surprised. Although they never spoke of him much, Elizabeth and Darcy understood at that moment that finally they could put that history behind them forever.

Aunt Catherine, of course, was infuriated at the news of her nephew's wedding. She was especially frustrated with her servants for neglecting to bring her the papers that announced his engagement. She was sure that, had she seen the announcements in time, she could have stopped the wedding. Before she could berate the staff, however, her daughter asserted herself for the first time against her mother. Anne reminded her mother of the details of her father's will, entailing Rosings in its entirety to Anne upon reaching her majority at five and twenty. Anne was a year past that at the time of her cousin's wedding and warned her mother that she could move to the dower house at any time if she did not wish to welcome Elizabeth into the family.

Begrudgingly, and more out of a fear of moving to the smaller dower house than out of any love for her new niece, Lady Catherine de Bourgh placed an insincere smile on her face the next April when her nephew Fitzwilliam

Darcy brought his new bride along with him on his yearly visit.

That same visit, Colonel Fitzwilliam, who had always held an uncommon level of compassion and tenderness for his cousin Anne, was surprised and *more* to see her improved health. It appeared that her health had improved simply by asserting herself more with her mother, thus gaining back some of her vigor as she spent more time in the garden, on walks or driving her little phaeton and ponies around the park. His heart was shot with cupid's arrow from that moment on, and he spent much of his efforts afterwards persuading her to love him. They were married just before Elizabeth and Darcy's first wedding anniversary, its being the moment Anne first decided to gain control of her life as she agreed to help her cousin keep his wedding a secret from her mother.

Twelve Years Later

Darcy's rich baritone laugh echoed through the house as he entered accompanied by his eleven- and nine-year-old boys at his side. His six-year-old daughter, Anne Elizabeth, named after the girl's mother and his, was on his shoulder.

Both boys were exact images of their father, though the eldest and heir, William Thomas, was closer in temperament than was the younger, Alexander George. William was pensive and more reserved than his younger brother, whose personality more resembled the mischievous one of his mother and Uncle Richard. Although the boys had very different personalities, they seemed more akin to best friends than brothers most of the time.

Bending over to place his daughter on the floor, Darcy helped to assist her out of her cloak. He handed them with a smile to the waiting servants and divested himself of his own outerwear. Having just returned from doing some holiday shopping, the children and their father were eager to return to the warmth of Darcy House.

"Now boys, go on and see that you hide those packages well. You know how your mother can be quite curious when it comes to her presents."

The boys laughed, and William said with a serious tone, "Yes, Papa." He took the suggestion to heart and was already thinking through where he could hide the packages.

"Can I give Mama my present now, Papa?" Anne asked, her dark brown eyes sparkling so like her mother's and tugging at her father's heart.

Darcy smiled indulgently at his daughter. She was his darling, and he could no more deny her anything than he ever could her mother, especially when she looked at him with such beguiling eyes. He reached to smooth out her long chocolate curls and drew her into his arms for a quick kiss on the cheek.

Before he could give in to her request, his housekeeper spoke up, "Come, Anne, my dear, we must not spoil Christmas by giving your gifts too early. I know just the spot to hide your gifts, so run along with nanny, and I will be up to the nursery in a moment to hide them with you."

Darcy gave Mrs. Carroll a thankful glance for helping him avoid having to tell his little girl no. He watched as their nanny led the children up the stairs to the nursery, Anne's curls bouncing down her back as she skipped up the stairs. Overwhelmed with love and fatherly pride for his family, Darcy stood there a moment, watching until they were out of sight.

Maudlin thoughts about the wonderful blessings his wife had given him in their time together made Darcy suddenly very eager to see her. With a swelling in his chest, he turned to his butler with a smile.

"Mr. Carroll, might you know where my wife is this morning?"

"I believe she said she would be in the library, sir."

Darcy smiled. "Thank you, Mr. Carroll," he said, even as he began to walk in that direction.

His eagerness to see his wife mounted with every step he took towards her location. When he reached the library door, he paused just outside with his hand on the knob. A thought occurred to him, and he turned and headed back to the entryway to speak to his butler again.

"Mr. Carroll, do you remember my wife's exact words?"

Mrs. Carroll joined her husband at that moment and said, "I do, sir. I believe she said she would be in 'your library.'" Mrs. Carroll shook her head and continued, though Darcy was already walking away at a quickened pace. "Though why, after all these years of marriage, she would still not see it as her own library as well is beyond me."

Darcy did not stay to hear the rest of his housekeeper's words; instead a grin spread across his face, and he walked quickly towards his study door, pulling off his cravat as he went, pausing only long enough at the door to finish removing his coat and open his collar buttons. Smiling like a Cheshire cat, Darcy quietly opened the door to his study.

His breath hitched in his throat at the sight of his wife sitting behind his desk. It still had the same effect on him that it did the first time he saw her thus occupied so many years ago. Closing the door quietly behind him, Darcy leaned against its frame to watch her. Her legs were propped up on the surface of his desk, drawing his eyes to her bare feet and ankles, just visible past her skirts. She was so charmingly situated, with her head dipped down while she read her book, seemingly unaware of his presence. If it were not for the budding blush of her cheeks, the longer he stood there watching her, he would have thought his wife had not noticed his entrance. After twelve years, he had not grown tired of looking at her. Her features, softened slightly with age, still delighted him. Her figure, still light and pleasing, though maybe a touch rounded from bearing his children, also captivated him. While he watched her quietly, he folded his arms across his chest, his one leg moved to cross the other at the ankle. Sighing, Darcy wondered whether he had ever loved his wife more than he did at that moment.

He took the time to memorize every inch of the scene she presented and realized for the first time that he had never drawn her thus. The thought surprised him, and he vowed to himself to sketch her as soon as the opportunity arose. Having made his vow, he decided another thorough perusal of his wife with his eyes was necessary, so that he could capture the scene perfectly in his memory. While he allowed his eyes to drink in her beauty, her cheeks reddened further. She drew her lip under her teeth as she attempted to affect an air of indifference to his presence or his gaze.

Darcy swallowed; still uncommonly roused by her, he reached up to pull at his neck cloth and smiled to himself when he remembered it was no longer there, and the restriction around his neck was something altogether different.

MR. CARROLL LOOKED DOWN AT his wife and smiled. She was still mumbling about the mistress and her reference to the master's library.

"I believe she was referring to his study, dear."

Mrs. Carroll shook her head, seemingly unable to understand the ways of the gentle class. "Well, now that the master is back from his shopping and they are together, I might as well see to the Christmas dinner menu's approval." She stepped forward as if to go to the study to speak to Mr. and

Mrs. Darcy.

Mr. Carroll reached forward in time to pull her back by her apron ties.

"Mr. Carroll, unhand me; I need to get these menus approved!"

Mr. Carroll's smile grew wider as he simply shook his head. "Not now, my dear."

"And why not, might I ask?" she queried as she placed her hands on her hips.

Mr. Carroll remained silent but shook his head again. Then lifting his head, he resumed his post in the regal manner in which he always stood, his smiling face his only breach of decorum.

His wife stood looking at him until realization dawned on her, and she gasped as she looked down the hall towards her master's study and then back up at her husband, who peered down at her at that moment to give her a wink.

Giggling, she blushed and stammered, "I suppose I ought to check in on the children now, then."

"Excellent idea, my dear."

AFTER SEVERAL ENJOYABLE MOMENTS OF watching his wife read at his desk, Darcy's composure and patience could not wait a moment longer. He cleared his throat to attract her attention.

Elizabeth looked up to her husband at the sound, blushing further when she could see that she had not fooled him. Immediately, her eyes took in his casual attire, and she smiled. Looking towards the chaise lounge where he discarded his cravat and coat upon his entrance, she remembered all too clearly the first time she saw him so informally attired.

"Good afternoon, Mrs. Darcy," he drawled, drawing her eyes back to him.

"Good afternoon, Mr. Darcy. Did you enjoy your shopping?"

Reaching behind him, Darcy clicked the lock to his study door, causing his wife to draw a sharp breath, her lips pulling up in a small smile. Darcy pushed himself off the door frame with a shove from his shoulders as he casually walked closer to his wife. He felt satisfaction as he noticed her swallow and lower her feet to the ground when he drew near to the desk.

"We did, indeed. The children found some delightful things for you."

Elizabeth's brows rose, and excitement passed across her face, causing Darcy to laugh. He loved discovering, through the years, how much his wife enjoyed receiving presents from him, no matter how small. Giving her gifts was one of his favorite pastimes as well. He stepped closer still until he reached her side as she sat in his desk chair.

"I am glad to hear it," Elizabeth mumbled as she looked up at her husband's tall frame. She smiled when he shifted and leaned against the desk to face her.

Elizabeth slowly closed the book on her lap, placing it carefully on the desk beside him. She knew that look in his eye and secretly smiled to herself. With love in her eyes, she said, "Well I am glad you are back, Fitzwilliam." She boldly returned his look of longing. "It is good you are here, my dear. I believe we have some estate matters to discuss."

Darcy surprised his wife by capturing her wrists and pulling her up against him. He wrapped his arms securely around her, trapping her. She laughed and placed her hands on his chest.

Looking at him, she said cheekily, "Hello to you, too, sir."

Darcy smiled as he bent down and kissed her just below her ear. "What estate matters did you wish to discuss, my dear wife."

Elizabeth shivered. "There is the matter of a succession," she said suggestively.

Darcy groaned, but placed another soft kiss at her temple. "We already have an heir in William, my dear."

Elizabeth pushed gently away from him, and with an innocent, sweet voice, said, "Well then I guess we have nothing to discuss after all." She halfheartedly attempted to disentangle herself from his embrace. She laughed when his arms tightened and pulled her close to him again.

Leaning down to whisper into her ear, he said, "Someone I know once said to me that a wise man knows when to agree with his wife. I am a wise man, my dear. If you say we have estate matters to discuss, then by all means, let us discuss them. Let no man say Fitzwilliam Darcy is neglectful of his estate."

The Darcys then spent an uncommon amount of time discussing the estate.

CPSIA information can be obtained
at www.ICGtesting.com
Printed in the USA
LVOW08s1750171116

513437LV00001B/122/P